dangerous passion

Also by Lisa Marie Rice

DANGEROUS SECRETS
DANGEROUS LOVER

dangerous passion

LISA MARIE RICE

red

AVON

An Imprint of HarperCollins*Publishers*

DANGEROUS PASSION. Copyright © 2009 by Lisa Marie Rice. All rights reserved. Printed in the United States of America. No part of this book may be used or reproduced in any manner whatsoever without written permission except in the case of brief quotations embodied in critical articles and reviews. For information, address HarperCollins Publishers, 10 East 53rd Street, New York, NY 10022.

HarperCollins books may be purchased for educational, business, or sales promotional use. For information, please write: Special Markets Department, HarperCollins Publishers, 10 East 53rd Street, New York, NY 10022.

FIRST AVON PAPERBACK EDITION PUBLISHED 2009.

Designed by Diahann Sturge

Library of Congress Cataloging-in-Publication Data

Rice, Lisa Marie.
    Dangerous passion / Lisa Marie Rice.—1st ed.
        p.   cm.
    ISBN 978-0-06-120861-4 (acid-free paper)
    I. Title.
PS3618.I2998D365   2008
813'.4—dc22   2009002483

09 10 11 12 13   OV/RRD   10 9 8 7 6 5 4 3 2 1

This book is dedicated to my best friend,
the sister I never had, Lorena Rossi.
Thanks for all the years of friendship.
This one's for you, Lorenchen!

Acknowledgments

As always, a heartfelt thanks to
May Chen, my editor,
and Ethan Ellenberg, my agent.

Prologue

Feelings kill faster than bullets.

Former Russian army colonel Dmitri Rutskoi had drummed that saying into his troops' heads in Chechnya.

It was true.

Stay the finger on the trigger at the sight of that cute dark-haired little boy. Why, he can't be more than eight years old. And the next thing you know, that cute little boy has pulled out an AK–47 and turned you into human hamburger.

That nice old grandmother in the burqa? She has seven pounds of explosives strapped to her thick waist, just waiting for the moment to go to Allah and take you with her.

And what to say about Africa? Whole armies of cute little twelve-year-olds, carting AK–47s bigger than themselves, wearing amulets they are certain make them bulletproof, willing to cut you down because you looked their way.

The entire world is your enemy.

So Rutskoi taught his men ruthlessness, taught them to switch their feelings right off, because feelings are deadly. Feelings make you vulnerable, make you hesitate when action is called for, make you soft instead of strong.

The deadliest feeling of all is love for a woman. A woman is like a sword aimed straight at the heart.

Rutskoi had never hoped to be able to use that in bringing Drake down. Viktor Drakovich didn't have human weaknesses, certainly not women. He trusted nobody, he was nobody's friend, he loved nobody.

No one had ever seen Drake with a woman on his arm.

Of course not.

Drake was smart. He knew a woman would be a chink in his armor, a liability. He'd survived five attempts on his life over the past ten years by presenting no weak spots at all.

Rutskoi was sorry that he would be the one to bring Drake down. It didn't have to be that way. He'd moved to America to partner up with Drake, not kill him.

He'd been fascinated by Viktor Drakovich since he'd met him, as a young Russian army lieutenant in Chechnya fifteen years ago. He'd heard various versions of Drake's story. He was Russian, he was Ukrainian, he was Moldovan, he was Uzbekistani, he was Tajikistani. No one really knew. He just rose up out of nowhere in the nineties, an immensely smart and immensely strong young man who built a powerful empire that spanned the globe.

Drake had been supplying arms and ammo both to the *Obshina*, the Chechen mafia, and the Russian army fighting them. When weapons supplies from Moscow ran out, Rutskoi turned to Drake and found him to be utterly reliable. Drake delivered what he said he'd deliver, exactly on time, exactly where he said he would, all in perfect working order. And he had his own fleet of planes and helos and ships to do it with.

Drake was a legend. A man who dealt straight but who made a vicious, deadly enemy if you double-crossed him.

Rutskoi had had no intention of double-crossing him. In fact, he went out of his way to help Drake. When he left the Russian army, Rutskoi headed straight for the United States, where Drake had taken up residence.

Drake was one of the richest and most powerful men in the world, now living in the richest, most powerful nation in the world. Rutskoi wanted a piece of that, badly.

And why not? Drake ran a multibillion-dollar enterprise, single-handedly. Like any good general, he needed a lieutenant. And who better than Rutskoi, who knew the business from the ground up and who had deep, long-standing contacts of his own in Africa and the large land mass of splinter countries that used to be known as the Soviet Union?

It was a new world, and in this new world, a man had to dream big and take risks. He was ready.

Rutskoi had brokered a major arms deal and had socked away over a million dollars. He took half out of his Swiss bank account and had landed in New York a month ago. He spent the entire month in a suite in the Waldorf Astoria, familiarizing himself with Drake's new turf.

America—ah, America. So sweetly, deliciously decadent, yet cleanly and efficiently so. There was no pleasure you couldn't buy—all wrapped up, clean and sanitized and payable by credit card. Rutskoi wallowed in it. Well, he deserved it, after all. The long, hard years in an impoverished army, the subhuman conditions of the war in Chechnya, the constant danger—all forgotten.

Who could remember hard times on a soft bed with an even softer woman under you? At the end of the month, refreshed and ready to go, Rutskoi contacted Drake. Drake was nothing if not swift and businesslike. The appointment was for the next day.

Wonderful. Rutskoi could feel the power moving through him. The second half of his life was about to begin. He'd survived the worst that life could throw at him and had come out stronger. Soon, he would be rich and powerful and feared, the second-in-command of an immensely rich, powerful and feared man.

He was going to team up with a master of the universe and live forever. He knew where to buy new hearts and livers and kidneys.

He could still remember the feverish excitement he'd felt as the limo dropped him off in front of Drake's building. He knew how to school his face to impassivity—God knows he'd had enough experience dealing with drunken, incompetent generals—but inside he was bouncing with elation.

It took Rutskoi half an hour to work his way through Drake's security, which at the time had pleased him. The man was invincible, impregnable. Each layer of security, executed with perfect, polite professionalism by Drake's bodyguards, reassured him. This was truly the big time. He imagined that the only other man so well-protected could be the president of the United States, who arguably was less powerful in his world than Drake was in his. Drake's world was no democracy.

Finally, Rutskoi was led into a room with a door that closed like a steel vault behind him.

Ah. The smell of leather, fine whiskey and excellent cigars. The scent of the big room came to him before his eyes had a chance to adapt to the semidarkness. There were only a few lamps on, but the impression was of a huge room with an immensely tall ceiling. And comfort. Everything was built for the comfort of a man. Big leather armchairs; thick, plush carpets. An array of expensive-looking spirits in cut-crystal decanters. A brass-and-wood humidor.

"Come in," came a deep voice from within. And there he was. Drake.

Rutskoi wasn't easily impressed and he wasn't easily scared, but Drake impressed him and frightened him, at the same time. Of average height, he was immensely strong. His huge hands and feet were stippled with yellow calluses. Rutskoi had seen him punch a man so hard it was as if he had been hit with a bullet. He'd also seen Drake massacre a man with one kick.

He was adept at both SAMBO, the Russian martial art, and savate, French kickboxing. He could not be bested in hand-to-hand combat. He simply took his opponent to the floor and demolished him. And he was frighteningly intelligent. At times it was as if he were plugged into some secret intelligence system only he had access to. He was never caught by surprise, ever.

The story was that the killing of Ahmed Masood on the tenth of September, 2001, was a clear enough signal for him to start immediately dismantling his arms supply chain to the Taliban.

By the twelfth, he had moved his entire business to the States and teamed up with the CIA to funnel in arms to the Northern Alliance. He never sold another weapon to an Islamist or jihadist after that.

Though he was on every international list of outlaws, wanted by the UN and Interpol, he became untouchable, protected by the Americans. His pilots had stones the size of refrigerators. They ferried in arms to U.S. soldiers in Iraq, the only pilots brave enough—or crazy enough—to fly into Baghdad International on a daily basis, no matter the danger.

When Drake walked up, every hair on Rutskoi's body stood up. He swallowed his fear and awe, pushing them away. He had to meet Drake as an equal or this wasn't going to work.

"Sit down, Dmitri," Drake said and listened politely. The next thing he said, quietly, was "Get out," after Rutskoi explained what he wanted.

Without pressing a bell or making any sign, Drake's bodyguards came and frog-marched him out. He was literally thrown out the door by two huge bodyguards.

Rutskoi vowed revenge, but it was hard to take revenge on a man who didn't even notice you.

He spread the word that Drake's head was worth 50K and sat back and waited. And waited. And waited. Drake clearly paid his people so well that 50 grand wasn't an incentive. Either that or they were shit-scared of him. Probably both.

Rutskoi studied and waited and planned in vain, until he got the call. Not just any call. The Call. The one that was going to change his life.

Finally, a little of the money he was throwing around stuck somewhere. Rutskoi had left a Hotmail address and received an anonymous message.

If you want information on Drake, transfer $50,000 to this bank account.

At the bottom of the email was an IBAN, the first two letters, CH. A Swiss account.

Rutskoi's bank in the Caymans was efficient and fast. Half an hour later, he had mail.

Drake slips out of his building on the first and third Tuesday afternoon of every month, without bodyguards, and has done so for a year.

There were a number of attachments. Hands trembling, Rutskoi opened them, and—there it was. Information on Drake. Even better—information on a *weakness*.

At last! A chink in Drake's armor, straight through to the heart of the man.

Drake went to a well-known art gallery on Lexington every other Tuesday afternoon from two to three. Of all the things Rutskoi knew about Drake, a passion for art was not one of them. Going to a gallery wasn't breathtaking news.

No, what was incredible was that, month after month, Drake never entered the gallery. He waited outside, in the darkness of an alley, and observed what went on inside the gallery through a small window, watching from the shadows. What went on every other Tuesday of the month, regular as clockwork, was the arrival of a young artist, Grace Larsen, bringing her new work to show.

The work that was bought punctually by an unknown buyer. Every damned piece. For a year now, a lawyer representing a company incorporated in Aruba purchased by phone all new work by Grace Larsen, price no issue.

Rutskoi recognized the name of the company. It was one of the many shell companies Drake used to run his airlines. Drake was buying the paintings, no doubt about it.

Unsurprisingly, the gallery owner's prices for Larsen's work had been hiked 300 percent over the past year. And yet still she sold. To the same single buyer.

Rutskoi clicked his way impatiently through the attachments, trying to figure out how to use this information. Then he stopped. And stared.

Ah.

There were five attachments, JPEGs of the artist. Rutskoi sat back, pleased.

This was more like it. He was looking at a weakness that was going to finally bring Drake down.

Rutskoi felt adrenaline course through his veins as he leaned closer to the screen to get a good look at the photographs. After examining each one, he hit PRINT and examined the photographs carefully.

Grace Larsen was an unusually attractive woman, of medium height, slender without being bony like so many women in Manhattan. Wavy auburn hair, refined features, pearly white skin. She had an old-fashioned kind of beauty. She was undoubtedly why Drake was buying all her work and why he stood outside a window in a dark alley every other Tuesday afternoon.

To see her.

Though, granted, it was weird to think of Drake . . . What would be the American word? *Pining.* Drake was not a man to pine, after anything. Whatever he wanted, he obtained, by whatever means necessary. There was nothing he couldn't have. If he wanted the woman, all he had to do was buy her. Why wait outside in an alley, exposed, for a couple of hours a month just to see her?

She didn't appear to wear makeup on and her clothes were ordinary, but on such a woman, makeup was almost superfluous and she didn't need clothes to emphasize her beauty.

She looked utterly natural, quietly beautiful, serious, un-painted and unenhanced. Not Drake's type at all. Though, come to think of it, who knew what Drake's type was? Who knew if he even *had* a type?

Drake could afford the best, and though the woman was stunning, she didn't have "mistress" written all over her, as many women did. Rutskoi had bought enough women to be completely familiar with the type. The kind of woman who looked at a man's watch and shoes before she looked at his face. The kind of woman who was hooked on Tiffany and Armani the way street thugs were hooked on crack.

This woman didn't look that way at all. She didn't look expensive. She didn't look like she was in the market to be bought.

What was Drake thinking? With his money and power, he could have beautiful women lined up around the block, patiently waiting in line to serve him, in whatever way he wanted. He could have an entire harem, trained to fuck him in every possible position, exactly as he liked. There was nothing sexual he couldn't have or couldn't buy.

Standing in the shadows in the cold of a Manhattan winter or the steamy furnace of a Manhattan summer for an hour or two a month, without his bodyguards, without any security whatsoever, for a glimpse of a woman . . . it was madness.

Everything about the woman was a negative. No known drugs. No sex life that the informant knew of, either with men or women. Was not hooked on clothes or jewelry. There was a one-time credit card payment of three hundred dollars to the GAP, which any elegant Manhattan matron would have laughed at.

Rutskoi opened the attachments again and stared at her.

Why risk it? Drake was the most security-conscious human

Rutskoi had ever seen. More than any of the *Mafiya* bosses back in Russia. More than Putin.

Why risk being defenseless for several hours a month? What could possibly be worth it? Drake was vulnerable not only while in the alley, but traveling there and back.

For what? *Why?*

It couldn't be the paintings and watercolors and drawings themselves. He was scooping them up already. Wherever he had them stored, if he wanted them, he had access to them. No, it was more than the artwork. It *must* be for the woman.

Drake wanted to be able to observe the woman, unobserved. To risk so much, he must be obsessed. And he couldn't afford to let that obsession show to his men. They were loyal, it was true, but loyalty in their world was bought. Drake didn't have friends, he had employees. And employees could become disloyal. Look at the informant. He had just opened a huge hole in the armor plating surrounding Drake for a miserable fifty thousand dollars.

So here Drake was, obsessed with a beautiful woman who was unaware of his existence, completely defenseless, several hours a month. Grab the woman, force Drake to give up his codes, kill Drake and the woman, become one of the most powerful men on earth, all in one stroke.

This was it.

The decision was made. It was Thursday. He could have everything in place in a few days. This time Tuesday evening, he could be sitting in Drake's place, king of the world.

Rutskoi picked up his phone. It was time to recruit a partner.

One

Alleyway outside the Feinstein Art Gallery
Manhattan
November 17

Feelings kill faster than bullets, that old Russian army saying, raced through Viktor "Drake" Drakovich's mind when he heard the noise behind him. It was barely audible. The faint sound of metal against leather, fabric against fabric and the softest whisper of a metallic click.

The sound of a gun being pulled from its holster, the safety being switched off. He'd heard a variation of this sound thousands and thousands of times over the years.

He'd known for a year now that this moment would come. It was only a question of when, not if. He'd been barreling toward it, against every instinct in his body, completely out of control, for a full year.

From his boyhood living wild on the streets of Odessa, he'd survived the most brutal conditions possible, over and over again, by being cautious, by never exposing himself unnecessarily, by being security conscious, always.

What he'd been doing for the past year was the equivalent of suicide.

It didn't feel that way, though.

It felt like . . . like life itself.

He could remember to the second when his life changed. Utterly, completely, instantly.

He'd been in his limousine, separated from Mischa, his driver, by the soundproof partition. In the car he never talked, and used the time to catch up on paperwork. It had been years since he'd driven anywhere for pleasure. Cars were to get from A to B, when he couldn't fly.

The windows were heavily smoked. For security, of course. But also because it had been a long time since the outside world had interested him enough to glance out the windows at the passing scenery.

The heavy armor-plated Mercedes S600 was stopped in traffic. The overhead stoplight continued cycling through the colors, green-yellow-red, green-yellow-red, over and over again, but traffic was at a standstill. Something had happened up ahead. The blare of impatient horns filtered through the armored walls and bulletproof glass of his car, sounding as if coming from far away, like the buzzing of crazed insects in the distance.

A motorcycle eased past the cars like an eel in water. One driver was so enraged at the sight of the motorcyclist making headway, he leaned angrily on his horn, rolled down the window and stuck his middle finger up in the air. He shouted something out, red faced, spittle flying.

Drake closed his eyes in disgust. Even in America, where there was order and plenty and peace—even here there was aggression and envy. Humans never learned. They were like violent children, petulant and greedy and out of control.

It was an old feeling, dating from his childhood, as familiar to him as the feel of his hands and feet. Humans were flawed and rapacious and violent. You used that, profited from it and stayed as much out of their way as possible. It was the closest thing to a creed he had and it had served him well all his life.

Oddly enough, though, lately this kind of thinking had made him . . . impatient. Annoyed. Wanting to step away from it all. Go . . . somewhere else. Do something else. *Be* someone else.

If there were another world, he'd emigrate to it. But there was only this world, filled with greedy and violent people.

Whenever he found himself in this mood, which was more and more often lately, he tried to shake himself out of it. Moods were an excellent way to get killed.

Strangely out of sorts, he looked again at the spreadsheets on his lap. They tracked a 10-million-dollar contract to supply weapons to a Tajikistani warlord, the first of what Drake hoped would be several deals with the self-styled "general." There was newfound oil in the general's fiefdom, a god-damned lake of it right underneath the barren, hard-packed earth, and the general was in the mood to buy whatever was necessary to hold on to the power and the oil. When this deal went through smoothly, as it certainly would, Drake knew there would be many more down the line.

Years ago, if nothing else, the thought would have given him satisfaction. Now, he felt nothing at all. It was a business deal. He would put in the work; it would net him more money. Nothing he hadn't done thousands and thousands of times before.

He stared at the printouts until they blurred, trying to drum up interest in the deal. It wasn't there, which was alarming. What was even more alarming was the dull void in his chest as he reflected on his indifference. Not being able to care about not being able to care was frightening. Would have been frightening, if he could work up the energy to be frightened.

Restless, he glanced to his right. This section of Lexington was full of bookshops and art galleries, the shop windows more pleasing, less crass than the boutiques with their stupid, outlandish clothes a block uptown.

And that was when he saw them.

Paintings. A wall of them, together with a few watercolors and ink drawings. All heartbreakingly beautiful, all clearly by the same fine hand. A hand even he recognized was extraordinary.

Though the car windows were smoked, the gallery was well lit and each work of art had its own wall-mounted spotlight, so Drake got a good look at them all, stalled there in a mid-Manhattan traffic jam. And anyway, his eyesight was sniper grade.

He did something he'd never done before. He buzzed down his window. The driver's mouth fell open. Drake flicked his gaze to the rearview mirror. The driver's mouth snapped shut and his face assumed an impassive expression.

The car instantly filled with the smell of exhaust fumes and the loud cacophony of a Manhattan traffic jam.

Drake ignored it completely. The important thing was he had a better view of the paintings now.

The first painting he saw took his breath away. A simple image—a woman alone at sunset on a long, empty beach. The rendering of the sea, the colors of the sunset, the grainy beach—all those details were technically perfect. But what came off the surface of the painting like steam off an iron was the loneliness of the woman. It could have been the portrait of the last human on earth.

The Mercedes lurched forward a foot then stopped. He barely noticed.

The paintings were like little miracles on a wall. A glowing still life of wildflowers in a can and an open paperback on a table, as if someone had just come in from the garden. A pensive man reflecting himself in a shop window. Delicate female hands holding a book. The artwork was realistic, delicate, stunning. It pulled you in to the world of the picture and didn't let you go.

Drake had no way to judge the artwork in technical terms; all he knew was that each work was brilliant, perfect, and called to him in some way he'd never felt before.

The car rolled forward ten feet, bringing another section of the wall into view.

The last painting on the wall jolted him.

It was the left profile of a man rendered in earth tones. The man's face was hard, strong-jawed, unsmiling. His dark hair was cut so short the skull beneath was visible, which was exactly as Drake wore it in the field, particularly in Afghanistan. Far from even the faintest hope of running water, he shaved his head and his body hair, the only way to avoid lice. The face of the man didn't exactly look like him, but the portrait had the look of him—features harsh, grim, unyielding.

Running from the forehead over the high cheekbone and down to the jaw, brushing perilously close to the left eye, was a ragged white scar, like a lightning bolt etched in flesh.

Reflexively, Drake lifted a hand to his face, remembering.

He'd been a street rat on the streets of Odessa, sleeping in a doorway in the dead of winter. Some warmth seeped through the cracks in the door, allowing him to sleep without fear of freezing to death in the subzero temperatures.

Emaciated, dressed in rags, he was perfect prey for the sailors just ashore from months working brutal shifts at sea, reeling drunk through the streets. Sailors who hadn't had sex in months and didn't much care who they fucked—boy or girl—as long as whoever it was held still long enough. Most of the sailors didn't even care whether who they fucked stayed still because they were tied down or dead.

Drake came awake in a rush as the fetid breath of two Russian sailors washed over his face. One of the sailors held a knife to Drake's throat while the other dropped his pants, already hauling out a long, thin, beet-red cock.

Drake was a born street fighter and fought best when he was close to the ground. He was born with the ability and had honed it by observation and practice. He scissored his legs, bringing the man with the knife toppling to the ground, then hurled himself at the knees of the second man, hobbled by his pants. The man fell heavily to the ground, his head hitting the broken pavement with a sickening crack.

Drake turned to the first man, who'd scrambled to his feet and was holding the knife in front of him like an expert, edge down. The chances of surviving a knife fight barehanded were ludicrously low. Drake knew he had to even the odds fast, do something unexpected.

He flung himself forward, into the knife. The blade sliced the side of his face open, but the surprise move loosened the sailor's grip. Drake wrenched the knife out of his hand and jabbed it into the man's eye, to the hilt.

The sailor dropped like a stone.

Drake stood over him, panting, his blood dripping over the man's face, then pulled the knife out of his attacker's skull and wiped it down on the man's tattered jacket.

He took both men's knives. One was a *nozh razvedchika*, a scout's knife. The other was a Finnish Pukka, rare in those parts and very valuable. He bartered both along the Odessa waterfront for two guns, a Skorpion and an AK–47— including clips and shooting lessons—sold cheaply because they were stolen.

He was on his way.

Later, as soon as he could afford it, he had plastic surgery on the long, jagged white scar on the left side of his face. He was known for being able to blend into almost any environment, for turning himself invisible, but a very visible scar was like a flag, something no one forgot. It had to go.

The surgeon was good, one of the best. There was nothing visible left of his scar. Besides himself, only the surgeon could remember the shape of the long-gone scar. But there it was, in a painting in a gallery in Manhattan, half a world away and two decades later. However crazy it sounded, the scar in the painting was the same scar the surgeon had eliminated, all those years ago.

Traffic suddenly cleared and the Mercedes rolled smoothly forward. Drake punched the button in the center console that allowed him to communicate with the driver.

"Sir?" Mischa sounded startled over the intercom. Drake rarely spoke while they were traveling.

"Turn right at the next intersection and let me off after two blocks."

"*Sir?*" This time the driver's voice sounded confused. Drake never left the car en route. He got into one of his many vehicles in his building's garage and got out at his destination.

The driver caught himself. Drake never had to repeat himself with his men. "Yessir," the driver replied.

Once out of the limousine, Drake continued walking in the direction of the car until it disappeared into the traffic, then ducked into a nearby department store. Ten minutes later, satisfied that he wasn't being followed, he doubled back to the art gallery, having ditched his eight-hundred-dollar Boss jacket, Brioni pants, Armani cashmere sweater and scarf and having bought a cheap parka, long-sleeved cotton tee, jeans, watch cap and sunglasses. He was as certain as he could be that no one was tailing him and that he was unrecognizable.

The art gallery was warm after the chill of the street. Drake stopped just inside the door, taking in the scent of tea brewing and that mixture of expensive perfumes and men's cologne typical of Manhattan haunts, mixed with the more down-to-earth smells of resin and solvents.

At the sound of the bell over the door, a man came out from a back room, smiling, holding a porcelain mug. Steam rose in white fingers from the mug.

"Hello and welcome." The man transferred the mug from his right hand to his left and offered his hand. "My name is Harold Feinstein. Welcome to the Feinstein Gallery."

The smile seemed genuine, not a salesman's smile. Drake had seen too many of those from people who knew who he was and knew what resources he could command. Everything that could possibly be sold—including humans—had been offered to him, with a smile.

But the man holding his hand out couldn't know who he was, and wasn't presuming he was rich. Not dressed the way he was.

Drake took the proffered hand gingerly, not remembering the last time he'd clasped another man's hand. He touched other people rarely, not even during sex. Usually, he employed his hands to keep his torso up and away from the woman.

Harold Feinstein's hand was soft, well-manicured, but the grip was surprisingly strong.

"Have a look around," he urged. "No need to buy. Art enriches us all, whether we own it or not."

Without seeming to study him, Feinstein had taken in the cheap clothes and pegged him as a window-shopper, but wasn't bothered by it. Unusual in a man of commerce.

Drake's eyes traversed the wall and Harold Feinstein turned amiably.

"Take my latest discovery," he said, waving his free hand. "Grace Larsen. Remarkable eye for detail, amazing technical expertise, perfect brush strokes. Command of chiaroscuro in the etchings. Quite remarkable."

The artist was a *woman?* Drake focused on the paintings. Man, woman, whoever the artist was, the work was extraordinary. And now that he was here, he could see that a side wall, invisible from the street, was covered with etchings and watercolors.

He stopped in front of an oil, a portrait of an old woman. She was stooped, graying, hair pulled back in a bun, face weatherbeaten from the sun, large hands gnarled from physical labor, dressed in a cheap cotton print dress. She looked as if she were just about to step down from the painting, drop to her knees and start scrubbing the floor.

Yet she was beautiful, because the artist saw her as beautiful. A specific woman, the very epitome of a female workhorse, the kind that held the world together with her labor. Drake had seen that woman in the thousands, toiling in fields around the world, sweeping the streets of Moscow.

All the sorrow and strength of the human race was right there, in her sloping shoulders and tired eyes.

Amazing.

The door behind him chimed as someone entered the gallery.

Feinstein straightened, his smile broadened. "And here's the artist herself." He looked at Drake, dressed in his poor clothes. "Take your time and enjoy the paintings," he said gently.

Drake smelled her before he saw her. A fresh smell, like spring and sunshine, not a perfume. Completely out of place in the fumes of midtown Manhattan. His first thought was, *No woman can live up to that smell.*

"Hello, Harold," he heard a woman's voice say behind him. "I brought some india-ink drawings. I thought you might like to look at them. And I finished the waterfront. Stayed up all night to do it." The voice was soft, utterly female, with a smile in it.

His second thought was, *No woman can live up to that voice.* The voice was soft, melodic, seeming to hit him like a note on a tuning fork, reverberating through him so strongly he actually had to concentrate on the words.

Drake turned—and stared.

His entire body froze. He found himself completely incapable of moving for a heartbeat—two—until he managed to shake himself from his paralysis by sheer force of will.

Something—some atavistic survival instinct dwelling deep in his DNA—made him turn away so she wouldn't see him full face, but he had excellent peripheral vision and he watched intently as the woman—Grace—opened a big portfolio carrier and started laying out heavy sheets of paper, setting them out precisely on a huge glass table. Then she brought out what looked like a spool of 10-inch-wide paper from her purse.

Goddamn. The woman was . . . exquisite. More than beautiful. Beautiful was nothing nowadays. Beauty—the crassest kind possible—could be easily bought. Americans could afford the best of everything. Girls grew up with good nutrition, good dentists, good plastic surgeons, good hairdressers, good dermatologists. It seemed that all of them had good teeth, healthy hair, clear skin. All of that was nothing.

She wasn't very tall, but had long lines to her. Long legs, long neck, long, supple fingers. She moved easily and well, more with the light grace of a dancer than the strength of an athlete. Her shoulder-length hair looked as if it had just been washed, but not by a hairdresser. Washed and left to dry in the air. There was no perfection to it, except for its glossiness and the color—an amalgam of copper-bronze and light brown. She moved into a ceiling spotlight and her hair came alive, a sunburst of shiny colors.

She was smiling at Feinstein but there was a melancholy air there, a sadness, as if she'd seen into the heart of the world many times and found it cold and black.

Drake recognized that look. He saw it in the mirror every morning.

She was unadorned—no makeup, no jewelry, no fancy clothes. But that was as it should be, because she was almost extravagantly beautiful. Any jewelry would simply distract the eye from the porcelain skin; green-blue eyes; high, perfect cheekbones; full, serious mouth.

Cool air, a bell ringing. Three people walked into the gallery, two men and a woman. They were immediately drawn to the artwork up on the walls, planting themselves in front of the paintings making *hmmm* sounds.

They made wonderful cover.

Circling slowly, making no noise whatsoever, Drake drifted until he was in the direct line of sight of what Grace was showing the gallery owner, flipping through the papers.

Miracles. That's what she was showing the owner. God-damned fucking miracles, each and every one.

Drawings of just about everything under the sun. The woman seemed to draw everything that came into her line of sight, and then, as if the world weren't enough for her imagination, there were some fantasies, like the carefully rendered dragon on a hilltop, as finely drawn as any Chinese classic.

Two small boys in Central Park. A cop on horseback, back erect, eyes straight ahead, ready for anything. A hot-dog vendor looking to the side with a slight smile on his face. Overblown roses in a crystal vase, a petal caught just as it fell . . . one by one she laid them out for Feinstein, who examined them carefully, his face giving nothing away, though if Drake owned the gallery, he'd have been hopping with joy just before pulling out the checkbook.

That wasn't the way business was done, no one knew that better than Drake. You play it cool and always underbid. Never show your hand. Never let emotions interfere with a business transaction. But this art was way outside any rules governing commerce.

It was magic.

But there was more to come.

She gave one end of the big spool to Feinstein, then started walking backward, unrolling it, smiling as Feinstein's eyes widened.

Neither of them was paying him any attention, so Drake let himself take a good look, forgetting to breathe for a second.

They were unspooling the Manhattan coastline, rendered in architectural detail in black ink. On and on and on the spool unrolled, each stroke of each building precise, perfect. He recognized every inch of the work and could even see his own building. Just the last floor was visible, the penthouse, where he lived. Rendered in perfect detail. He'd never seen anything like it.

Had she spent months on a boat, at anchor, drawing? What was remarkable was the fineness of the strokes, without one mistake.

She stopped unrolling the spool and held it by the end. It was at least twelve feet in length, each detail perfect.

The three newcomers gathered along the strip, oohing and aahing, walking slowly along it, eyes glued to the miniature coastline, pointing out familiar buildings.

Feinstein pulled the strip more tightly so they could see better and Drake nearly had a heart attack. Fuck, a little more pressure, the paper would rip, and something irreplaceably precious would be lost.

Drake barely stopped himself from attacking the gallery owner. He had to consciously freeze his muscles and hope Feinstein understood enough to pull with only enough power to pick up the slack and not rip the strip apart.

Otherwise Drake would rip *him* apart.

Whoa. Where had that thought come from? The man was portly, elderly, with the soft mottled hands of the old. An art gallery owner, for Christ's sake. Drake didn't attack civilians and he certainly wouldn't attack an elderly gentleman, particularly not one who'd been instinctively kind and was this remarkable artist's friend.

But still. For a second there, when he thought that miracle strip of paper was going to be ruined, he could feel his hands closing around the man's neck, dewlap and all. He wouldn't have lasted a second. Drake had known how to snap a man's neck since he was ten and he'd only gotten better with the years.

The trio was shuffling along the strip, pointing out landmarks, excitement in their voices.

"Franco," the woman drawled, her red-painted lips pursing at the final O, "this would look just divine in your studio, wouldn't it? All along the yellow wall."

"*Sì, cara.*" Franco shook his head admiringly. "I'd frame it simply, not to distract from the clean lines. *A giorno.*"

No! Mine! Drake clamped his lips together tightly or he'd have shouted the words.

They reverberated in his chest, rolling around like huge granite stones, pinging off his rib cage.

Mine.

He couldn't remember the last time he'd desired something this intensely.

He'd been rich for a long, long time now. There was nothing material he couldn't buy. Nothing. He'd even been offered his own country, a minute island. More a speck of land barely rising above the water, really, but still.

He owned an entire skyscraper in Manhattan, plus villas scattered around the world. He had expensive planes, expensive cars, expensive clothes, expensive women, though lately he'd been off sex.

It had been years since he'd felt that burning in his chest that meant he coveted something. In his childhood, it had flared particularly strongly in winter, when he wanted a warm room. And always when he caught the whiff of a restaurant and his empty stomach growled.

How he'd *wanted* then. Ferociously. But that was a long time ago, another life ago.

So the intensity of this wanting took him completely aback, the echo of a child's desperate need in a man's mind.

Things shifted in his head, taking in this new, completely unexpected desire, making it fully his. At times, it was as if the very concept of desire had fled his life and he welcomed it back, a little gingerly. An old foe who had somehow morphed into a friend.

He looked around at the walls and knew that he had to have everything on them. Oils, watercolors, drawings. Everything. It all had to be his, there was no other way.

It would have to be done anonymously, through one of his many lawyers, using one of his shell companies.

He turned his head slightly, to where Grace Larsen was watching the three patrons and Feinstein, full lips slightly upturned. He had the distinct impression she didn't smile much. Which he understood completely, because neither did he.

The gray winter clouds outside must have parted, because suddenly she was suffused with light, making her skin glow, picking out an incredible play of colors in her shiny hair. She stood in the center of the rectangle of light painted on the hardwood floor, as if on a stage.

Feinstein was starting to roll the strip up. He glanced over to her and said, in a quiet voice, "Well done, my dear. Bravo."

Her head bowed just an instant, a knight accepting a king's just praise.

The word *mine* roared in Drake's head again, reverberating, nearly flooring him with surprise.

If it had been years and years since he'd wanted things, he had never wanted *people*. Not specific people.

He didn't have lovers, he had sex partners.

He didn't have friends. He had employees.

He hired the best at what they did, paid them more than market price and let them do what they did best.

Women came and went, rarely staying in his life for more than a night or two. He didn't pay for sex. He didn't have to. The women who came to his bed understood very well what he could offer. A thank-you gift the next morning was always sent from Tiffany or Fendi or Armani, chosen in rotation.

Having one woman in his life—even if he'd wanted one, which he didn't—would be insane.

He had his layers of security for a reason. He had enemies. Smart, ruthless enemies, some stretching back twenty years. A woman he cared about would have a huge bull's-eye painted on her forehead, a fast and easy way to break through his defenses. She would be the softest target in his world.

There wasn't a woman alive who would be willing to live beneath his heavy blanket of security, never being able to walk around, never being able to do her own shopping, not even allowed to go for a walk, because he sure as hell would never allow his woman to be a target.

And what would be the point of being able to buy all the clothes and jewelry you wanted if you could never be seen in them?

Not to mention the possibility of children.

God, just the idea of having a child made him break out in a sweat. He'd seen too many children die violent deaths. He'd go insane if there were a child of his somewhere out in this cold and violent world, a target for someone bent on vengeance.

So occasional safe—very safe—sex with occasional partners was as close as he ever got to another human. He had very little recollection of the women who'd trooped through his bed. If he closed his eyes, he could remember little details. A mole on the underside of a breast. A shaved pubis. Pretty knees. An artistic tattoo. That kind of thing.

That was it, though. The women the details had been attached to—gone. He couldn't remember their names or their voices. He could barely remember their faces even right after fucking them.

But he remembered *her* face. Oh, yes. Every detail.

Everything about her was so perfect. Just . . . perfect. Large eyes the color of the sea, hair that seemed to have a thousand colors in its glossy depths, pale, perfect skin.

And an air of melancholy over all that.

She bewitched him. She didn't know of his existence, but hers filled his life in an instant.

Grace Larsen was indeed her name, and she came to the Feinstein Gallery every other Tuesday afternoon, as Drake found out soon enough. When he got home he made it his business to know everything about her. So every other Tuesday afternoon, Drake was there, too. In an alleyway, in the shadows, hidden and alone, watching through a small window that only gave him a narrow view of the gallery and that afforded him only isolated snatches of Grace.

It was folly, it was insanity, but he couldn't have stayed away had a gun been pointed at his head.

And now one was.

He was going to pay the extreme price for his folly.

At the sound of a round being chambered, he reacted instinctively. He had superb hearing and was able to triangulate the position. About a yard behind him and slightly to his right.

Time went into slow motion, though his body moved faster than thought, instinctively, violently. He still had fractions of a second before the trigger could be pulled, enough time to remove himself from any possible trajectory.

Drake was a ground fighter. He dropped instantly to the cold, oil-stained concrete. Whoever the man was, Drake knew he was concentrated exclusively on the shot, therefore his balance would be top-heavy. All the attention in his body would be concentrated in his eyes and hands. He probably wasn't even feeling his feet.

Drake had trained himself to be aware of all parts of his body in combat, but he knew that ability was rare. He dropped, shot out his leg; his heel hooked the shooter's foot and brought the man down with a foot lock.

He'd learned SAMBO from one of the Russian masters. Once he got an opponent on the ground, the man was his.

The man toppled and fell. He was as tall as Drake had instinctively calculated from the source of the sound, but the shooter was heavier than Drake had imagined. He fell badly, right on Drake's left knee. A blast of pain shot through his knee, red-hot, almost unbearable. For a second, he wondered if it was broken, then dismissed the thought. If it was, there wasn't anything he could do about it.

But he didn't think so. He knew the feeling of deep injury and this wasn't it. It was just pain. Pain could be ignored.

Drake had the man in a half guard, elbow against his neck, but he couldn't block the man's lower body with his wounded leg. Through the thick down jacket, Drake could feel that his opponent was large, bulked up with solid muscles. Unusual for a shooter, and his damned bad luck.

But though Drake was less bulky, he was strong and fit. His hands were very strong from a lifetime of judo. Grunting, sweating, he walked his right hand down to where the shooter was holding his gun, trying to wrench it around.

The shooter was strong. But Drake was stronger.

He dug his thumb into the tendons of the shooter's inside wrist, feeling muscle then bone beneath his fingers. He tightened his grip as the man got off a shot. Luckily, he was holding the gun away from himself and it pinged silently off the brick wall, shards of brick spattering against the plate-glass window, then raining down on them.

Drake dug his thumb in deeper, felt the man grunt in pain. One more second and the man's grip loosened, dropping the gun to the concrete with a clatter. Drake broke the man's wrist and picked the gun up. A SIG P229.

A side door opened, an elongated rectangle of light falling onto the filthy alleyway.

Two people stood in the doorway, two other men behind them.

A pale, beautiful woman with the muzzle of a Beretta 84 dug so hard into her temple a rivulet of blood ran down the side of her face. The man holding the gun to her head was a tall, long-haired Latino with bad skin and cold, cruel eyes, wearing a long leather coat. Behind him stood two other Latino-looking men, smaller but no less vicious. Gangbangers.

And all bets were off. Because the woman with blood streaming down her face was Grace Larsen.

"Drop the gun. Now." The tall Latino's voice was cold, slightly hoarse.

Drake hesitated. He was armed beyond the SIG. He had a Glock 19 in a shoulder rig and a Tomcat in his waistband, but giving the SIG up went against every instinct he had. If he was to get Grace Larsen out of this situation alive, he needed every advantage he could get.

"Throw it," the man growled. He tightened his arm around Grace's beautiful neck. Her nostrils were white and pinched, her lips turning blue. He was cutting off her oxygen.

Drake could blow his arm off. It wouldn't be the first time. But he couldn't guarantee that the man wouldn't move at the last second, that he wouldn't hit Grace instead.

"Throw it!"

Drake opened his hand and let the SIG tumble to the ground.

Two

"Your secret admirer is going to love this," Harold Feinstein said to Grace, holding up a pastel. She'd worked on it for an entire day, not eating, not drinking, stopping only to go to the bathroom, working feverishly to catch every stingy ray of winter sun that drifted down through her skylight.

She'd seen the image when she'd woken up and gone to the window to raise the blinds. A seagull, escaped from the ocean to the concrete of Manhattan, feathers a pristine white in the smoky city air, great wings outstretched, riding a thermal up the side of the nineteenth-century brick building across the street.

The building across the street from her apartment was worn, old, used up. It was slated for demolition soon and looked it— boarded-up windows, broken front door, the shell of a building no one lived in and no one loved anymore. A dying artifact.

In contrast, the bird had epitomized newness, freedom, lightness—the ability to simply pick up and leave troubles on the ground. She'd watched, entranced, for a few minutes as the bird reveled in its flight, wheeling in the sky above the street, lightness and grace. Utterly inhuman yet symbolizing the best of the human spirit.

How hard she'd worked to capture that magic moment of utter freedom.

Harold lay the pastel reverently on the big glass table in the center of the gallery, next to the watercolors she'd brought, lining her work up like brightly colored soldiers. It was a ritual they'd been following for well over a year now, ever since she'd walked into his gallery with a portfolio under her arm and 150 dollars left in the bank.

Harold touched the edge of the paper with his index finger, then moved on to touch a watercolor of a drake in last week's snow in Central Park.

"He's going to love these," Harold murmured. "And I'm going to love selling them to him." His eyes gleamed behind his thick glasses. "I'm raising your prices again. He's not going to complain. Not when he sees this."

Grace tried not to smile. "Harold, you don't know it's a he and neither do I. The man who buys my work on this other person's behalf is a lawyer, for heaven's sake. His client could be anyone. Man, woman. Could be a *Martian*, for all we know."

What did she care? Whoever the lawyer's client was, s/he was buying Grace's entire output and didn't so much as blink when Harold kept upping her prices. After years of struggling, trying to make it as an artist, she was finally supporting herself and more—socking money away. Real money, to her astonishment. After a lifetime of living like a student, she got a huge thrill every time she checked her bank statements.

Whoever was buying up her work had turned her life around. She didn't even really mind that whoever was scooping up her work wasn't showing it anywhere. Harold had told her that anyone who spent that much money and who had that amount of work of a single artist was usually planning a major show and in any case would want to publicize the collection, for investment purposes. But her unknown client was keeping her work tightly under wraps. Abroad, apparently.

Grace didn't care. She wasn't in the business to become famous. She was an artist because she couldn't be anything else, not and remain sane. She had a lousy record of being fired from temp jobs, waitressing, teaching, trying to entice women she didn't care about to buy things she found absurd and useless in her very very brief stint as a shop assistant at Macy's.

"Ah. Him again." Harold stopped and picked up a portrait. A small full frontal portrait in oil of a strong-featured man with dark eyes and short dark hair. Unsmiling and powerful, with a jagged white scar along the side of his face. "Different but the same." Harold's eyes were shrewd as he slanted a glance at her. "Nightmares back?"

Grace looked away, ashamed that once, when she'd been exhausted because she hadn't slept, she'd confessed to Harold that she had nightmares, often.

Not nightmares, not really, not always. Just . . . very vivid dreams—full of color and sound. Often steeped in danger and heartache. So utterly unlike the calm progression of her days, her nights were etched in blood and turmoil.

She often dreamed of a man. The same man, every time,

though each time his features were different. She never clearly saw his face anyway, just rough glimpses, as if through a thick fog.

A strong jawline, narrow nose, hooded eyes. By day, when she tried to capture the man on paper, his features would melt. Each portrait she did of him was different. The only things common to all the men were harsh features, dark eyes, short dark hair and a white scar like a lightning bolt on the left side of his face.

She saw him often from behind, walking away. And every time he walked away, there was a keen sense of aching loss in the air. She could never run after him, though she wanted to. She was always somehow mired in the horrible paralysis of the dream world.

The nightmares were due to stress, she knew that. She'd read every book there was on the subject because going to an analyst was out of the question. She didn't have the time or even, really, the inclination.

What was a shrink going to tell her she didn't already know? That she came from a highly dysfunctional family? Check, no secrets there. That her father's abandonment when she was nine years old and her mother's decline and indifference to her had colored her early years? That she immersed herself in her art because she didn't function well in the world? What else was new?

No, analysis would be a huge waste of her time and money. Grace thought she had a pretty good handle on herself. On what she could do and couldn't do.

" . . . framing?"

Oh God, she'd done it again. Zoned out while someone was talking. And that someone was Harold, no less. He cared for her, it was true. He was estranged from his only son, and treated her like a beloved child. They'd grown to be great friends. In fact, Grace probably talked more to Harold in the couple of hours a month she spent in his gallery than she did with any other human being.

But Grace was also very *very* aware of the fact that every cent she earned came through him. Not listening while he spoke to her was incredibly rude and—worse—stupid.

"Sorry, Harold. I didn't quite—"

He gave his characteristic bark of laughter, placing a light hand on her shoulder. "Don't worry, my dear. Wherever it is you go when you do that, it must be a much more interesting place than my blathering on about the matting and framing."

Grace smiled, ashamed. The matting and framing in question was of *her* work. Harold worked really hard to make sure each painting, watercolor and drawing was presented in the best possible way.

Though it was also true that her mysterious buyer was snapping up everything she produced, no matter the matting, no matter the framing.

"Come," he said gently. "Let me make you a cup of tea." Harold's remedy for just about everything.

"Okay, I—" Grace turned at the sound of the bell over the door. Customers. She drifted away. Customers meant sales for Harold. They could have their tea afterward.

Only . . . they didn't look like possible buyers of art. As a matter of fact, they looked dangerous.

Grace moved back to Harold's side.

Grace lived alone in New York and she knew the look of dangerous men, enough so that she'd never been in trouble because she knew enough to avoid the dangerous places they congregated. The Feinstein Art Gallery was the last place on earth she'd think of in terms of trouble.

But trouble was walking through the door, right now.

Three men, one tall, broad, with bad skin, dressed in a long black leather coat, the other two short and wiry, one dressed in an expensive fleece track suit, the other in jeans and a bomber jacket. They came into the gallery in single file, footsteps echoing on the hardwood floor, then fanned out, as if covering territory. They didn't look alike but they shared a look of cold menace, staring at her and Harold like sharks eyeing minnows.

Something cold and nasty had just entered Harold's bright and civilized gallery.

In here, both she and Harold could forget for a moment what was out there, cocooned in art and hot tea.

But now the outside world was in here, lined up in front of them like gunslingers awaiting the signal to shoot. There was a moment of utter and complete silence as the three men stared at them, menace coming off them in almost visible waves. Fear made her senses diamond bright. Her heart kicked up its beat, sounding loud in her ears, like a drumbeat.

Grace moved closer to Harold in an instinctive attempt to protect him, though there was nothing she could do against three tough-looking men. But Harold was so vulnerable, so fragile. He was elderly and had a heart condition. Her shoulder touched his and she could feel that he was trembling.

At least she was young and strong. And had a can of Mace in her purse. She clutched the strap of her purse, surreptitiously fingering the clasp. She kept the Mace handy, in a side pocket. No sense in having a weapon if you had to dig down to the bottom of a purse to find it.

With a strong indrawn breath, Harold drew himself up and looked the men in the face. "May I help you gentlemen?" he said. She was so proud of him for his firm voice.

It happened so fast, she had no time to react.

Subconsciously, she was waiting for them to respond. Centuries of civilization had drummed it into her DNA that a query requires a response. Whatever bad thing the men might be bringing into the gallery, it would be after answering a question posed to them.

What happened next had nothing to do with civilization. It came straight out of the caves. Not a word was spoken. Shockingly, Leather Coat stepped forward, punched Harold in the face, then stepped to the side, hooking a big, beefy arm around her neck in one smooth motion.

Harold fell to the floor like a puppet whose strings had been cut. Blood lined his mouth and his nose spattered blood with each heaving breath.

With a cry, Grace lunged toward him, but was brutally restrained by the huge arm around her neck, holding her so tightly he was cutting off her air. She brought her hands up to claw at his sleeve but could find no purchase against the sleek leather and the hard, ropy forearm muscles underneath.

The man shifted, lifting her until her toes could barely reach the ground, tightening his arm until she saw stars dancing in front of her eyes. Inside she was screaming, scrabbling madly to get to Harold, but she was held as contemptuously as a doll off the ground, and only a high-pitched mewling sound escaped her lips.

An icy metallic ring dug into her temple. She shifted her eyes to the right to understand what it was.

A gun. A huge, black, terrifying gun, held against her head.

"Stop," the man said simply. His voice was deep, guttural, inhuman, the tone one of utter command. There was nothing Grace could do. In another thirty seconds, she'd be unconscious anyway from lack of oxygen.

Resistance was not only useless, but any hope she had of helping Harold required her to be conscious and upright.

She stilled instantly.

"Good," the man grunted, rewarding her by letting up a little on the pressure against her throat. Her feet hit the floor at the same moment her throat spasmed, wheezing as air burned its way back into her lungs. If she'd been free, she would have bent forward in an effort to breathe better, but the man maintained his hold around her neck, letting her know exactly who was boss.

The rim of the gun tightened against her temple until the skin broke. A trickle of warm blood dripped down the side of her face.

With every choked breath, she breathed in a nauseous combination of rank sweat overlaid by an expensive men's cologne. The combination was so horrible she was almost sorry she could breathe again.

Outside the window, a businessman hurried by, coat whipping in the wind. A few heavy drops fell to the sidewalk and he put a burgundy leather briefcase over his head to shield himself from the rain that was beginning to pelt down.

He could have been on the moon for all the help he was.

Fleece Track Suit checked his watch, then looked at Leather Coat. "It's time."

The man simply lifted her off her feet again and, as compact and disciplined as a phalanx, the three men—Leather Coat holding her as if she were a doll being carried to another part of the playground—walked together quickly to a side door, the one that Grace knew gave onto an alleyway flanking the gallery. She'd once helped Harold dump cartons in the alleyway, a dank, dark cul de sac, the feral urban counterpoint to the airy grace and light of the gallery.

There was one small window set in the gallery's north wall, overlooking the alley. She looked through it and gasped. There were two men there, one aiming a big black gun at the back of the other. The man holding the gun was tall, heavy, with long reddish-brown hair, his victim shorter, broader, with close-cropped dark hair.

The long-haired man with the gun tightened his grip on the trigger. Grace was horrified to think that she was about to witness a cold-blooded murder. If she could have, she'd have screamed a warning to the victim, but she barely had enough air to breathe. And even if she could scream, not much sound bled out through Harold's thick windows.

Instinctively, though, she fought against the man holding her, trying to get some kind of sound out. Maybe if she kicked the wall . . .

The dark-haired victim suddenly dropped from sight and Grace stilled, stunned. He was there and then . . . he wasn't. He'd just disappeared.

The goon holding her moved forward, together with the other two thugs, to the small window. There was a clear view of the alleyway and she could see that the man hadn't disappeared. He had simply dropped to the ground like a stone. Grace would have thought that he'd been shot, but it looked like he was . . .

Oh my God, yes. He wasn't down for the count. He was fighting. From the *ground*. And winning, too, from the looks of it. He had his attacker in some kind of complicated hold, completely paralyzed.

The victim's legs tightened around his attacker's middle and he held the attacker's neck in the bend of his elbow, squeezing. One hand was squeezing the gun out of the attacker's hand. The attacker was kicking madly, like a pig in a slaughterhouse, but nothing he did could dislodge the dark-haired man. The gun clattered to the ground and the dark-haired man snatched it up, handling it with familiarity.

One of the thugs in the gallery kicked open the door to the alleyway and the man holding Grace moved forward until they were spotlit in the doorway.

The two men on the ground looked up, both breathing hard, muscles straining.

"Drop the gun. Now." Leather's Coat's voice was hoarse, as if he didn't talk much, with a heavy Hispanic accent. He lifted his arm until her feet dangled again. The gun barrel cruelly ground into the skin of her temple. The entire right side of her face was covered in blood now. She could smell her own blood—a dark metallic smell. "Drop it or I pop her one right in the head."

God. Watching the attack in the alley, she had, for a second, completely forgotten about the man holding her tightly against him with a gun to her head. She started trembling. She had no idea who the victim of the attack was. How could using her as a threat possibly work? It hit her like a sledgehammer to the heart that she was one second away from dying.

She twisted in her captor's hold, trying to kick him, suddenly desperate now to get away. There wasn't enough oxygen in her head to make plans, she only knew she didn't want to die without putting up some kind of fight.

The arm around her neck was like steel, the muscles she could feel against her side and back thick and hard. He probably outweighed her by over a hundred pounds. Fighting was insane.

But the animal part of her refused to die without a struggle. Grimly, she clawed again at the arm around her neck and kicked as hard as she could at his shins, but all she encountered was something stiff and unyielding. The man was wearing boots that went to his knees.

Her tormentor growled low in his throat and squeezed. Tight, tighter.

Oh God, she was going to die. Right here, right now. All the things she had left to do with her life, all the paintings she wanted to create, the music she wanted to listen to, the walks she wanted to take—it was too late.

"Throw it," her tormentor rasped.

The dark-haired man kept his gaze fixed on Leather Coat, unblinking in the rain that threw a scrim over the scene in the alleyway.

Her vision was failing, spots revolving in front of her eyes. There was a dull blackness at the edges of her vision. "Throw it," her tormentor said again.

Throw what? What was he talking about?

A clatter on the ground. Her tormentor hadn't been talking to her. He had addressed the dark-haired man, who had thrown the gun he'd wrested from his would-be assassin onto the oily, pebble-strewn ground. He slowly stood up.

"Let up on her," the man said quietly. He had a deep, calm voice with a hint of accent. "You're choking her to death."

"Your other weapons first."

The dark-haired man reached inside his parka and pulled a gun out. He held it carefully by the muzzle. "Safety's on, as you can see. Now let her breathe."

Amazingly, that quiet voice held enough command to make the arm around her throat loosen. Her feet scrabbled, touched the ground for the first time in what felt like hours.

Grace took in a big wheezing breath, hoping it wouldn't be her last. Though the chokehold had loosened, the gun was still rock-solid against her head. She was still so close to the man who held her that she could feel the vibrations in his chest as he spoke.

"The rest of your weapons," he said to the dark-haired man.

The gun came away from her head, the cold barrel sliding horribly down her neck, trailing down over her arm to stop at her elbow. "Or I blow a hole in her elbow. Then shoulder. Blow her arm right off. First one, then the other. Then I kneecap her. She'll die piece by piece."

Grace was shaking so hard her teeth rattled. The man's low tone was matter-of-fact, not menacing, which made it even more horrible. He could have been ordering a drink in a bar, not threatening to kill her by slow degrees.

Fear set up a keening whine in her head. She looked around wildly, wondering if this would be her last sight on this earth.

A filthy alleyway in the rain, cloudy light at one end, dank darkness at the other. One of her few friends, Harold, lying behind her on the floor, wounded, if he hadn't already died from the blow. And four men, all violent, all dangerous, all armed. They wanted something from the dark-haired man and, crazily, were using her to get it.

Though she felt danger to her coming from the four attackers, she didn't feel that at all coming from the man who'd been attacked. The menace he radiated was tightly focused on the man holding her.

"Go on," Leather Coat growled. The gun tapped horribly against her elbow. "Give me an excuse to shoot."

Grace looked up at the man holding her. He was grinning at the dark-haired man. He never looked at her. She had a horrible feeling she barely existed for him. She was like a tool dangling from his arm, useful to get something he wanted, of no intrinsic importance. "I'm waiting. I hope you give me the excuse to blow her away bit by bit. I'll enjoy it."

No doubt he would. Cruelty was etched in every line of his face.

The dark-haired man reached around his waist, pulling a gun from behind him. Moving slowly, he placed it on the ground.

"Knives," her tormentor rasped. "And don't tell me you don't have any."

In a second, two sharp, gleaming knives clattered to the ground.

"I hear you carry a *karambit*. Out with it."

A wicked-looking curved knife that came to a surgically sharp point fell to the ground in a flash of steel. The man holding her grunted.

The attacker on the ground stood up, wincing, with a sneer of victory. He'd been bested in a fight, but now the odds were in his favor.

"Turn around," Leather Coat growled to the dark-haired man.

Grace's gasp was loud in the alleyway. The dark-haired man was unarmed and helpless. They'd already tried to kill him once and now they were going to finish the job.

She had no idea who he was, but she felt connected to him somehow. He had let himself be disarmed to spare her. She had no idea if he could have prevailed against four men, but the way he fought proved that he wouldn't die easily, not without inflicting a great deal of harm. The dark-haired man knew how to defend himself, not to mention the fact that he walked around with a small arsenal on his person.

Maybe he was a bad guy, too, just like the other four. Maybe she had stumbled onto some kind of turf war of drug dealers or something. Maybe this was a mob shakeout.

She could believe that, absolutely, of the other four but found it hard to believe of the dark-haired man, for no special reason her oxygen-deprived brain could conjure up, except that he had a different look.

Whoever he was, he'd pissed off the four criminals greatly and on the theory that your enemy's enemy is your friend, she was on his side. As he was on hers. He'd allowed himself to be disarmed and was probably going to die, right now, to spare her.

No. Every cell in her body rejected the notion. He wasn't going to die, slaughtered like an animal. She wouldn't let him. Apart from anything else, the instant he was gone, she would be dead, too. She'd seen the goons' faces. They weren't the kind to leave witnesses behind.

Together with some oxygen, an electric pulse ran through her, grounding her, giving her strength. She wasn't ready to die. Not here, in this filthy alley, and not now, two months from her twenty-eighth birthday.

And neither was he going to die. She met his eyes, the deepest brown she'd ever seen. His gaze was clear, direct and sad. Grace caught his gaze, willing him to look at her, to follow her thoughts, darting her eyes to her purse. He could see that the clasp was open. She looked deliberately at her purse, at him, at the man holding her. Over and over again.

He understood. The slight aura of resignation and defeat was gone. Grace watched as he turned back into a warrior, right before her eyes. His broad chest expanded as he took in deep breaths, like swimmers do before going a distance underwater. His stance changed, became springy as he balanced on the balls of his feet. The other men seemed oblivious to the change. They were gloating, sure that they'd won this battle, and weren't paying attention.

Which was perfect.

Grace had no idea how good a fighter this man was, but she was willing to risk everything to find out. And if he couldn't overwhelm four men, she'd rather die by a shot to the head trying to get away than by slow torture.

"Hey!" Leather Coat bellowed to him. "You heard me! Turn around right now, you fuckhead, or I'm blowing a piece of her away."

Leather Coat was distracted by the drama. Like all bullies, he relished control, imagining victory before victory was his, simply because it was unthinkable that he lose. She'd known people like that, who loved wielding overwhelming power over others because it fed their ego. And Leather Coat's ego must be really pumped right now, holding a gun on a woman, facing an unarmed man four to one. The kind of odds bullies loved.

Grace could feel him relaxing, letting down his guard, ready to enjoy the next couple of minutes. It was a done deal, as far as he was concerned.

Over her dead body.

She waited a beat, allowing Leather Coat's grip to loosen further, gave a sharp nod to the man, hoping he understood, reached into her purse with a lightning fast move, brought the Mace canister up to Leather Coat's face and sprayed him full in the eyes.

His bellow could be heard in New Jersey. The big black gun clattered to the ground as he brought both hands to his eyes, roaring with pain and rage.

What she saw next defied belief. Dark Hair had moved

almost too fast for her to track. Before her hand was in front of Leather Coat's face, he was in the air, twirling, foot lashing out, striking his adversaries with meaty *thunks!* Barely landing lightly on his feet before twirling again.

Grace staggered back, hoping the dark-haired man knew what he was doing, because she'd just put her life in his hands. Leather Coat would surely shoot to kill just like he said he would if he caught back up with her.

They went down like felled trees: one-two-three-four. She still hadn't registered what she'd seen when the man straightened, and—completely non-winded, completely in control—pulled out something sleek and black from his pocket and spoke into it quietly in a language she didn't understand, then flipped it closed.

Leather Coat lay on the ground in a fetal position, his desperate gasps for breath echoing off the walls of the alley. The man who had attacked Dark Hair was on his side, eyes rolled up in his head. The man in the fleece track suit lay still, unconscious, his arm bent at an unnatural angle. The man in the bomber jacket had gleaming white bone showing through his jeans, blood pooling under him. The kick had smashed his femur. He was bleeding profusely, the rain sluicing the blood-red water under him into the drains.

Grace stood in the rain, shocked and shivering.

The dark-haired man looked down at the four men for a heartbeat, his face cold and remote, then bent calmly and snapped their necks with an efficient twist of his huge hands. She could hear cartilage crack, four times. Then he calmly scooped up his two guns and his knives.

Grace bent over, ready to vomit her guts out, when a strong hand took hold of her arm. "We don't have time for that," the dark-haired man said. "Sorry."

She straightened and looked him full in the face, wincing, expecting a monster, expecting to see brutality and savagery. What she saw instead was a weary kind of gentleness and what looked an awful lot like remorse.

"I'm so sorry." His deep voice was low as he wrapped a huge hand around her arm. "For everything. But now we must go."

Though his voice was calm, he moved fast. In a moment, they were at the mouth of the alley, moving out into the street. He still had his hand around her arm. He wasn't holding her tightly enough to hurt, but he seemed to be able to propel her forward through the rain as if she had wheels instead of feet.

In an instant, they were out on the sidewalk and the man was checking the street carefully, the kind of survey a soldier would give to enemy terrain.

The bell over the gallery door rang and Harold appeared in the doorway. He clutched the doorjamb for support. One eye was swollen shut and his face was blood streaked. He blinked, then saw her. Grace's heart clenched as she saw relief flood his face. His free hand reached out to her, shaking, half in and half out of the doorway. "Grace. Oh my God, you're alive." Harold's trembling voice cracked, barely audible over the rain.

Tears flooded her eyes. Harold, her friend. She started forward and was held back by the dark-haired man's strong hand around her arm.

She met his eyes. "Let me go." She wanted to shout, but her voice came out a hoarse whisper. She pulled against his hand, but it was like pulling against a steel pillar. He wasn't letting her go.

"Grace," Harold quavered, hand outstretched.

Every muscle in her body was tense and shaking, including the muscles in her throat. She had to cough to speak. "Please." She was trembling so hard she could barely stand. "Let me go to him. He's wounded, he needs help."

The rain was pelting down hard now, moving in sheets down the street. She was soaked and chilled to the bone. She was scared and she wanted to get to Harold *right now*. If she was scared and hurting, he would be doubly so.

The man had maneuvered himself so that he was between her and the street. His shoulders were so broad she couldn't see around him, he blocked off her entire visual horizon. He scrutinized the surrounding buildings again.

The rain was making the blood on Harold's face run, his white shirt splashed with pale pink color, plastering his sparse gray hair against the skull. He swayed.

"Oh God." Grace's heart was pounding. She put her hand over the man's where he was grasping her upper arm, his hand so big it met around her arm, coat and all, and nearly snatched her hand away at the heat. It was freezing cold outside, but his huge hand was so hot it felt like an iron against her wet coat. "Let me go to him, please."

Another tug, the man's hands tightening further, and then suddenly . . . Harold disappeared. Or his head did. Where his head had been there was a pink mist dissipating fast in the rain. Half a second later, Grace was facedown on the sidewalk and a ton of male was on top of her. Something was pinging, gouging holes in the pavement, in the walls of the gallery. Shards of concrete rained down on her.

Grace was so shocked, it took her long seconds to realize what the sharp cracks were.

"Goddammit. A sniper." The deep, low voice was speaking right into her ear, so close she could feel the puffs of his breath. He lifted and pulled her closer to the curb until she was resting against the front fender of a big black vehicle. "The engine block should stop a bullet. Stay here and don't move."

Another crack sounded and his heavy body jolted.

Grace lifted her head slightly to look at him. She didn't process his words in any way. She looked back down the street to where a limp collection of clothes lay sprawled across the doorway to the gallery, the rain washing red, then pink, into the gutter. None of this made any sense, least of all the remains of her best friend, a shattered mass of pink-and-gray flesh.

"Harold," she whispered, her voice shaking so hard she could barely articulate.

"Is dead," the man said brutally. "Now we have to stay alive. No, dammit." He brought an arm like iron over her back. She'd been blindly trying to rise up, putting her shaking hands on the ground to lift herself up to . . . to go to Harold.

To do *something*.

"Stay *down*, dammit," the man on top of her hissed. One huge hand covered the back of her head and pressed until her cheek lay on the rough pavement. She watched the big raindrops ping and bounce off the concrete, her mind completely blank, empty.

The heavy man on top of her shifted and started talking in a low, deep, urgent voice. What was he saying? Whatever it was, there was no possible response in her. She was too shocked to make out more than a few words here and there. *Sniper . . . west side of Lexington, second-story window, come from Park . . .*

It took her several seconds to realize that he wasn't talking to her but into a cell. He was discussing some kind of strategy. The words flew into her head and then right back out again. The only thing that penetrated the fog in her head was the deep calm of his voice, the assurance. He could have been a man discussing the menu of that night's meal. It was amazing to think that voice came from a man under fire.

Even his body was calm. His coat must have been open because she could feel the heat of his wide chest against her back. His heartbeat was strong and steady, unlike her own trip-hammering one, beating wild and high in her chest. His breathing was calm, regular, while she was gulping in great gasps of air that choked her and burned her lungs.

A click and the cell phone closed.

Tears were running down her face, lost in the rain.

"My men are coming." That deep, calm voice next to her ear again. It was insane, but somehow it calmed her, just a little. "I'll get you out of here, I promise."

A huge hand planted itself next to her face on the pavement. He was holding his gun, big and black and oily-looking. Something else caught her attention. A big pool of deep red forming underneath her, spreading and turning pink in the rain.

She was shot! Oh my God, she'd been *shot*!

Grace stopped breathing for a moment, trying to take stock through her shattered senses. She was freezing, lying in a puddle of red-tinged water, her cheek grinding against the rough pavement, trying to breathe, though the man on top of her weighed a ton. She was cold and shocked and terrified.

But not wounded.

The amount of blood that was now flowing freely down into the gutters was from a serious wound and wasn't coming from her. Couldn't. She'd have felt a wound that deep.

"You're—" Her voice wasn't coming out at all. She tried again. "You're wounded."

He grunted in answer and shrugged, the movement sending a fresh welling of red onto the pavement.

Grace chanced a look upward, trying to gauge how badly he was wounded. God, if he was dying, what could she do?

But he didn't look like he was dying. His face didn't in any way betray that he was wounded. He wasn't grimacing in pain, he wasn't pale. His skin was that same smooth olive tone as before and he looked as if he were trying to figure out a particularly difficult chess problem, not as if he were in a life-or-death situation with a hole in his chest and a man with a rifle just waiting for them to show. Shockingly, when he met her eyes, he even smiled.

It was faint and over almost before it began, but it was definitely a smile. Dying men don't smile. Or at least she imagined not.

Only one way to find out. "Are we going to die here?" she whispered.

"No." His jaws clenched. "Nothing will happen to you, I swear. I won't let it."

He rolled away from her, gun at the ready. Grace twisted her head to watch him. His parka had a big hole in it and underneath that, a big hole in the shoulder, oozing blood.

"My God," she whispered. "That's serious." Her fingers scrabbled for her purse. It had fallen in the middle of the sidewalk, the long strap facing them, thank God. She caught the tip and started pulling it toward her. "I've got a scarf in my purse. I can use it as a pressure bandage to stop—"

The world blew up in her face. One second her purse was inching its way to her and the next there was a big crater in the pavement and tiny pieces of black leather floated in the air.

Grace's ears rang as all outside sound was cut out. Her face and neck hurt. When she put her hand to her face, it came away wet and red.

All her senses were gone. She was screaming but she couldn't hear herself. She'd lost all sense of up or down and it was only when the man's face came into view that she realized she'd been blown on to her back.

His mouth was moving, the strong cords in his neck were standing out, so it was entirely possible he was shouting, but she couldn't hear a thing. It was like being dead, or halfway into a coma. Large hands were frantically touching her all over. His long fingers sifted through her hair, feeling every inch of her skull.

She winced when he touched the back of her head. It was incredibly painful. Maybe she wasn't dead, after all.

The man threw his black parka onto the sidewalk and when that was blasted away, he lifted himself up, big black gun in hand. He grasped the gun with both hands, sighting over the top of the roof of the car, and shot three times. She couldn't hear anything but she could see his hand buck slightly with each shot, then come straight back to the position it had been in before. Three pretty, bright brass casings twirled in the air. One fell on her hand and she jerked to roll it off. It was hot and burned her.

Then suddenly she was lifted to her feet, an iron arm around her waist, and she was half carried to a waiting car on the street. Men were all around her now, in a tight circle, backs to her. Big men, dressed in black, all carrying weapons.

She was literally thrown into the backseat of a large car, her head banging against the far window. Another body piled in, the door slamming closed just as the car took off so fast it pressed her against the seat.

A second later, the car took a corner violently. She bounced off the door and would have fallen to the floor if an arm hadn't come around her shoulders, anchoring her to a hard male body.

The car raced through the streets, veering wildly around corners. Grace would have been tossed brutally around if she weren't clamped to the man's side.

She burrowed into him, the one steady thing in a wildly careening universe. She'd seen five men killed, she'd seen her best friend's head blown off, someone had shot at her. It was as if she'd entered another dimension, a world of darkness and danger, feral and lethal.

A deep, calm voice sounded in her ear. "It will be all right."

No, no it wouldn't be all right. Not ever again.

She closed her eyes and clung to him as they raced through the streets. The big car had excellent suspension and the driver was superb. They were traveling as fast as an ambulance or a police car racing after a suspect, but of course without the siren, so the driver had to zip around other cars like a crazed man. It was a miracle they didn't crash and burn.

Grace was in a fog of pain and shock, with barely the energy to hope that the car wouldn't run into a light pole or overturn at a corner. She rocked against the man holding her as his blood soaked through her coat. When she felt the wetness she pulled away, horrified to see the front of her coat wet with his blood. She looked up at him, at that calm, strong face. He looked as if absolutely nothing was wrong. As if he hadn't been assaulted, shot at, wounded.

But the wound was real, she could see the mangled flesh. "You need to close that wound with something or you'll bleed out."

What to use to staunch the wound? The scarf in her purse was long gone. A shrug and her coat was off. The lining was a silk and polyester blend. Maybe that would do as a pressure bandage, though she didn't know the absorption properties of polyester. Still, it was the only thing she had, so she started ripping the lining. Her hand was covered by his broad, olive-toned one.

"Not necessary."

"You're bleeding!" Grace could hear the hysteria in her voice. Of all the horrible things that had happened since she'd walked into Harold's gallery, this was one she could do something about. Not much, but something. "We have to stop the bleeding." She batted his hand away, crumpled up the back panel of her jacket, pressed it against his wound and held it tightly.

Surely she was hurting him, but he gave no sign of that, not even a grunt. He just closed his eyes when she pressed against his shoulder.

"Sorry," she whispered. He looked a little pale now, though it was hard to tell in the darkened cabin of the car. "I know I'm hurting you. But we'll be at the hospital soon and they'll stitch you up. It will be okay, you'll see."

She threw his words of comfort right back at him. The usual cheery words, words that were often overused and were often untrue. Life sometimes opened wounds that never healed. She hoped this one would. He'd saved her life.

The man leaned his head back against the headrest and

closed his eyes. One big hand came up to cover hers. It was still shockingly warm, considering they'd been in the freezing rain and that he'd lost a lot of blood. "Not going to the hospital," he said softly. "Not safe."

Grace waited a few beats while what he said penetrated her weary brain, then jerked when she realized what he'd said. "That's insane. Of course we have to take you to the hospital. You've been *shot*."

His eyes opened suddenly, looking at her intently. Their faces were only inches apart. His eyes were chocolate brown, intelligent, weary. He reached up a hand to touch the scrapes and cuts on her face. His fingertips came away red and he held them up, studying them. "And you've been shot at." Something flashed in his eyes, something hot and dangerous. "I'd kill them again for this. I'm sorry it was quick."

Grace shivered. It was as if someone had opened a window and let in the chill winter air. "Never mind that, they're all dead. Now we have to deal with your wound."

"Yes, and yours. Just not in a hospital."

Grace blinked. "If not in a hospital, then where?"

He glanced out the window, jaw muscles jumping. "Here."

The car took a sudden turn into a garage entrance, plunging full speed down a ramp, braking inches from a concrete wall. Grace would have fallen to the floor if the man hadn't braced her. The car was still rocking when the passenger doors were wrenched open and Grace was lifted out by two men.

Armed men surrounded the car and she found herself in the middle of a little phalanx, together with the dark-haired man. The armed men moved fast, as a unit. In an instant they were in an elevator. It was large enough to accommodate the team, and rose quickly. Grace looked up above the door to see what floor they were going to, but there was nothing. No indication of what floors they passed. She glanced to the side, to the big shiny brass panel with the CLOSE DOORS button. It was the only button on the panel. They were in an elevator that only stopped at one floor. At the top of a building, apparently, because they rose at an ear-popping pace.

The men stood at attention, surrounding them with their bodies, weapons drawn.

One of the men, tall and very fit, with a white streak in his black hair, turned to the man with her. "Glad you're safe, Drake." He glanced down at the shoulder wound, unflinching, as if he'd seen many of them. "Dr. Kane's on his way, just like you asked."

Drake. The man's name was Drake. She had no idea if that was his first name or his last name.

She had no clue who he was, or where she was. All she knew was that she had been caught in the middle of what looked like an assassination attempt in which her best friend had violently lost his life. She was now in an elevator in the middle of a group of hard-looking armed men and had no idea what plans they had for her.

All of a sudden, it occurred to Grace that she was a witness. A witness to four murders. Five, counting Harold. Actually, six, assuming this Drake had killed the sniper. And they were definitely not headed toward the nearest police station so she could testify to what she'd seen.

She looked around, her heart starting to pound. Every man there was taller than her, way bigger than her, immensely tougher. They looked strong and dangerous, none more than their boss, the man they called Drake.

He hadn't threatened her in any way, it was true. Indeed, the threat of harm to her had been used against him.

But she was in an enclosed space with him and this small

army of men, who looked perfectly capable of violence, and she knew for a fact that Drake was capable of terrifying, swift and terrible violence.

If he meant her harm in any way, she was as good as dead. Nothing she could do could stop him or even slow him down. She didn't even know where she was, and no one else knew where she was.

For an instant, Grace regretted her quiet life. She had a few friends, but they didn't meet up that often. Everyone was busy, no one more than she was. She essentially worked around the clock, eating and sleeping at odd hours. She could be missing for several weeks, even a month, before anyone really took notice.

The person she saw the most was dead, his head shattered by a sniper's bullet.

She'd had lunch with one of her best friends, Alice Restrepo, the day before yesterday. They only saw each other about once a month. How long would it take Alice to report her missing to the police? When Grace didn't answer the phone, Alice would just assume she was consumed by a painting. The bell of worry would ring eventually, but by that time, Grace could be long dead. Could be at the bottom of the Hudson River or in a concrete piling in New Jersey. Could be raped, tortured to death, her mangled body buried where no one would ever find her.

She shivered, looking down at her feet, wishing she were invisible. Though no one was paying particular attention to her, she had no illusions that she could make a run for it. A private elevator spoke of lots of money buying lots of privacy.

With a ping, they arrived at wherever it was they were going. The elevator doors opened with the quietest of *whoosh*es. In front of them, across a very large hall, was a door worthy of the gate of a fortress. Twelve feet high at least, made of shiny steel.

The men around her filed out, fanning out into a security perimeter, but Grace stood still, eyes fixed on the ground, trying to control her trembling. Drake stood beside her, unmoving.

"Boss . . ." one of the men said. The men were obviously quivering with eagerness to get him behind that huge steel door.

"Go now, I'm fine," Drake said quietly. They didn't look happy, but they did it. They were used to obeying this man.

Drake pushed a button and the doors of the elevator closed again.

Grace stepped back and looked him full in the face. He winced a little at what he saw on hers.

"You're frightened." The deep voice was soft. He lifted a large, blood-stained hand to her cheek. His touch was soft, though she could feel the calluses on his fingertips. "I'm sorry about that. I'm sorry about everything. More than I have words for. You've become involved in . . . a business dispute through no fault of your own. You've lost a friend and you're hurt. I cannot tell you how much I regret this. But it's done. And now you need to be kept safe from my enemies and you need medical care. All of this exists and is waiting for you behind that door you saw."

She stared at him numbly. Though his touch had been fleeting, she still felt the warmth along her cheek.

For all she knew, this was a serial killer just waiting to entice her into his fortress. Certainly he had dealings with criminals. It was entirely possible he was a criminal himself. But the regret in his voice sounded sincere. And he wasn't pushing her out of the elevator and into whatever was behind that door. Something in his stance told her that he would be willing to stay here forever, dripping blood on the floor, until she left the elevator of her own free will.

He swayed slightly, then brought himself back upright. The muscles in his jaw worked. There was a soft plop and when Grace looked down, another drop of bright red blood joined the small puddle on the floor.

Oh my God. He was badly wounded, he'd lost a lot of blood. He was barely standing, his forehead was beaded with sweat. And yet here he was, standing with her until she took a decision, patiently waiting for her.

Grace wasn't too good with people, but like many introverts, she was an observer. What she saw before her was patience and regret with an overlay of pain and fatigue. No cruelty or craziness.

"Okay," she said softly. "Let's go in."

Three

Drake kept himself upright by sheer willpower. That, and searing, devastating guilt that he'd ruined the life of this beautiful woman. It wasn't a coincidence that his attackers had come while he was out in the alley watching her in the gallery and that they used her to get to him. He knew who they were, too. Undoubtedly, Dmitri Rutskoi was behind this.

Rutskoi had come prancing into his office expecting to be made Drake's lieutenant and hadn't taken it well when Drake had thrown him out. Drake knew Rutskoi. He was a true soldier. If he'd made it his mission to go after Drake, he wouldn't stop until one of them was dead. And he'd undoubtedly partnered up with Drake's direct competitor in the Americas, Enrique Cordero. Drake had recognized two of Cordero's goons.

Somehow Rutskoi knew about Grace, which meant that Rutskoi and Cordero were willing to go through her to get to him.

The thought terrified him. It was worse than the wound in his shoulder. He'd been shot before and he knew this was nasty but not serious. A few days of rest and he'd be fine. But the thought of Grace falling into the hands of his enemies, of being maimed or tortured or killed because of him—it drove him crazy.

It had taken all his willpower to stay still in the elevator to allow Grace to choose to enter his domain. He and only he could offer safety. Offering her a choice was the only gift he could give her and it was a false one, because if she had balked, he'd have ordered his men to carry her in by force, even kicking and screaming. He'd have hated it, but he'd have done it, no question.

The alternative, letting her go, was unthinkable. Right now, the only safe place for her on this earth was by his side. Anywhere else, and she was a gorgeous target, a bull's-eye painted right on that smooth forehead.

He watched her face, making sure nothing showed on his.

She was swaying a little, shaking with adrenaline aftermath and cold, arms locked around her midriff, as if she needed comfort only she could give herself. Some flash of intuition told him that she often did this—held herself because no one else did.

It was one of the most shocking things he knew about her. Her essential solitude, so unusual for a woman who looked like her. From what he'd been able to see, her closest friend had been Harold Feinstein and now he was dead. She'd watched his head explode.

The harsh overhead elevator light showed up every scratch, every drop of blood on her pale skin. He could clearly see the broken skin at her temple where the muzzle and front sights of the SIG had ripped a hole. Her left cheekbone was rubbed raw from where he'd tried to grind her face into the pavement in an effort to make sure she didn't present a target.

She was shocked, pale, hurt and bleeding. Shaking, hair wet and muddy, clothes dirty and torn.

Even so, she was the most beautiful woman he'd ever seen.

He punched the button and the doors of the elevators opened. Drake couldn't see any of his men but he knew they were close.

Grace looked as if she would shatter if he touched her. Her skin was waxen, the bruises shockingly dark against the preternaturally pale skin. Did he dare put his arm around her? He didn't want to scare her, but she looked as if she would fall down in the next minute if he didn't do something fast.

He compromised by taking her arm and walking forward. She came along, stumbling slightly.

They crossed the big, empty hall. It was brightly lit and had security cameras all around the ceiling molding, watched over 24/7 by a team of nine men in the basement, working in shifts of three. Drake punched in a seven-digit code, then put his palm against a glass panel in the wall. The panel flashed a brilliant green. Putting a hand to the big steel door, he swung it open easily, testimony to the excellent hinges, considering the fact that it weighed 1,000 pounds. It was built to the exact same specifications as the vault in the basement of most Citibanks.

They crossed the threshold.

"Welcome," he murmured and watched her eyes widen at the three-story atrium.

If at any time in the past year Drake had dared to imagine crossing his threshold with Grace Larsen on his arm, it would have been after a date, though God knows he didn't date. But still, at times he allowed himself dreams in his own head. Who was to know? So he had imagined a nice dinner in the private rooms of an elegant restaurant, afterward perhaps a drink at a private jazz club, then home.

Home. In his home. It was only in the deepest stretches of the most sleepless nights that he allowed himself to imagine Grace in his home. He never brought women here. This was his sanctuary.

There was another luxury flat in another building where he brought his women. Smaller, because he didn't live there, just fucked there. Anonymous as a luxury hotel room, which was fine, because the women were anonymous. Good for sexual release, but that was about it. He rarely had sex with the same woman twice. Lately, it simply hadn't been worth the possible breach in security and he'd substituted his fist. And even that had become rare.

He'd have said that his sex drive had died before its time if it weren't for the fact that just touching Grace Larsen's torn jacket, knowing her arm was underneath, made his cock twitch. If he hadn't lost a whole shitload of blood, it would have been a full-blown erection.

Grace turned to him, her beautiful mouth an O. She clutched his arm, as if ready to take his entire weight if he collapsed, though she never could. "You've got to sit down while I call an ambulance. We should have gone straight to the hospital, I don't know why we were brought here, you've lost so much blood—"

The ringing in his pants stopped her in mid-sentence. Drake placed a finger against her mouth as he pulled out his cell phone with his other hand. He flipped it open, grimacing at the sight of his blood-stained finger against her mouth. He pulled his hand away from her.

"Yes?"

"Dr. Kane is on his way up, sir."

Drake closed his eyes in relief and flipped the cell closed. "A doctor is on his way up right now," he said gently. "He'll take care of you."

"*Me?*" Those beautiful eyes opened in astonishment. "I don't need taking care of, for heaven's sake. It's *you* who's been shot. You've been bleeding like a stuck pig. In fact," she said, frowning, "it's a miracle you're still on your feet. How—"

She was interrupted by the big steel door opening. The man walking through was one of the very few men on this earth Drake would allow direct access.

"Drake!" Benjamin Kane came in fast, still wearing his white coat. White coats usually conferred an aura of authority on doctors, but Kane's wild, unkempt white-blond hair, gangly, undernourished-looking frame and patchy blond goatee made him look more like a South American kidnap victim than the brilliant trauma surgeon he actually was. "I came as soon as I got the call. Christ, man," he continued, giving Drake a quick, professional up-and-down glance, "you need to stay out of trouble. You're too old for this shit. Let's get to the clinic right now. Good thing I stocked up on several bags of O. Come on, come on."

After a brief, surprised glance at Grace, Ben ignored her. Drake knew he was trying to be discreet but would be pumping him for info later. Ben walked ahead of them down the long corridor to the clinic, white coat flapping around his skinny knees.

Drake and his men were in a dangerous business. One of the first things he'd created after moving to America was a headquarters with its own infirmary. Hospitals, by law, had to report gunshot wounds, so he'd seen to it that he could deal with most of them himself.

He'd created an actual clinic—a big room, kept sterile, with everything a medical team could possibly want, though only Ben used it. He'd stocked it with all the equipment necessary to deal with injuries, including imaging machines, and Ben could manage most nonfatal injuries with what was in the room.

Drake let him go on ahead. Ben was fast—he'd be set up for surgery by the time Drake made it to the clinic.

Drake walked slowly down the corridor, gritting his teeth against the horrible feeling of weakness. He *hated* it. He'd always hated it. For all his life, any weakness—physical or emotional—could get him killed. Not showing any weakness at all was second nature.

The corridor looked a mile long, and the glare of the lighting hurt his eyes. It felt like he were walking uphill. Up a steep hill.

He would have expected Grace to follow Ben, but she stayed by his side. He didn't want her there. He wanted her in the clinic with Ben.

"Go on ahead," he said. His voice came out almost a whisper. He cleared his throat. "I'll catch up."

It was disconcerting to be on the receiving end of her gaze, intense, direct, like a blue-green spotlight. "No, I'll stay here with you." Her voice, though soft, was firm. Though he didn't remember her doing it, he was now aware that she'd put her arm around his waist to brace him. She walked slowly, matching him, pace by pace, watching him carefully.

Damn it, she needed medical attention. "Go!" he said harshly.

She merely shook her head, tightening her arm around his waist.

Fuck. Fuck, fuck, *fuck*. He needed her there as fast as possible, so Ben could start taking care of her. He gritted his teeth and tried to speed up, but tripped over his own damned feet.

"Here." Her voice was low, soft. She positioned her shoulder under his arm. "Put your arm around me."

Drake was close enough to smell her. He was intensely sensitive to smells. Once he'd thwarted an assassination attempt because he smelled smoke on the man's clothes in his hotel room. He'd turned down a number of women because of what he could smell underneath the perfume and lotions. He was absolutely convinced that emotions smelled.

He knew the smell of fear, of danger, of hatred. Grace's smell was utterly different. She had the smell of woman. A woman in springtime. Clean, through and through.

He stumbled. Grace held him, but barely. She was shaking with the strain and breathing heavily, the sound loud in the corridor.

Drake forced himself upright again and concentrated like a laser beam on the clinic's door ten feet away. He could do this. He'd done harder things and he could do this. A minute later, he was sitting on a hospital bed breathing hard, and Ben, scrubbed and gloved, was bent over him. Surgical instruments lay gleaming on a tray and Ben held a big pair of sharp scissors to cut Drake's shirt off.

"Okay, buddy. Let's take a look at what we've got here. I've got the X-ray machine up and running if we need it." The scissors came closer and Drake batted them away.

"Check the woman first."

Ben froze and looked at Grace, whose face was a mask of astonishment.

"What?"

"You heard me. And it's not like you to need information twice. You're wasting time and that's not good for a trauma surgeon. You're not touching me until she is stitched up."

Ben took in a deep breath. "Okay, this is how it goes. This is what I got all those med school debts you paid off for me for. In school they teach you something called *triage*. That's French for selection, the idea being that you select out cases on the basis of the severity of the wounds and treat the most severe cases first. And that, my dear Drake, is you."

Drake sat back, tipped his head back and closed his eyes. "No. Her first."

Ben made a strangled sound of frustration. But he knew better than to argue. "Okay. Have it your way." Drake opened his eyes to watch Ben settle Grace into a chair. "Damn man," he grumbled to her. "Okay, okay, let's see what we have here."

Grace tilted her head up to look Ben in the eyes. "He's been bleeding badly," she said, whispering. She was trying to talk to Ben without him catching on. "He has a gunshot wound. I've just got cuts and scrapes. Please attend to him first."

"No." Drake put the last of his energy into his voice.

Ben's sigh was loud. "Head like a rock," he told Grace, raising his voice to make sure Drake could hear him. "What can I say? He's the one pays the bills. So, tell me where it hurts." He was swiftly gathering together the instruments he'd need for her on a tray, the clatter of steel on steel bright in the room.

She smiled at that. "More or less everywhere. Mainly here—" she pointed to her head, "here and here." She indicated her neck and elbow. "I hate this. I hate being treated while he's over there bleeding." Grace's eyes slid to his. Drake simply stared at her and she looked away.

"Well, my dear . . . What's your name, by the way? If I'm going to clean you up, I should know your name. I'm Ben, by the way." Ben was gently cleaning the scrapes on her hands. Grace hissed in a breath at the sting of the antiseptic.

Drake couldn't help it. He jerked as if he'd been buzzed by a cattle prod. "Ben . . ." he growled.

"Sorry." Both Ben and Grace spoke at the same time. She laughed, a soft little huff.

Ben slanted him a glance, then focused back on Grace. He was a good doctor, the best. Drake had to back off. She was covered with cuts and scrapes, there was going to be some discomfort while Ben cleaned her up.

But damn, he hated to think of her hurting. *Hated* it.

"So . . ." Ben had sterilized tweezers and was working on something in her hand. "Back to my question. What's your name? I need to work on my bedside manner, or so everyone tells me, so I need to have a name to do that."

"Grace," she said softly, then sucked in a breath. Ben stopped immediately. "Sorry. No, that's fine. I don't mean to be a wuss. Grace Larsen."

"Uh-huh." Ben had that distracted voice that meant he was intensely concentrating on what he was doing. "And what do you do, Grace Larsen?"

"I'm an artist."

"Artist, huh? I . . . see." Ben's hands stilled and he shot Drake a look. He knew what was in the study. He concentrated again on her, cleaning up the side of her face. He peered closely at her temple, gently lifting her hair away. "What happened here? Someone grind something into you?"

"You could say that." Her voice turned dry. "A gun muzzle. It wasn't fun."

"No, I bet it wasn't. The sights tore your skin. I don't want to put stitches in, though. I'm no plastic surgeon and you're too beautiful for me to mess your face up. But you might want to have that looked at later. I'll put in butterfly stitches. How we holding up, boss?" Ben raised his voice without looking over at him. "I'm wrapping this up."

Grace peered around Ben to look at him and he saw her eyes widen. "Listen, I'm fine now. Go to him, please."

Ben carefully placed the last butterfly stitch and looked at Drake, who was holding himself up by sheer willpower.

Ben scrubbed his hands carefully but fast, snapped on new latex gloves and came to him, holding a big syringe.

"Okay, my man, it's your turn, and it's about time." He cut away Drake's shirt, looked carefully at the wound without touching it. "Ricochet," he said finally, "you lucky bastard. If the force hadn't been almost spent by the time it made its way into your tough hide, you might have been a goner. As it is, it's shallow and it's going to be easy to get out. You got a free one there, Drake, my man."

Ben was carefully filling the big syringe with anesthetic.

"Not very much anesthesia," Drake said. "I don't want to lose the use of my shoulder and arm."

Ben looked at him, shocked. Drake nearly smiled. It took a hell of a lot to shock a trauma surgeon.

"You're crazy. I can't stitch up a bullet wound if it's not completely numb. You can't hold still for me. We're not out on the Afghani plains, Drake, we're in midtown Manhattan. Cleaning bullet wounds requires probing and debriding. It's going to fucking hurt if I don't pump you full of anaesthesia."

"No." Drake kept his voice firm, but only through a huge effort. "Just the bare minimum."

He couldn't lose the use of his shoulder and arm, not even for an hour. He had no idea how far his security had been breached. Every instinct he had told him that he was safe here, but there had to be a mole and he could be close by. The thought of Grace in danger while he had lost the use of his arm and shoulder was too frightening even to contemplate.

"So how the hell am I supposed to work on you if I'm fucking hurting you?" Ben asked in exasperation.

Drake closed his eyes and went away.

Four

It was just amazing to watch. Before the doctor could inject the anesthetic, this man, this Drake, as everyone called him, simply closed his eyes and . . . disappeared. It was as if he put himself into a deep sleep—actually it looked like more of a coma, though he remained sitting upright—in a second.

"What—what happened?" she asked. Her voice sounded shaky.

Ben looked up at her and frowned. "Don't go into shock on me," he warned. "At least not yet. I need to take care of Drake now."

"Of course," she said, ashamed. The man's wound was much worse than anything she'd suffered and he'd insisted she be treated first. The least she could do was not distract the doctor.

"Amazes me every time," the doctor said conversationally as he made three injections of anesthesia around the wound. He started cleaning the area, bloody gauzes dropping steadily into a steel receptacle. He took something that looked like cooking tongs and, after a few moments' fierce concentration, dropped a flattened piece of metal into the receptacle. "Hmm. Boat-tail Sierra MatchKing. Don't see too many of those in city shootings. Came from a military rifle."

He brought out a scalpel, needlepoint scissors and a curved needle with thread in it. Grace's stomach lurched.

"Are you—are you hurting him?" Grace asked.

"God knows. He's got this incredible control over himself and when he has to, he just disappears. Poof! He's gone." He shook his head. "Strongest son of a bitch I've ever met." There was raw admiration in his voice.

Grace had to look away, think of something else besides what Ben was doing to Drake's torn flesh. She looked around and took in the big room for the first time. "What is this? A private hospital?"

"You could say that." Amusement colored Ben's voice. "Yeah, you could say that. I like the idea. Drake Hospital. That's what I'm going to call it from now on. Drive him crazy."

Grace watched Drake's face. It was completely impassive. Even his eyes behind the closed eyelids were still.

"Can he hear you?" she whispered.

"Maybe. Maybe not. Who knows? I admire him tremendously, but he's an enigma. Who knows what goes on in his head? I sure don't."

Grace eyed what looked like a CAT scanner. "So. Where are we? Are we—are we in a private home?"

"Yep." He was bent over Drake's shoulder. She heard snipping sounds and swallowed heavily. "Drake's."

"So, um, there's this clinic in a home? How does that work? And are you the boss?"

She saw his mouth curve up even while he was intently focusing on what he was doing. "The boss? Me? With Drake anywhere within a hundred-mile radius? No ma'am. Absolutely not. I'm the hired help. Highly educated and highly skilled, it's true, but just the help."

"I—uh," she floundered, feeling suddenly weary. She hurt all over and was keeping herself from keeling over only by gripping the edges of the cot, intensely aware of the fact that she was alone in a building with God only knew how many men. Armed men. And alone in this room with two men she didn't know.

Something of what she was feeling must have shown on her face. He flicked a quick glance her way. When he spoke again, his voice held no teasing note at all. If anything, he sounded . . . kind.

"You must be frightened. Drake hasn't told me what happened, but it looks like the two of you were attacked. But you had Drake with you and he's the smartest, toughest, bravest man I know, so you were okay. As for this room, yes, it's sort of like a private clinic. Drake employs a lot of men and sometimes they're . . . injured. In the line of work they do. He's very private, so he decided to set up a sort of field hospital of his own."

"What line of work?"

Silence. When it became obvious he wasn't going to answer, Grace changed tack. "Have you . . . have you known him long?"

His mouth curved in a slight smile. Clearly, he felt this was something he could answer. "About four years. I was a surgical resident in my last year, with over a hundred thousand in student loan debts, when I came across a man who'd been shot. I patched him up as best I could and got him to the nearest hospital. He was one of Drake's men and the surgeon told Drake I'd saved his man's life. The next day, my debts were wiped out and Drake asked me to set up this clinic, with no limits to what I could spend. A young doctor's dream."

"And you work here all the time?"

"No, good God, no. I'd never keep my hand in. No, I work full-time in a hospital, but I'm on call for Drake. When he needs me, I come." He picked up the curved needle and thread. "You know what? I'll bet you anything that wherever he's gone to, he'd feel better if you held his hand."

"His hand?" Grace asked, startled. "I don't know him, he doesn't know me. How could my holding his hand bring him any comfort?"

Ben stopped and looked at her directly. "I'm just guessing here, but . . . he saved your life, didn't he?"

She nodded, numbly. "Well, maybe it wouldn't be too much to hold his hand, then."

Put like that . . .

Grace jumped down from the cot and nearly fell to the floor as her knees buckled.

"You okay?"

It was unthinkable that Ben be distracted from patching up Drake's wound. She stiffened her knees and straightened her spine. "Yes. I'm just a little . . . Yes. I'm okay."

She walked slowly over to the two men. Drake was utterly still. Though Ben was bent over Drake, she was aware that he was following her progress.

Grace took a hard metal chair, brought it close to the bedside and sat down. Acutely aware of Ben's attention on her, she reached out for Drake's hand. She stopped just before touching him, her hand hovering an inch above his.

His hand was huge, maybe the largest human hand she'd ever seen. Sinewy and rough, with odd-looking, tough yellow calluses along the sides of his hands. They were definitely not the hands of an office worker.

Most professions left signs on the body. Even clerical workers had bodies that became soft and round and stooped. She had no idea what business Drake could be in to have hands like this.

Ben's hands were those of a doctor, a surgeon. Though the skin looked soft, his long, elegant fingers were strong and supple.

Drake's hands looked like tools, immensely strong, sturdy, indestructible.

Slowly, she moved until her hand touched his, her palm covering the back of his hand. His skin was warm, almost preternaturally so. Her skin was chilled—like most operating rooms, this clinic was kept very cold and she'd been soaked by the rain. It felt like she was touching a small furnace. The heat crept up her arm.

Suddenly, Drake's hand turned until his palm was clasping hers, the grip warm and tight but not painful.

Startled, Grace looked at Drake's face. It was utterly expressionless, in the stillness of deep sleep. There was no sign of consciousness at all. And yet he was now holding her hand.

Ben was smiling slightly as he took stitches in Drake's shoulder.

Grace chanced a look. The wound was looking much better as Ben closed it into a neat, stitched line.

Now that his shoulder wasn't such a bloody mess that she had to avert her eyes, she looked at the rest of Drake's torso. She'd have had to be dead not to.

She'd never seen a body such as his. Dressed, you only noticed that he had unusually broad shoulders. But now that he was naked from the waist up, she could see what she'd only sensed before when he'd been lying on top of her on the sidewalk outside the gallery.

The man was raw, naked male power. He didn't have the bulked-up muscles of gym rats or wrestlers. His muscles were lean, so stripped of fat she could actually see the striations of muscle tissue under the skin. She knew her anatomy and could see the muscles, one by one, how they fit over one another, worked together. He must put himself through incredible workouts to have muscles like this, deep and toned.

He was almost frighteningly powerful. She'd seen how fast he could move, how deadly he was in a fight, how proficient with a gun. This man would make a formidable enemy.

He wasn't *her* enemy, though. Certainly not now. Now he was a wounded man, holding her hand for whatever comfort she could provide.

Ben snipped the last thread and started applying gauze to cover the wound.

She squeezed Drake's hand lightly. "It's going to be okay," she murmured. "The wound looks so much better now that Ben's stitched it up. Don't worry, you'll be fine."

She felt like a fool, talking to a man who couldn't hear her. And yet . . . his grip tightened slightly on her hand, a warm pressure, so slight she might have imagined it, but she didn't. She sat quietly, her hand in his, hoping she was providing some comfort.

By the time Ben straightened, Grace's head was nodding. God, she was tired. She felt like resting her head on the cot and going to sleep, simply letting herself black out, but she couldn't afford to rest yet. There was still the trip home to negotiate. How could she get home? Her purse was gone. She had no money for either a bus or a taxi. Maybe she could convince someone here to drive her.

Home. She wanted to go home. To seek comfort in her familiar surroundings. Fix herself a cup of tea, step into a hot tub of water. Try to wipe out the sight of Harold's head exploding.

Mourn him, in private. Nurse her wounds.

Her eyes hurt, her face hurt, her head hurt.

Her heart hurt.

It felt like some huge hole had been ripped in the universe and monsters had come rushing through it. Monsters who could attack a woman, use her to get to a man and, above all, blow a man's head off.

Every time she closed her eyes she could see Harold's death, as graphically as when it happened. And every time, her heart gave a huge kick in her chest. She'd been conditioned from childhood to understand that there was no justice in the world. The fact that Harold was kind-hearted and had a wonderful eye for art was no shield in this world, none at all. But his violent passing was hard to grasp. It was so difficult to contemplate a world without Harold in it.

Grace had so few things in her life, really. They could be counted on the fingers of one hand. Her art, Harold, her few other friends, her apartment. Her life revolved around these few elements, and now one of them—hugely important to her in every way—was gone, wiped out in a bloodbath.

Her eyes stung but she refused to let any tears fall. They would be saved for later, for when she got home. All through her childhood, she'd learned to control her tears, learned the hard way that they were for private moments only.

She yearned for the safety of her home. It wasn't luxurious, certainly nothing like the few glimpses she'd had of this penthouse apartment, with its eighteen-foot ceilings and plush carpets and antiques and artwork. Her home was modest, the most extravagant thing about it the skylight in her studio, which let in as much light as Manhattan ever offered. It was simply, even sparely, decorated, filled with works in progress.

She yearned for it the way a thirsty man yearns for water.

She felt exposed, naked here. Though she tried to control it, her hands were shaking, even the one in Drake's warm clasp. She was shaking all over.

Ben administered a syringe of what she assumed was an antibiotic. It was done. She was patched up, Drake was stitched up, she could go.

She stood. "Uh, Ben?"

He had pulled off the gloves with a snap and was putting his surgical instruments in an autoclave. "Yeah?"

"I wonder if—if it wouldn't be too much trouble . . ."

He turned, bright blue eyes direct. "Do you need something?"

Grace hated asking for favors, *hated* it. There hadn't been anyone to ask things of growing up and now, as an adult, she found she'd much rather do without than ask. That way she was never disappointed. But now she was forced into asking for help.

She could feel her face becoming warm. "I, um, I need to ask a favor. Could you perhaps lend me the money for a cab to get home? Or have someone here drive me? My purse was—" *blown up*, she almost said, but didn't. "Lost. I need to get home somehow."

"Okay," Ben said. "I'm sure Drake will—"

Drake's eyes popped open. "Absolutely not," he said in a low, deep voice.

Five

Shit shit *shit!*

Rutskoi closed his cell phone with a snap and hurled it against the wall of the apartment he'd rented under an assumed name in the Bowery.

It shattered into a thousand bits that fell to the floor with a clatter. At the Waldorf, it would have fallen to the lush rose-patterned carpet and there would have been maids to vacuum the mess up. But he'd had to leave the Waldorf. Going into the operational part of the mission, he'd left the soft world of luxurious living behind and entered the iron world of warfare.

Drake's driver had picked him up at the Waldorf, so Drake knew where Rutskoi was. If Rutskoi was foolish enough to continue staying there, his life wouldn't be worth shit.

Drake's revenge was always swift and lethal.

Rutskoi had realized it would come to this the instant the big street door of Drake's skyscraper had closed behind him with an audible *click*. He'd been so sure Drake would say yes to him—goddamnit, the man *needed* a lieutenant—that he hadn't really thought through the consequences of a no.

He had just made an enemy of one of the most deadly men on the planet. He needed help. He couldn't take on Drake alone, it would be suicide. And if there was one thing Rutskoi knew, it was that he wanted to live.

Large.

So he'd called in Enrique Cordero. Cordero had essentially run the Central and South American arms trade B.D. Before Drake. Cordero was smart—though undisciplined—and had avoided drugs and women, the markets the cops zeroed in on. He'd had a neat little business supplying Central and South America with arms before Drake came and sucked up all the oxygen.

Enrique would be up for payback, oh yeah. Up for getting his market back. Rutskoi could share. Hell, there was enough in Drake's business to keep ten men, a hundred. Word on the street was that Drake's deals raked in a cool billion a year in profit. Not to mention the value of the fleet of planes and ships and helos he used to transport them. Yeah, there was enough for two. He and Cordero could split up the markets, like one of those Renaissance Popes splitting up the New World.

Rutskoi would take North America, Europe and Asia. Cordero could take Central and South America and Africa, and be welcome to them. Rutskoi had had enough of third-world countries to last him the rest of his life. He wanted to do business where there were toilets and beds and sidewalks.

He'd had it planned down to the finest detail, with Cordero's sniper in an empty apartment across the street. The sniper had been lying in wait, prone, on sandbags on the little terrace, with orders to shoot everyone who could interfere with the kidnapping of Drake and the woman, this Grace Larsen.

Rutskoi had been inside the apartment with binoculars, away from the windows, directing the kidnapping.

The plan had been to wing Drake, shoot him full of Rohypnol, grab him and the woman and take them to a safe location. Tie Drake up and let him watch Cordero's goons rough the woman up until Drake coughed up his bank codes and passwords.

It all hinged on how much he cared for the woman.

Out of this entire fiasco, there had been one good bit of solid intel. Rutskoi had observed Drake with the woman. Drake had put himself in danger to protect her. Drake couldn't know that the sniper had orders not to kill him. In protecting her, he had been willing to sacrifice his life.

She was the key. This Grace Larsen was somehow the key to Drake. The man with no chinks in his armor now had one. A beautiful woman. The biggest chink in the world, a classic.

Get Grace Larsen, you got Drake. Once Drake was his, Rutskoi would become one of the most powerful men in the world.

Not bad for a former Russian army colonel. Not bad at all.

If there had been anything even remotely funny about the situation, Drake would have laughed at their expressions. Ben's jaw simply dropped and Grace's lush mouth opened in astonishment. They both looked utterly blindsided.

Well, what the fuck did they think?

They *weren't* thinking, that was the problem. Smart as Ben was, as talented as he was as a doctor, he didn't think like a soldier. It simply wasn't in him. And Grace was an artist, an incredibly gifted one who, from what he could see, lived a simple life, mainly inside her own head.

Neither of them could think strategically, carry the complex geometry of violence in their heads without it affecting their thought processes. Drake was born to this world, was at home in this world, was a goddamned *king* in this world.

He was born with the ability to think four, five, even ten strategic moves ahead. While his enemies were busy reacting to his first move, he saw straight through to the endgame. The endgame he inevitably won.

He remembered the exact second when he'd heard the sound behind him. His body prepared itself to react, but it was meat and bone and blood. Bound by the laws of physics and gravity.

His mind, however, held no such limitations and it saw, as clear as day, the consequences of what was happening.

His obsession with Grace had left him open, a man who'd never given anyone an opening. Right now, Grace Larsen was a huge opening through the heart of his life.

Time and again over the past year, he'd told himself that what he was doing was dangerous. He took every possible precaution, evading his own security, but nothing was perfect. So in this imperfect world, someone had somehow found out where he was going.

Though he'd lectured himself to be content with buying up all Grace's paintings and drawings, somehow it wasn't enough. Even knowing he was putting himself in danger, he persisted in seeing her.

He'd observed her twice a month for over a year now and though he was insane to hide in an alleyway which was a cul de sac, though he understood with half his brain that he was endangering his life twice a month, the other half of his head loved his obsession. He'd make his circuitous way back to his building each and every time walking a little lighter, head filled with images of her. He could see her in his mind's eye for days afterward, all the expressions that crossed her face. Laughing, serious, relaxed, tense in the few moments she showed new work until, inevitably, Feinstein smiled.

She was unlike any woman he'd ever known. In the past year, he'd handed over several hundred thousand dollars for her paintings. Her work was worth every penny and of course the money was nothing to him.

Still, he knew how poor she'd been. He'd checked her bank account and she'd had next to nothing. But all the money he poured into her artwork didn't change her lifestyle at all. The greed gene seemed to have passed her by completely.

Every single beautiful woman Drake had ever met wanted to enhance her beauty. Make it bigger and bolder, to wield more power over men. Above all, women wanted to stop the clock. They were obsessed with it.

They'd starve themselves, put themselves under the knife, inject themselves with a lethal toxin to smooth out their faces. None of it had anything to do with health and strength, it was all vanity.

Over the course of the year, Grace hadn't changed one bit. Though she could now afford designer clothes, the best hairdressers, she could probably fucking move into the most expensive spa in Manhattan and spend all her time there . . . she stayed exactly the same. He hacked her credit card accounts and the only thing she spent more money on than before was art supplies.

There was no vanity there. None at all, that he could see. She didn't buy herself new friends with her new money. If anything, at times she seemed a little lonely.

Christ, he knew what that felt like. Knew it in his bones.

Every time, he came away from watching her feeling a deep connection. It was insane, of course. The only connection was in his head. But even there, it was such a rare thing, he cherished it. Cherished just the notion of the existence of Grace Larsen, who seemed to have no ambition other than to make beautiful paintings, who seemed to have no greed or aggression in her.

It made him feel better just to know she was in the world. Because his world *was* full of violence and greed and treachery.

And today, tragically, his world had crashed into hers, changing it forever.

Ben was the first to recover. He turned to Grace. "Do you live alone?"

She looked startled, then uneasy. "Yes, I—I live alone." She clearly didn't like saying it.

Good girl, Drake thought. *Don't give out any personal information to anyone.*

She could to him, though. He'd rather rip his own throat out than hurt her. She didn't realize that yet, but she would.

"You have some nasty gashes in your head," Ben said. "I don't think you're concussed but I wouldn't swear in court that you're not. I think you should stay here for the time being, under observation. You'll be cared for here." He shot a look at Drake, who nodded his head slightly, amused that Ben had already taken her under his wing.

Drake hopped down from the hospital cot and walked over to Grace, standing so close to her she had to look up, not so close it would set off her alarms. Her face tilted up to his, expression wary, and weary.

"I've ordered some food brought up," he said gently. He reached out a hand and stroked the back of his index finger down her cheek. Her skin felt incredibly soft but chilly. She was in a state of mild shock.

Drake looked into her sea-green eyes, amazed at what he found there. Pain, shock, sadness. Those were to be expected. But other expected emotions were missing.

No hatred, no hostility, no animosity, even though she'd lost a friend and had been threatened and shot at because of him.

Above all, he saw absolutely no calculation in her sad, weary gaze. He couldn't remember the last time a woman had looked at him and seen a man and not a walking bank account.

She'd seen the car, the men he commanded, parts of his living quarters, including a private clinic. She hadn't seen it all, of course, but she'd seen enough to know he had . . . resources. None of that seemed to make any difference to her. While Ben had been stitching him up and he'd sent himself away from the pain, her slender hand in his had grounded him. He'd actually felt the human connection of solidarity from her, felt very strongly the comfort she'd wanted to give.

Drake couldn't remember the last time someone had offered him comfort. Certainly no woman in his life had ever tried to offer him anything, least of all comfort. They all wanted things from him, the bigger, the brighter, the shinier the better.

She was swaying on her feet, cold and wounded, and he snapped out of his reverie. Just being near her seemed to slow his thought processes down, make him clumsy and stupid. He couldn't stand to see her like this, hurting and sad. She was his responsibility, now. He had to start taking care of her.

"I need to go home," she whispered, eyes searching his. He didn't know what she was looking for. Permission? Or was she seeking some sign that he meant her harm?

"Grace," he said. "May I call you Grace? I heard you telling Ben your name."

As if he didn't know her name. As if it weren't engraved on his mind.

She nodded, eyes huge.

"All right then, Grace." Slowly, Drake drew in a deep breath, a prelude to what he had to tell her. He was only going to give her a small part of the truth, but even that was going to be hard for her to take. The whole truth would wipe her out. He'd have to portion it out to her over the next few days. "I think you should stay here, with me, for a . . . while. Until we're sure it's safe for you to return." Her eyes widened. "The men who came after me, they can easily find out where you live. They could come after you and probably will."

He made it sound like a probability, whereas it was a certainty. No one would have made a move like that without knowing everything about the players. They knew enough to use her as leverage against him. No fucking way they didn't have her address. No fucking way there wasn't an army camped out on her doorstep, just waiting to take her down.

What little color Grace had in her face left. She was the color of ice. "I hadn't even thought of that," she whispered.

No, she wouldn't have. This wasn't her world. Her world was full of beautiful shapes and colors. She swayed again and Drake caught her gently by the elbow.

"Ben," he said, without taking his eyes from hers, "leave the medicines we should be taking on the table. Thanks."

Ben understood that for the dismissal it was. A moment later, the door closed quietly behind him.

Drake waited for him to leave his apartment, then opened the door into the corridor. His quarters were seven large rooms making up one side of a skyscraper, all opening out onto a big corridor.

Drake ushered Grace out. This was in many ways a dream come true. All this past year, he'd caught himself wishing he could be with her. Wishing they could eat together, spend time together. And deep down, where no one could possibly know his thoughts, wishing that this beautiful woman could be his.

She was his now, all right. But not for long, because fate had dealt him a cruel, cruel blow. Thanks to him, this gentle, beautiful woman's life was now over.

Thanks to him, Grace Larsen was a dead woman walking.

Six

Grace was freezing cold. The temperature in the house was normal but she seemed to have a frozen core that simply wouldn't warm up.

It was all starting to catch up with her and she longed for the comfort and familiarity of home. Yearned for it with all her heart.

But when Drake told her that whoever had come after him would come after her, she'd felt a shock of recognition. She'd seen with her own eyes how ruthless the men who'd come after Drake were. How they hadn't hesitated to use her to get to him.

Finding her address would be easy. Harold's office had her address on file. If they knew her name, she was in the phone book. She shook at the thought of being alone in her apartment with killers coming for her.

Drake took her elbow and again, where his skin touched hers, heat bloomed. He bent his head to hers, face still, voice low and courteous.

"Would you like to wash up before eating something? It might make you feel better."

Oh God, a bath! Right then, Grace wanted a bath more than she wanted food or the oblivion of sleep. Sinking into clean, warm water, soaking her aching muscles—bliss. She nodded, clenching her jaws so her teeth wouldn't clatter.

"Come with me." He led her down the enormous corridor. Ben had disappeared and they were alone. She looked around, really noticing her surroundings for the first time.

It was the most . . . sumptuous home Grace had ever seen. And filled with color. They were walking on antique Persian rugs in the deepest reds and greens and blues she'd ever seen. Huge enameled vases in deep, bold hues held thriving plants as big as trees. They passed an open door that obviously led into the living room, so enormous the other end of it was lost in shadows, with comfortable, masculine-looking furniture arranged in groupings, one around a huge lit fireplace.

Finally, they reached a big wooden door. Drake reached around her to open it, then ushered her in.

It was a bedroom. His bedroom. "The master bathroom's through there," he murmured, nodding his head at another door at the end of the huge room. "I've had the bath drawn for you." He looked at her torn and dirty clothes and smiled faintly. "You'll want to change, but nothing of mine would fit you so I had one of my *gi*s laid out for you. I hope you'll find it suitable. It's brand new, I've never worn it. It's the only thing I can think of to give you. At least it will be comfortable and clean."

"Thank you," she said politely. "That's very kind. What's a *gi*?"

Again, that little half smile. "A *gi* is a training uniform for a number of martial arts. It has a kimono-like top and pants with drawstrings, so you can just cinch everything more tightly around you. You'll find it on top of the towel cabinet, together with everything you'll need for a bath."

He obviously had somehow found the time to give instructions to the army of servants he undoubtedly had to run such an enormous household. But when? She'd have sworn that she'd heard every word he'd uttered since arriving here.

"Okay, thanks."

He nodded his head and, cupping her elbow, led her toward the door on the far side of the room.

It felt like it took half an hour to cross his bedroom. She'd never seen a room so large. It was at least as large as the loft of one of Harold's sculptors in Tribeca. Only this wasn't minimalist black-on-white Manhattan décor; it was almost barbaric in its splendor.

There was a huge antique four-poster that could sleep a basketball team, with rich emerald-green sheets made of expensive polished cotton. And they'd definitely have to have been custom-made: no commercially made sheets would fit that huge bed. Her hands itched to touch the material, it looked so thick and soft. With an emerald-green custom-made down comforter on top.

Her own bed was nice. She'd splurged on a big bed with an orthopedic mattress, and she liked pretty sheets, but it was nothing like this.

Plants here, too. Huge and lush and thriving. The air had that freshness only plants could give a room.

Plush carpets in jewel tones were everywhere, and living-room sets were scattered throughout the huge space, creating intimate little corners.

They passed by a hearth made of black marble that was big enough to roast an elephant in. Someone had lit the fire at least an hour ago, because the fire was mature, its smokeless red-orange flames licking greedily upward.

Colors. There were so many rich, deep colors everywhere, and she realized how color starved she was in Manhattan, where everything seemed to be either black or white or—when designers went really wild—taupe and ecru.

Color was a gift from the gods, and how anyone could live in a black-and-white environment puzzled her endlessly. Here there was no dearth of colors. Colors and textures and—she had to keep from gasping—a view to kill for. They were very high up. The lights of Manhattan were spread out like an array of diamonds all across one wall. Thick green curtains hung at the edges of the big windows. At midday, the place must be flooded with light. She could see the Chrysler Building and the Empire State Building in the distance, and a deep black square close by that must be Central Park, so they were in a serious money zone. This kind of space in these zip codes was way up there in the mega-rich category.

She'd been so busy taking in her surroundings she hadn't spoken, but Drake seemed perfectly comfortable with silence. This was unusual. Most men weren't comfortable with silence. They wanted to hear the sounds of their own voices and they wanted to hear women echoing what they were saying. Luckily, Drake seemed as immune to that as she was.

They'd reached the far wall and a big white laminated door with a shiny brass handle. "Here we are," he said, opening the door.

Grace nearly gasped. It wasn't a bathroom, it was . . . it was an apartment. Certainly as big as her own apartment, with acres of rich green marble countertops, emerald green tiles, several amazingly elaborate shower stalls with an array of nozzles and . . . yes, a tub as large as a small pool with fingers of steam rising from it. And about a billion jets around the rim, promising a water massage guaranteed to ease the ache in her muscles.

Every cell in her body yearned to be in that tub, but there was something she absolutely had to know first.

She turned around to look Drake full in the face. She'd been stealing glances at him, fascinated by his hard face, but had been too embarrassed to stare. Now she studied him openly, studied those firm, almost ascetic features, the features of a strong man who'd seen and done hard things.

She looked him straight in the eyes. Eyes that were dark brown, with no striations at all. Just that solid color, as if a child had filled in his pupils with a crayon. The whites of his eyes were the clear white of someone who lived healthily. But one never knew.

She wrapped her arms around her midriff, a little scared because if he gave the wrong answer to her question, the answer she was dreading, she was in big trouble. Terrible trouble. Alone in a building with a man who seemed to be so powerful in so many ways, so very capable of crushing her.

Here goes nothing.

She drew in a deep breath, the words coming out in a trembling rush. "I'm sorry to have to ask this, but I can't stay here a second longer without knowing the answer. Please tell me that whatever all that violence was about, it wasn't about drugs. That this—" She waved her hand, encompassing the baronial splendor of the apartment. "—this isn't about drugs. I—I need to be certain about that."

Because otherwise, she'd just vomit her misery up and leave immediately, though she had no idea where she could go. Not with thugs possibly gunning for her. Assuming he even *let* her go.

Drake didn't say anything for a long moment, just watched her, eyes cool and calm. Her heart drummed wildly, like that of a trapped bird's.

Then he took her hand and placed it against his chest, right over his own heart. He'd had a clean black shirt waiting in the clinic and she could now feel that it was made of thick raw silk. Underneath she could feel slabs of hard muscle, his wiry chest hairs and the slow, strong beat of an athlete's heart.

"Put your mind at ease. What happened today had absolutely nothing to do with drugs," he said in a low, even voice. His gaze held hers, steady and direct. "I abhor drugs as much as you do. Maybe more. I would die rather than have anything to do with them."

Grace was an observer, used to living on the sidelines of life. She'd developed a good understanding of people. He was either telling the truth or he was a world-class liar.

"However," he said softly, "what you saw had everything to do with money and power."

"Money and power." She shrugged her shoulders, hand still on his chest. All of New York ran on money and power. "That's nothing. I just couldn't bear the thought of being in the home of someone who is involved in drugs."

"I'm not." He dipped his head briefly, eyes locked on hers. "You have my word."

Christ, she must be insane, because she was buying this, totally. She had the distinct impression he rarely gave his word and when he did, he kept it. Whoa, maybe she *was* concussed. She searched his eyes for a moment longer and found nothing but directness, some sadness and some pain.

Against all the odds, she believed him.

"Okay. I'm sorry I asked, but I had to." A huge weight had been lifted from her chest.

He dipped his head again. "I understand completely."

Slowly and carefully, he lifted her hand from his chest and brought it to his mouth, placing a gentle kiss on the back. Even his mouth was hot, the soft brush of his lips painting a small circle of flames on the back of her hand.

Her body blossomed.

She drew in a deep breath and he released her hand.

She felt behind her blindly and grasped the shiny brass handle. "So I'll, um, take a bath. And I think you should sit down, right now. Are you in pain?"

He looked surprised at the question, eyes flaring briefly. "Nothing I can't handle. Don't worry about me, you go take your bath and soak your muscles. You were tossed around pretty brutally. I'm going to take a bath of my own in another room. And here—" He dug into his pants pocket and held some kind of electronic device in the huge, callused palm of his hand. She looked it over carefully. It was sleek and essentially featureless save for a big button on one side. "Take this with you. Put it on the side of the tub within easy reach. If the hot water makes you feel faint in any way, just press it and I'll come. Don't lock the door. I'll come as fast as I can."

Well, she was going to be naked in that tub, so there wasn't much of a chance of her pressing that button. She was a big girl. If she felt faint, she'd just get out. Still, to make him happy, she grasped one end. He held on to the other. They were linked by five inches of plastic.

"Call me if you need me." His voice was insistent. A muscle rippled in his jaw, as if he were clenching his teeth against saying something more.

She looked at the lines of his face—harsh, strong, totally unlike any male she'd ever met—and realized something terrible. Something that shook the foundations of her world.

Oh God.

She was attracted to this man. Massively. Wildly.

This was clearly insane. Being shot at had made her crazy. That was the only explanation possible. This had never happened to her before, ever. She had to be in bed with a man for her body to bloom as it had just done, by the simple touch of his lips to her hand.

A hot flush had shot through her, head to toe, and it wasn't menopause. It was the real deal. As if by merely kissing her hand, he'd speeded up the rate at which the blood circulated in her body. Actually, that sounded about right because her heart had speeded up as well and was now pounding so hard it was a miracle he didn't hear it.

Pools of that heat centered in intense flashes in her breasts and between her legs. When his lips touched the skin of her hand, she'd clenched tightly between her legs, the first time that had ever happened to her, so startling it took her a second to even recognize it as desire.

Desire for a man who was scary. She knew nothing about him except that he appeared to be rich and powerful. Powerful enough to have men gunning for him. Powerful enough to have men with guns protecting him.

In her experience, rich and powerful men were obnoxious creatures, completely concentrated on themselves, oblivious to others. This man, Drake, had proved himself to be the exact opposite. He'd disarmed himself for her, shielded her with his body, insisted that she be treated for scrapes and bumps before Ben dealt with his bullet wound.

Rich, powerful men had obnoxious vibes coming off them in almost palpable waves. She wasn't getting this from Drake at all.

What she was getting from him was desire. Rich, powerful *sexual* vibes, like some intense spice, centered on her.

And—whoa—she felt them right *back*.

This was absolutely nuts. What did she know about him except that he was lethally dangerous? He'd fought like a trained soldier, yet he didn't act like one. Soldiers were trained to obey and this man looked like he would obey no one. An army of one.

Whatever he was, whoever he was, he was way too rich for her blood. She was going to get mangled. She had no defenses whatsoever against the solid male power she could feel streaming from him.

Desiring him was suicide.

She stepped back from him, as if backing off from a force field, clutching the electronic device in her hand.

He stepped back, too. Maybe he sensed how rattled she was and knew he had to back off. He nodded at the device.

"Keep that close to you at all times and don't hesitate to use it if you feel faint. Don't lock the door," he repeated, as she started closing the door in his face.

No, she wouldn't lock the door. It was his home and anyway, he looked like the kind of man who could pick any lock in a heartbeat.

She wanted him.

Drake eased himself into the steaming hot water in the bathroom off the living room, careful not to wet his bandages, sighing at the hot jets massaging his sore muscles.

Grace definitely wanted him, which was good, because

they had to start their affair soon. Fucking her was a strategic necessity, something he knew he had to do, but it wasn't a sacrifice. It was his deepest desire. Only now that he'd been close to her, touched her, could he admit openly to himself how much he wanted her. Like he wanted his next breath, that's how much he wanted her.

And now she was here, in his home, naked, right this minute.

His jaw clenched, imagination running riot at the thought of Grace naked in his tub.

That long, white neck tilted back over the lip of the tub, all the jets firing, clouding the water, revealing then hiding that lovely pale body. He could almost see her beautiful face relaxing, the lines of pain and stress slowly disappearing.

It wasn't like him to have to imagine a naked woman. Most women he'd wanted naked were only too willing to comply.

He'd noticed a change in naked women over the years he'd lived here. There was no softness anymore. Most beautiful women took pains to become buff, tightly muscled. *Hardbodies*, the Americans called them. It puzzled him so. Who wanted a hard woman in this hard world? The whole point of having a woman of your own—not that he'd ever wanted one—was to have some softness in your life.

But the women he'd been with over the past few years had been hard, inside and out. Totally invulnerable. The complete opposite of Grace Larsen, with her smooth, soft skin and even softer heart. She was right to keep away from the world, because the world was one giant hammer, just waiting to come smashing down on someone like her.

It had almost smashed her today.

He clutched the rim of the tub tightly, feeling a little flare of pain in his shoulder. Not much. Ben had given him something that dulled it, while letting him have as much use of his hand and arm as possible. And anyway, pain was nothing. Learning how to disregard pain had been his first lesson learned.

The biggest pain in his body right now was his straining erection at the thought of a naked Grace in his home. More nights than he cared to think about, he'd jacked off to thoughts of her. All he had to do was conjure up the fleeting glimpses of her from the alleyway and instant boner, as the Americans would say. And that was when what he knew of her was those brief flashes in the gallery, separated by heavy plate glass, as she talked to Harold Feinstein. There had been no way for him to know how amazingly soft her skin was, how the touch of her hand could send his pulse racing, how every cell in his body came to a point in her presence, like iron filings to a magnet.

God, she was beautiful. She was smart and brave and kind, but fuck, she was so beautiful, too, with the kind of beauty that didn't dissipate with wear and tear. Muddy, bloodied, wet and bedraggled, she'd simply taken his breath away.

Everything about her seemed designed specifically for him, starting from her eyes, the most beautiful he'd ever seen. Large, slightly tilted, not blue, not green—the exact color of the Mediterranean at noon.

Or her breasts, clearly visible underneath the wet sweater she'd been wearing. It had also been clear that she wasn't wearing a bra, because she didn't need it. Her breasts were perfect as they were.

Grace Larsen was so fucking dangerous. Just wanting to see her had placed him in mortal jeopardy and now a big part of him understood how much she was going to cost him.

Everything. Everything he'd built and worked for, gone.

She was going to cost him everything he had, including life as he knew it. Thirty-four years of existence, gone.

He couldn't mourn his life, though, because there wasn't enough room in his head for that. Right now the most intense sensation in his body was the tightness between his thighs. He looked down at himself and sure enough, he was as hard as stone.

He held himself with his uninjured hand and gave an experimental tug, running his hand from the base to the tip, imagining that Grace held him, and he nearly came out of the tub from the intensity. God!

His jaw clenched. He sometimes jerked off when it was too much trouble to find a woman. He found it a pleasant stress reliever. But touching himself now, with the recent, up-close images of her right there in his head—it felt like he'd lost a layer of skin.

Another pull and he clenched his jaws at the intense sensation. He'd seen her, touched her, breathed her air. It wasn't hard at all to imagine that they were in bed together. She'd look at him out of liquid eyes, naked on his bed, and open her legs for him. He could see it behind his closed lids, he could *feel* it.

Feel her arms coming around him, the soft huff of breath as he mounted her. She'd be soft and slick for him, because in this half-dream state she wanted him just as intensely as he wanted her, which meant that she was weeping in her cunt for him, just as he was weeping for her.

He'd push into her, fast, because though he was known to be a controlled lover, he wasn't feeling in control at all. Just mount her, pull her legs apart and shove in fast, feeling every delicious inch . . .

Whoa. Rewind.

That wouldn't work. He knew it wouldn't work from fucking hundreds of women. He was big and he had to take care. In his world, he'd seen way too much brutality to women. Even the thought of hurting a woman made him nauseous. And this was *Grace*. So no, he wasn't going to open her legs and thrust as hard as he could.

First he'd touch her, softly, gently. Carefully feel her cunt in all its soft folds, while kissing her breasts. Feel her open up, soften for him. Hear her sigh with longing—

No, that wasn't working, either. Because he couldn't get the image of fucking her out of his head. He was in her, fucking her hard, hands clasped to her hips, watching her head move up and down on the pillow with his thrusts.

His hand was moving faster now as he saw the two of them on his bed, her pale slender legs curled around his as he pumped in and out of her. His fist worked hard and fast as the images of them intertwined on his big bed burned in his head.

He closed his eyes, hand working faster and faster in the water, as he imagined moving in a hot and slick Grace, listening to the puffs of her breath in his ear, her low moans, her arms tightening as she screamed and her cunt started clenching around him—

It was too much. Overload. Hot prickles raced down his spine, his toes curled and his jaw clenched as his cock swelled in his hand. It was impossible to resist the heat, like trying to stop a freight train. The climax just barreled right through him. He started spurting hot jets into the water as he arched his back with a pleasure so intense it was almost pain, one of the most explosive orgasms he'd ever had.

It took long, long moments for him to settle down, for his breathing to go back to normal, for him to be able to open his eyes and see his bathroom and not the naked pair of them on his bed.

He lingered in the water for far too long, contemplating the ceiling, feeling his new reality shift around him. His life was changing more quickly than even he could keep up with.

Christ, he was in a shitload of trouble if jacking off to the thought of Grace was much more exciting than any of the sex he'd recently had. He was so used to having his life tightly under his control, master of his surroundings and himself. This scared him a little. There was no place in his head for these new sensations, for the feel of another life joining his. Grace was now in his life, not by choice but by violence, thrust there by circumstances beyond his control and hers. He could deal with the responsibility—he bore the responsibility of a goddamned empire on his shoulders. What he couldn't deal with were the emotions attached to her. Brand-new emotions. Uncontrollable ones. Not much frightened him, but this did.

He sat in the tub while the water cooled and his cock relaxed to a semi-erect state, contemplating the massive changes in his life.

Finally, he shook himself back into action, standing up in the tub, letting the silvery water wash off him. His life was now not completely his own, he thought as he toweled himself dry. There were steps to be taken, and step number one was to take care of Grace.

He'd brought in clean clothes, a sweater and jeans, and dressed. Back in the bedroom, he pressed a button on a small console.

"Sir?" a disembodied voice answered immediately.

Drake smiled. He'd found Shota on the streets of Tbilisi, an underage conscript who'd been wounded and abandoned by his teammates. He'd taken Shota back to his hotel, patched him up, and when he would have sent him on his way, discovered that Shota didn't want to leave. Shota was hopeless as a soldier, but he turned out to be a superb butler.

Drake had had households in Odessa; in Ostende, Belgium; in Johannesberg and now in Manhattan, and Shota made sure everything ran smoothly. He had six maids, four chefs and an underbutler working for him, making sure that Drake lived in clean and comfortable circumstances and that his needs were met instantly.

For an instant, Drake ran through his mind the possibility that Shota had betrayed him. He let the idea lie there, turning it over gently, looking at it from all angles, then dismissed it. Not only was Shota fanatically loyal, he wasn't greedy at all. Shota lived in the building, two stories down, like all his employees. He paid no rent, no utilities, ate on the premises and seemed very content. Drake had had to force him to accept a raise last time.

Drake knew that he treated Shota well and he felt that Shota's loyalty was real.

Humans are capable of many things—no one knew that better than Drake—but by the same token, they were always true to themselves. Shota was loyal to the bone. So he wasn't the one.

Drake was going to go over every single employee he had. Only someone working here could possibly know his movements. All in all, Drake had a permanent staff of forty-five men and six women, amongst them a traitor. He had finely tuned instincts and he kept his surveillance camera recordings forever, so if necessary, he could go over every single employee's movements over the past year.

He'd find the man and make him sorry, but right now there were other, more important, things to see to.

"Sir?" Shota's voice held some puzzlement. "Did you need something?"

Christ. He was so wiped out by the orgasm he'd forgotten he'd buzzed downstairs.

"Yes, Shota. I'd like dinner brought up to the dining room, set on the table in front of the fire. Something warm and nutritious, with a sweet dessert" —Grace was going to need warmth and sugar to overcome her shock— "and a good bottle of red. One of those Argentinian merlots you bought would be nice."

"Yessir," Shota's voice came back. Drake could imagine him already bustling about, beginning the preparations.

"For two," Drake said, a slight smile lifting one side of his mouth.

"*Sir?*" Shota sounded shocked and well he should be. He'd been with Drake for years and Drake had never, ever had anyone over for a meal. Any meals with women were consumed in private clubs with adequate security measures or catered in his flat on Fifth. He never ate over business deals, one of his many hard and fast rules. Food and alcohol were distractions he couldn't afford during negotiations, and the possibility of poisoning always had to be factored in.

"Dinner for two, Shota. And tomorrow morning I need for you to go to . . ." Drake tried to think of the clothes he'd seen Grace in. She had classic tastes, nothing overly trendy, and she liked clean, bright colors. "Valentino," he decided. "And Ralph Lauren."

How much of what? Well, it was going to take at least a week to do what he had to do, not to mention seducing her into what had to be done. "Five sweaters in blues and greens and reds, cashmere, five pairs of pants, cashmere and wool, five simple wool dresses, cashmere, ten silk shirts. Colors for a woman with auburn hair and blue-green eyes. Then go to La Perla and buy underwear. Silk, of course. No thongs." Some instinct told him she wouldn't wear thongs. She didn't dress to seduce.

"But—but . . ." Shota sputtered.

"I don't know what size, but specify it's for a woman who is five five and weighs one hundred twenty pounds. Oh, and shoes. Fur-lined boots, flat-heeled shoes. Lots of them. Try Ferragamo. Size seven." Drake was entirely used to sizing up competitors. He'd be surprised if he were one inch or five pounds off the mark.

God, what else would a woman need?

"Go to somewhere like Bergdorf or Saks and buy creams."

"Creams, sir?" Shota sounded resigned.

"Yes." What kinds of creams? Fuck if he knew. "Day creams, night creams, body creams . . ." And shit, didn't that create images in his head? "And, and intimate products."

Shota coughed. Drake smiled. "You know—things women need at times."

A choked sound came over the intercom.

Drake suspected Shota was gay. Personally, he didn't give a shit about anyone's sexual orientation. Whatever Shota's was, he kept his private life discreet. But Drake knew he'd have an excellent eye for the clothes and underwear, which is why he'd chosen him. Female hygiene products might stretch his expertise some, but he'd manage. Shota prided himself on providing excellent service to him.

"And Shota?"

"Yessir."

"I want dinner in fifteen minutes." Of the four chefs, two were always on duty. His men often ate on the premises. There would be excellent food ready at all hours.

"Absolutely, sir." Shota sounded relieved at being on familiar terrain. The cooks could provide a superb meal for fifty at the drop of a hat.

"Good man," Drake said. "And one more thing."

"Sir."

"From now on, until I order otherwise, you are the only person who enters my personal quarters unless I invite them up. You bring in the food and the other things I asked for, personally. Have someone help you get it to the door but you are the only one to cross that threshold, is that clear?"

He knew Shota would read it as testimony of Drake's faith in him, and it was.

"Perfectly clear, sir. And . . ." Drake could almost imagine Shota blushing. "Thank you, sir."

Drake switched the intercom off. He got up and went to a sideboard holding liqueurs and cigars in a humidor. The cigars were a monthly courtesy from Fidel and he idly wondered what would happen when Fidel went. No doubt the shipments would stop. Times changed. They were changing right now.

He poured himself a stiff glass of Courvoisier XO and sat down on the couch with a sigh and took a long slug.

What excellent medicine alcohol was. Unless you were a slave to it, as most of the Russians he knew were, it was one of life's great pleasures.

He sipped, enjoying everything about the moment. Extreme danger did that—heightened his senses, made him aware of the fullness of life.

The fire crackled pleasantly, the flames licking upward in intense colors, bathing the room in a warm pink glow. Two floors below, chefs were readying his dinner, which he was certain would be superb. The Courvoisier was a warm pool in his stomach, radiating heat outward.

He sat and basked in the firelight, savoring the clean taste of the cognac; safe in his fortress, he emptied his mind of all cares, all worries, and waited for the most beautiful woman in the world to come out of his bathroom.

How long would it take for him to shed this life? To effectively die? A week? Two weeks?

Whatever, as the Americans said.

At some point she was going to have to get out of this sinfully, outrageously luxurious tub. It was simply too wonderful, wallowing in the water, feeling the strong jets massaging her aching muscles.

She'd looked, but there had been no essential oils, so it was just unadorned New York water, which was fine.

Actually, though the bathroom was beyond sumptuous, she was astonished at the lack of personal care products.

Drake was obviously well-to-do. Filthy rich, actually. He could afford every skin care product in the world. But looking for some oil to put in the tub, all she'd found was masses of thick, blindingly white towels, something like fifty unused toothbrushes, ditto toothpaste, a year's supply of a very ordinary soap, shampoo and an electric razor. That was it.

Amazing.

A few months ago she'd briefly dated the guy in her bank who took care of investments. She'd been called into his office, wondering whether she'd done something wrong, only to find that the bank had been tracking her swelling account.

Their investment expert, Lawrence Kelsey, had wanted to explain a number of investment opportunities guaranteed to make her money grow.

In the end, it all seemed like a vast amount of work and more of a distraction than anything else. But at the end of the session, while shaking her hand, he'd held it tightly and asked her out to dinner.

And, in a moment of weakness and loneliness, totally against her better judgment, she'd accepted.

Dinner had been at a posh Japanese restaurant, where the food was excellent. She'd been able to concentrate on the food because Lawrence had kept up a running commentary on his banking career, with a little hour-long detour on his new plasma TV. She hadn't had to do anything but stay awake, nod occasionally and enjoy the fantastic tempura.

She'd even accepted going back to his apartment, fully understanding that they might end up in bed together, testimony more to her worry that she'd forget what sex was like than to his powers of seduction. She'd asked to use the bathroom and had found herself simply openmouthed with amazement at the vast array of skin care products and cosmetics and eau de colognes in an enormous white lacquer vanity. She'd felt quite ashamed of her own miserly collection. A quarter of an hour later, pleading a vicious headache, she was on her way back home.

Drake had nothing like that. For all the sybaritic luxury of the room, it was definitely a very masculine man's bathroom.

She tilted her head back over the rim and emptied her mind, feeling her muscles relax slowly, one by one. Someone had set the jets at maximum and she relished the gentle pummeling. Her mind drifted. She might even have fallen briefly asleep, because she suddenly jerked upright, noting that her fingers had become as wrinkled as prunes.

She felt no sense of hurry, though. Drake hadn't given her any feeling that he expected her to be quick, which was good. She was overwhelmed with exhaustion and found she could only move slowly.

The white towels were the thickest she'd ever seen. Once she'd toweled herself off and dried her hair, she noted the neatly folded black outfit on top of a cupboard. Opening the soft material out, she saw what a gi was. One of those pajama-like outfits she'd seen in martial arts movies. The material was thick silk.

Grace looked at her clothes on the floor. Muddy, bloody and ripped. Including the panties. Just the thought of putting any of her filthy clothes back on repelled her. With a shrug, she donned the jacket and pants. He was right, it was perhaps the only thing of his which could possibly fit her. In the movies she'd seen, the outfit's sleeves were three quarter length, but this covered her hands. She turned the sleeves up and wrapped the jacket around herself. The pants were too long, but not long enough to trip over. The drawstring waist was perfect. She contemplated her sodden shoes and opted to stay barefoot.

Okay. Time to leave the bathroom.

She realized that this time had been like a little respite for her. There were so many things she had to face once she went out into that bedroom, including Drake and this insane attraction he seemed to hold for her.

She knew nothing about him. The intense spike of fear she'd felt in the elevator had abated, but there was an underlying unease. No one knew where she was and she now realized she *couldn't* go home. In every way, she was in Drake's power. Being attracted to him didn't make things better, it made them worse.

Gathering her courage, she placed her hand against the white door and pushed.

Seven

Drake heard the bathroom door open. Steam escaped from the bathroom, curling around Grace in silver tendrils as she stood in the open doorway.

Christ, she was beautiful.

And scared.

He stood, a male's instinctive reaction in the presence of a beautiful woman.

Her entire body language spoke of distress. Eyes huge and fixed on him, not really knowing whether he was friend or foe, she was curled in on herself, seeking comfort from herself. She tucked her hands under her armpits to hide the fact that they were shaking. She was barefoot, one foot curled over the other. Her feet were extraordinarily pretty—pale, narrow and high-arched.

Drake walked up to her and untucked a hand from where it was clamped against her side. Slowly, watching her eyes carefully, he brought her trembling hand to his mouth.

Her eyes widened.

He smiled at her. "You're looking a little better. I'm glad. I've had some food brought up. You've had a bad shock and some warm food would do you good."

Drake released her hand and held himself utterly still. It was the only thing he could do. She must be feeling as if she'd fallen down a rabbit hole, only not into Wonderland but into Horrorland. He was lucky she wasn't screaming at him, calling the police.

Drake knew it was absolutely essential that he gain her trust and then bind her to him in all ways. This long journey they were undertaking together had to begin now. The only way he knew to take that first step was to remain still, opening himself to her.

Drake had spent a lifetime scaring scary men. At first out of desperate self-defense and then later—when he grew in strength, prestige and wealth—as a tactic. He was good at it. He was strong, smart, rich. Utterly ruthless. Those qualities gave off an aura that usually was enough to tell any man confronting him to back off. The kind of man who didn't perceive it was usually stupid, inevitably on the losing end, and often ended up dead.

Intimidation was second nature to him. He lived in a feral world. He knew how to stay on top by being more feral than most. None of his weapons, though, were any help here, with Grace. He didn't want to intimidate her, he wanted—needed—to seduce her.

Step number one in seduction—make sure the woman doesn't fear you.

So he stayed perfectly still, moving only his lungs, holding her hand carefully. Not too loose, not too tight. He was close enough to smell her, but not so close he was invading the buffer space every animal needs.

They stood there, Drake watching her calmly, utterly still. Slowly, her breathing evened out and she straightened. At some level, deeper than words, she realized she didn't need to guard her vital organs, which is what she'd subconsciously been doing in holding herself so tightly.

His stillness reassured her. Someone who means you harm gives off minute signals, muscles bunching and readying themselves for attack. He deliberately relaxed every muscle, cleared his mind of all thoughts, and made himself open to her, something he never did with anyone.

It worked. The vein beating in her neck took on a slower rhythm, her hand relaxed in his.

"Come," he said finally, tugging lightly. "Dinner is waiting for us. Let's go before it gets cool."

Grace stood for just a moment longer, watching his eyes. Whatever it was she was looking for, she found it. "Okay," she said softly, and stepped forward.

Drake looked down at her feet and frowned. "You're barefoot. I'm sorry I don't have any slippers that would fit you. Maybe one of the maids has a pair of slippers."

She smiled slightly. "Don't worry about it. The floor is mainly rugs and I'm used to going barefoot in my house. I'm okay."

He didn't like the idea, though he had to admit that he enjoyed looking at her pretty, bare feet. But she might catch cold. He made a mental note to tell Shota to add several pairs of Ferragamo slippers to the list of things to buy her.

They walked down the big hallway together. He didn't release her hand and she didn't tug it free. Drake was so taken by her presence at his side, by the feel of her soft hand in his, that he was almost at the door of the dining room before he realized that it was the first time in memory that he'd walked hand in hand with a woman.

Such a strange and intimate connection, in some ways more intimate than fucking. You can fuck a woman you don't particularly care for. Easy. But you don't hold her hand. Holding hands signifies an intimate connection, one of trust and affection.

They weren't there yet. But they would be. They had to be.

"Go on," he said, holding the door open for her. She looked up at him and, reassured by what she saw on his face, walked into the room.

Shota had outdone himself. Through his amazing radar, Shota had understood that this wasn't a business dinner. He'd brought out Drake's best china and what looked like all his silverware. Drake had no idea what make the china plates were. When they'd arrived in Manhattan, he'd simply told Shota to buy the best, and he had. Gleaming, delicate white plates with silver rims, crystal glasses, creamy white candles in silver candlesticks. The candles were lit. Together with a few low lamps, they were the only illumination in the huge room except for the enormous crackling fire.

The table looked appealing and intimate, not at all what it looked like when set for his solitary dinners. When he ate here, it was for fuel. This looked like a little ceremony.

It must have appealed to the artist in her, because as he watched her, a small smile curved her lips. "Very pretty," she said softly.

He nodded. It *was* very pretty.

No one had ever drummed manners into him. He'd grown up on the streets, fighting his way to the top. No one had ever told him how men are supposed to behave in society, with ladies. His formative years had been spent with warlords, generals and rebel leaders. Later, he befriended a few alcoholic war journalists and the odd rough CIA operative, none of whom had any manners worth speaking about.

But Drake knew how to observe, how to blend in. So he knew that he was supposed to accompany Grace to her chair, pull it out and wait for her to sit before sitting down himself. He'd seen it done. He knew how it was supposed to go.

But it wasn't to conform to some abstract society ideal that had him walking her to her chair and pulling it out.

It came utterly naturally, instinctively. From the deepest part of his being. It gave him enormous pleasure to take her to his table, to make sure that she was comfortably seated before taking a seat himself. It felt absolutely right. Nothing to do with manners and everything to do with gut-deep instinct.

His cooks had outdone themselves. Warm and nutritious, he'd asked. Apparently that meant soup. Soup that was . . . green, he discovered as he filled her bowl.

"I have no idea what this is." He filled his own bowl and waited until she picked up her spoon and delicately tasted the soup. "I hope it's good. My cooks seem to know what they're doing. Usually."

"It's delicious," she said softly. "And just for the record, it's watercress soup."

Watercress. Jesus. He knew every gun that had ever been manufactured. Every hold in every martial art. This was beyond him. What the fuck was watercress?

"An herb. It grows wild." She watched him with a small smile, answering his unspoken question. "Try it. You'll like it. It's really very good."

He did. It was.

They were both hungry and ate their way quickly through the food. Drake knew the food was all good, fantastic even, but he could hardly taste it. He was completely taken up with Grace Larsen. At his table, by his side.

In the past year that he'd taken extraordinary risks just to see her, telling himself he was an idiot, he'd never thought he'd actually ever be sitting beside her, except in the middle of the night, in his dreams.

He was a fast healer, almost preternaturally so. He felt much better already, almost normal. He could feel strength returning minute by minute to his body, he could feel the blood circulating more strongly in his veins. Alas, most of it went straight to his cock.

He'd deliberately put on tight, stiff jeans, hoping it would act as a sort of a chastity belt, but it wasn't working. Just watching her eat, move—hell, *breathe*—excited him.

Shit.

He had enormous mental discipline but mind games weren't working. Not when he had Grace less than a foot from him, his gi gaping slightly over her breasts, showing the dips and shadows of her breasts, her delicate collarbones visible.

He clenched his fist on the table. He wanted so badly to reach out and touch her that his hand itched. He understood his cock, trying to punch its way through stiff denim. His cock wanted to reach out and touch her, too.

Actually, his cock wanted *in* her, in the worst way. It was as if he'd never had sex before, it was so intense.

They were making polite conversation, about the food, the tableware, the candlesticks—he could barely keep his mind on what they were saying—and all the time his head was flooded with images of her in his bed.

He wasn't even fantasizing about foreplay—no, his head

had gone straight to the main course. Fucking. Fucking Grace. Who was—whoa—not more than a foot away from him. Close enough for him to smell her, a delicate fragrance under the sharper smells of the food and the wood from the hearth. Close enough to see how fine-grained her skin was, what a lovely glowing color she had, as if sprinkled with pearl dust.

She favored loose clothing, so all the times he'd seen her at the gallery, he had to guess at what was underneath, but now, dressed in his gi, which she'd had to cinch around herself tightly or the whole damned thing would fall off, he could see exactly how she was made.

Perfectly. That's how she was made.

She'd fit perfectly in his hands, fit perfectly under him. He could see them on his bed, long pale slender legs hugging his hips, arms around his neck, as he pumped inside her. She'd be soft there, too. Wet enough to take him, so that he could slide easily in and out of her. His hands—where the fuck were his hands in this scenario?

Holding that narrow waist, right at the sexy curve before it widened to her delicately round hips? But he also wanted to hold her breasts while fucking her, rasping a thumb across her nipple, feeling it turn hard as he moved inside her. But then he also wanted a hand in that glorious hair, feeling it curling softly over his arm like a female waterfall. But then what he *really* wanted was to hold her legs open with his hands, cup her knees and spread them so that he had full access to her cunt, nothing in the way, nothing between them . . .

Shit, he'd need four pairs of hands. How was that going to work?

Oh God, he was so hard it was painful. He found it next to impossible to banish the images of them on his bed, hard to soft, dark to pale. As he watched her avidly, watching each forkful go into her mouth—his cock envying the zucchini soufflé and gratin potatoes as they passed those lush lips, because that's where it wanted to be—he could feel an electric tingle in his spine. His balls tightened, his hips were unconsciously moving, wanting to be in her, thrusting.

Oh God, he was seconds from an orgasm, right here, at the dinner table. Not only would it be embarrassing, but also, she wasn't in any way ready to face the intensity of his sexual desire for her. It would alienate her, when he needed her by his side in every way.

So he called on every ounce of self-control he had and walked away. In his head, he pulled his cock out of Grace, got up from the bed and walked away.

One of the hardest things he'd ever done in a hard life.

And when the fog of lust retreated, he noticed what he should have noticed earlier.

Grace was making patterns in the white tablecloth with the tines of the dessert fork. The lost, lonely look was back.

Drake put a finger under her chin and turned her face to his. "What are you thinking?"

"I was thinking—wondering—where Harold is. Harold Feinstein. He was the gallery owner."

Whose head was blown apart by a sniper's bullet. "Yes," he said gently. "I know who he was. His body is in all likelihood in the city morgue, awaiting an autopsy."

Her eyes flared. "Autopsy? Why would they carry out an autopsy? I don't think there's any doubt about the way he died."

"No. Of course not. But it will take a coroner to study the bullet wound. The authorities will be able to tell a lot about the shooter from the trajectory, trace elements in the flesh and from the recovered bullet. Clearly, you don't watch *CSI*." The bullet would have gone through Feinstein's head like cream and had most likely ended up embedded into the hardwood floor of the gallery. The shooter wouldn't have risked running in and prying it out, so the police would have found it and studied it. Drake was going to break into the NYPD forensics lab computer to see their report on the bullet and the gun.

She flushed. "Oh, of course they'd need an autopsy. How stupid of me. Sorry. I don't actually have a TV, but even *I've* heard of *CSI*. I hope they find out who killed him. And who shot at us."

Drake had every intention of finding out before the police. And exacting his revenge.

He ran a finger over the back of her hand, feeling the soft skin, the delicate tendons, then lifted his eyes. "Don't apologize. I should think you've got better things to do with your time than watch dead bodies on TV."

Grace blinked. "That's—" She shut her mouth with a snap.

"What?"

Her jaws clenched as she shook her head, hard. He gentled his voice and placed his hand over hers, covering it completely. "What?" he asked again, softly. "What is it, Grace? There isn't anything you can't say to me."

She watched his eyes for a moment, looking for something, then took a deep breath. "I don't know if you'll believe it, but I think this is the first time I've ever said that I don't have a TV without being treated as if I were retarded or eccentric beyond belief. To most people it's too insane to even contemplate. But the thing is, I work all the time and TV would be a huge distraction for me. I'd rather read, anyway.

But in the end I'm not always up on the latest news and that's considered almost antisocial, like wearing mismatched shoes or—or going to an elegant restaurant in gym clothes. It's just not done."

He tightened his grip slightly, very carefully. His hands were immensely strong and he didn't want to hurt her in any way. He just wanted to emphasize his words. "I don't ever want to hear you call yourself stupid again. You're an artist. How could you waste your time watching the idiocies on television rather than creating? And I'll confess—I don't have a television set, either."

It was true. Drake's business depended on accurate information. He'd learned through bitter experience that the last thing television and the major newspapers dealt in was hard news. He used the internet, hacking into company and police reports for a clear picture of what was happening in the world.

He also had dozens of paid informers who would probably make a mint in journalism if the papers would ever print what they found out.

"Really? You don't have a TV either?" Her lips curved in a half smile. He found his own mouth instinctively moving and it took him a full second to realize he was smiling back. "Maybe we're both misfits, then."

Oh yeah. Though *misfit* wasn't quite what would describe him. He was the born outsider, the predator prowling on the margins of society. He always had been.

But it was a slightly shocking thought, all the same. The idea that he and this gentle, beautiful woman might have a basic element of their lives in common made him pause. He was used to belonging to no one, and to no place. To being like no one else on the planet. It was the deepest, truest thing about himself he knew. He was a loner and an outsider and nothing would ever change that.

His thumb slowly stroked the soft skin of her hand. "Maybe we are," he conceded, feeling a little shock go through him at the idea and at the feel of her. He looked down at her plate and frowned. She'd left half the dessert. She needed sugar to counter the shocks she'd had this afternoon and—and he wanted her to finish the dessert. It was delicious. She needed it, but more than that he found himself wanting her to eat food provided by him. Craving it.

"Here," he said suddenly, letting go of her hand and spooning up a bite of the lemon tart. "Finish this. You need it. Open wide."

She opened her mouth obediently. He fed her the morsel, watching as her full pink mouth closed over the spoon. He pulled the spoon out slowly, imagining very vividly that it was his cock pulling out of her mouth. The image just welled up, uncontrollable, unstoppable. A surge of blood rushed back between his thighs.

Oh God, everything about this was just so . . . delightful. The huge fire painted her skin a shifting pink glow, like the aurora borealis he'd seen in Vladivostock. The candles reflected in bright points of light in her blue-green eyes. He was close enough to smell her skin. There was complete silence in the room except for the crackle and pop of the flames and the occasional *swoosh* as one of the logs collapsed in the hearth.

Her eyes were fixed on his. He knew she was seeing his desire and he also knew she could see him curb it.

Sex was crackling between them. Her eyes were bright

with it. They were also bright with alarm. Though the air pulsed with sexual energy, Drake knew enough to bank his fires, because he didn't want to frighten her.

He'd have her. Oh yes.

Not tonight maybe, but soon.

Grace looked away, breaking the connection. "Do you think they'll release the body anytime soon? He has a son out in LA. They're not close, unfortunately. I think it was one of Harold's greatest regrets, that he wasn't close to his son. He never spoke much about him, but there was always a sad expression on his face when he did. I don't know what kind of memorial service the son will organize. Harold was Jewish but he wasn't religious. I hope I can find out when the service will be."

Every hair on Drake's body stood up.

"No," he said, and Grace's eyes widened. He had to clench his jaws against coldly ordering her to forget about even the thought of attending Harold Feinstein's memorial service. And then widening the ban by telling her that from now on, she was his Siamese twin, joined at the hip to him and that she wasn't to set foot outside his door without his express permission. And certainly never without him being a hand's span from her.

The words strangled in his throat. That wouldn't go over well for a woman who was used to being completely independent. At this stage, she'd rebel.

His mind whirred uselessly in the search for words to convince her, flailing. It was hard to concentrate on persuasive words when his head was filled with a very clear vision of her dead in a pool of her own blood, gunned down by Rutskoi or by one of Cordero's thugs. Or worse, with elbows and knees blown out just like Leather Coat had promised. It was a Cordero trademark.

No. They would never get their hands on Grace. Not while he lived.

Drake tried to modulate his voice, put some convincing in it, but it wasn't easy. He was used to commanding, not convincing.

"Grace, I'm afraid you won't be able to be at your friend's service." He bit down hard on the words *I won't let you*. "It's way too dangerous to show up at a specific place at a specific time. My enemies would know exactly where to get you."

Grace straightened in her chair. "If you believe that, then I can't even go back to my apartment."

Damn. He'd hoped it would take a day or two of stalling before she came to that conclusion. It was true. Like the title of an old American novel he'd seen in a bookstore, she could never go home again.

"I'm afraid that's—" His cell rang and he held up a finger. Only his men had this particular number and no one called him unless it was absolutely necessary. He looked at the number and frowned. Boris, the head of the four-man team sent to guard Grace's apartment.

"Yes, Boris?"

"Not Boris, boss." Ivan's image came on the small screen, voice grim. "He won't be calling you again. We came late." Ivan turned his cell around and the blood froze in Drake's veins.

It was a scene of utter destruction. A door blown off the hinges, a bloody mass on the floor, identifiable as Boris only by his black boots, utter chaos inside the apartment visible beyond Boris's bloody legs.

After an initial surge of rage at seeing his employee dead and Grace's apartment trashed, Drake felt himself go into combat mode. The switch was immediate, complete. He became a machine for combat, unhampered by emotions. Emotion held no place in this chilly land of calculation and maneuvering.

"Go further into the apartment," he said coolly, then turned the cell phone around so Grace could see it, too, see the wreckage of her apartment. She gasped, but he didn't touch her to comfort her, didn't shift his gaze from the screen. She didn't need to be consoled. She needed to be frightened. She needed to see this to understand what she was up against. It was brutal, traumatizing, but far more effective than any words he could possibly say. His words might not convince her, but this would. What was on his screen was one big danger sign that only an insane woman wouldn't heed.

Ivan walked slowly through the apartment, recording the destruction.

Interesting, Drake thought coolly. The wreckage was controlled and systematic, carried out with a knife. It wasn't vandalism, destruction for destruction's sake. There was an agenda here—pure intimidation. Whoever had done this wanted to terrify Grace, hit her in her most vulnerable points. All her artwork was destroyed, all her clothes, even her shoes. All personal things.

The message was clear. *We'll destroy you next. So be scared, because we're coming.*

Her eyes were riveted on the small screen. "My God," she breathed.

"Go into the kitchen," Drake ordered Ivan, not surprised when he saw that her plates and glasses were intact. Whoever had done this hadn't wanted to make any noise. Further proof that it wasn't a mad rampage, but a carefully thought out campaign to smoke Grace out of hiding, rattle her badly.

Or rattle him.

Fools.

Drake wasn't rattled, he was as cold as ice inside.

The attack outside Feinstein's gallery had been an attack on him. This was nothing new. His life had been threatened before, many times. He'd survived all the attacks and lived to have his vengeance.

But this—this was an attack on Grace.

Someone had just made a huge, huge mistake.

Drake narrowed his eyes. Grace had gone completely white, down to her lips. Her hands were shaking.

"Why—" Her voice was barely above a whisper and she swallowed heavily. "Why would anyone do that to my apartment? Why destroy my paintings? Why?"

He got up and went to a sideboard, coming back with two glasses of Jack Daniel's, a taste American officers had given him, his a double shot.

One thing the scene of destruction had done was make his hard-on disappear. Sex with Grace would come, and soon, but right now he had enemies prodding his defenses, representing a direct threat to her. She didn't need his arousal, she needed his focus to keep her safe.

"Here," he said, taking her hand and curling it around the cut crystal glass. Her hand was chilled and he held his hand around hers for a moment to warm it up. "Drink that down and I'll answer your questions."

She obeyed him, chugging the shot down in one long swallow. Good girl.

A touch of color came back to her face.

He drained his own glass and put it on the table, then moved his chair and sat down right across from her, their knees touching, holding her hands in his.

"Grace." He waited a second, to make sure he had her full attention. By sheer willpower he managed not to wince at the expression on her face.

This was not her world. She was as lost as if she had just landed on an airless, lightless planet and been attacked by wolves. She watched his face carefully, instinctively understanding that he was at home on this planet.

"Something bad has happened and unfortunately, you are caught right in the middle of it. Some very dangerous and, above all, very ruthless men are gunning for me and are now gunning for you. You saw what was done to your house, right?"

She nodded, eyes locked on his. He knew she was seeing the coldness in him; he could only hope she was seeing the regret.

"They wouldn't hesitate to do that to you. Slowly. As a way to get to me. I will keep you safe, I promise. But you must do as I say and you must stay in a fortified perimeter where I can protect you, which right now is this place. Access is by a code very few people know, and they are people I trust. Guards are posted outside at all times. The windows are bullet-resistant. No one can get to you here, trust me, but you're going to have to stay put. You can't go to Feinstein's memorial service, you can't go home, you can't go to any friends. As a matter of fact, until I start straightening this situation out, you can't leave this building. I wish with all my heart that things could be different, but they aren't. All I can say is that I will try to make you as comfortable as possible. I have staff on call twenty-four/seven, and all you have to do is express a wish and it's yours, as long as it doesn't involve you going out."

"I'm—I'm a prisoner?"

Damn. Yes, she was, but he didn't want her to think of herself in that way.

He brought her hand to his mouth and planted a soft kiss on her palm. Shocked and scared as she was, the pulse in her throat speeded up a little.

Thank God. Just as soon as was humanly possible, he was going to start fucking her, binding her to him with sex. He was going to get into her and stay in her as long as he could, until they breathed the same air, until their hearts beat together, until it would be unthinkable for her to leave his side.

"I want you to think of the outside world as a prison, Grace. And in here you can do exactly as you please. In fact—" Drake reached out to the intercom and waited for Shota's voice.

"Sir?"

"Shota, besides the other things I told you to buy tomorrow morning, I want to add art supplies."

"Sir?" Shota sounded resigned.

Drake watched Grace. "Art supplies. Everything a painter might need." Which was what? He floundered. "Ah, oil colors, watercolors, a complete range, ah—" Fuck, what were they called? "Canvases and the . . . thing they're placed on." He looked at Grace, eyebrows lifted.

"Easel," she said softly.

"Easel. Listen, just ask the owner to give you something of everything. Find out who the best supplier in town is, only not—" He leaned forward to her. "Where do you regularly buy your supplies?"

"Cellini's, on Broadway."

"Not Cellini's on Broadway. Stay away from there. Find out who is next best and go there. I want everything here by eleven tomorrow morning."

"Yessir."

Drake broke the connection.

Grace was sitting straighter in her chair, looking a little less like a truck had run over her. His respect for her went up another notch.

"I'll pay you back, Drake. I don't have my checkbook with me, it was in my purse, but I'll—"

Drake put a finger over her lips, horrified. "Stop. Please stop. Don't even think it. I'm the reason this is happening to you. All I'm trying to do is make you as comfortable here as possible."

"Okay." She drew in a deep breath. "I understand that I stepped into the middle of some kind of—hostile takeover." She gave a little laugh that turned wobbly. She bit her lips and waited a second for control. "Very hostile. But I don't understand why I'm involved. Why do they feel that some-how they can get to you through me? I'm nothing to you. I just happened to be in the wrong place at the wrong time. So why trash my house? Slash my paintings? What difference could that possibly make to you?"

Okay.

Drake had been hoping to put this moment off to when she was feeling better, when the adrenaline had worked its way out of her system and she wasn't shaking. To when she could be wearing clothes of her own and not his and was feeling less of a refugee from her own life.

But what you want and what must be are two entirely dif-ferent things. Drake understood that down to the bone.

"Words aren't enough," he said, rising from the chair. He put a hand on her elbow and lifted her gently up. "I must show you. Come with me."

They walked in silence down the long hall. Drake thought

briefly about somehow preparing her, but dismissed the idea immediately. It wasn't a moment for words.

His study was at the end of the long, wide hall, essentially across the entire footprint of the building. It took them minutes to get there. They walked in silence, Drake utterly conscious of her hand in his, of her presence at his side.

She was making no bones of her curiosity, twisting her head left and right, noting the furniture, the rugs, the tapestries.

Drake wondered what she thought of his home. It was as far from the current New York style as possible. He liked color, soft fabrics, fine antiques, rugs. He often thought that perhaps he had Mongol or Tartar blood in him, since he always set up households that looked like caravanserais.

He stopped outside the door to his study. His inner sanctum.

Drake looked down at Grace, standing quietly in front of the door. She seemed to understand that he needed a moment to gather himself, and though she must have been quivering with anxiety to discover what lay behind it, she stood and let him take his time.

He could see long lashes, the curve of a high cheekbone, lush mouth slightly downturned. Beauty and grace. Courage, even. A woman of great worth. He'd never thought to see her outside this door.

Drake reached out to the door, a beautiful mahogany veneer over stainless steel, and touched a small glass panel. He pressed his thumb against it; a bright green light flashed, and with a soft whirring sound, the door slid into the wall.

Grace watched the door disappear and then looked up at him for permission to enter. The door framed darkness that had a cavernous feel to it. It was the largest room in the apartment and the darkness inside was dense and black.

It had to be done.

Drake pushed gently at her back and reaching to the side, flipped the light switch of the chandeliers. There were three of them, from Murano, and they made the room and its contents glow.

Beside him, Grace gasped. He tightened his grip on her elbow as her knees buckled.

Eight

Enrique Cordero lived in Crown Heights, home of the Bloods. Cordero had come up out of the gang to form his own, a professional organization a million miles above the heads of the street gangs, though he used some of the old gang members now and again.

He hadn't used the excitable young punks forming the Bloods to get Drake, but he might as well have, for all the good they'd done.

Fucking amateurs.

Rutskoi had worked up a good head of steam by the time he made it to Cordero's home. Compound, really. Thirty thousand square feet of what looked like a Mexican adobe hacienda plunked down five thousand miles north in a more unforgiving climate. The compound was surrounded by concrete walls two feet thick, with only one way in—a set of big featureless steel doors set in the wall farthest from the street. You had to drive all the way around, being tracked by surveillance cameras every inch of the way, and announce yourself to the monitor.

Cordero's gatekeeper hesitated just long enough to be insulting, making Rutskoi wait a full five minutes. Finally, Rutskoi heard the loud metallic click of the gate's electronic lock disengaging. The big steel gates slowly swung open and Rutskoi drove his rental straight in.

Shitheads, he thought sourly.

The internal courtyard was lit up like a prison camp, huge 500-watt spotlights in each corner. He had to work to keep from shielding his eyes with his hand, not wanting to give Cordero's men the satisfaction. The overbright lights ruined his night vision, as they were meant to. He could barely make out two hulking figures looking like gorillas in jeans and parkas flanking the entrance to the house and knew that they could see him with almost brutal clarity.

Cordero thought he was so smart, but five of his men had let Drake go. He had fucking delivered Drake on a fucking platter and they had let him get away with hardly a scratch. The thought made him as angry now as it had five hours ago.

Rutskoi got out of the car, holding up his hands to show they were empty, and stopped right outside the door. The two men frisked him thoroughly, even feeling his balls and the crack of his ass. They were right to, a terrorist could hide a good four or five pounds of plastic explosive in underpants, but Rutskoi was no terrorist and they knew it. It was a power game and they had probably been ordered to do it by Cordero, who was an idiot.

"Go on in," one of the gorillas growled.

"I hope you enjoyed it," Rutskoi said, and both gorillas stiffened with rage while he walked through the door. That was petty. He didn't have time to play games with body-guards. It was a sign of his frustration and anger that he'd prodded the animals.

He stopped in the middle of the two-story atrium and tried to get himself under control.

Fuck! The one chance anyone had ever had to nail Drake, the one small piece of information on a weakness of his, and Cordero's men had blown it. That window of opportunity was never going to open again. Drake would be more tightly protected than the Kremlin now. And all because Cordero had sent second-rate men.

If only this weren't America. Rutskoi had no men here. If this had been back home and he could have taken care of it himself, Drake would be dead. After Drake gave him the codes, Rutskoi would be the sole proprietor of a kingdom and he wouldn't have had to team up with a shit-for-brains like Cordero.

But he *was* in America, and he *was* teamed up with Cordero. That was the bottom line and he had to deal with it. Rutskoi rarely wasted time wishing that things were different. It was a hard world and only hard men got by.

Under control now, he trotted up the stairs to the second floor under the watchful eyes of another pair of security guards posted at the top of the stairs.

"I have an appointment," Rutskoi said as he passed them. They grunted and swiveled their heads to watch him as he made his way down the hallway.

Before he got to Cordero's office, the door opened and a very young, very pretty dark-haired girl walked out. She was unsteady on her feet, dark red lipstick smeared over her lips, eyes unfocused, hair mussed. Rutskoi watched her stumble along the corridor.

He knocked briefly, then walked in, finding Cordero tucking his lipstick-stained cock back into his pants. White powder was scattered on the glass-topped coffee table.

Oh Jesus, Rutskoi thought. The fuckhead was *high*. A couple of hours after failing to kidnap one of the most dangerous men on the planet, he was getting himself a blow job while high. Did he *want* to get killed?

Rutskoi himself never did drugs, but he certainly understood why they helped in certain circumstances. In Chechnya, his men often shot up heroin. At a hundred rubles a shot, just a few dollars, they could spend a little time in a place inside their heads where dead Russian soldiers weren't rigged with IEDs. Where small kids didn't carry suicide belts. Where their officers weren't selling off their own equipment. Rutskoi always turned a blind eye as long as they did it on down time and not while they were on duty. They had to do something to help them maintain their sanity.

But Cordero wasn't in the world's worst hellhole, just praying to stay alive long enough to make it home, like Rutskoi's soldiers. No, Cordero had a high-profit business in a safe, stable country. He was a leader, or at least he was supposed to be.

Leaders kept clear heads at all times, were in control of themselves at all times. A leader wouldn't get sidetracked by sex and drugs when war had been declared against a frighteningly powerful man who was undoubtedly at this very moment planning his revenge.

Drake's revenge was terrifying. Rutskoi had seen it for himself.

The fact that Rutskoi was teamed with a man who was stoned and had just had sex when he should be fortifying his perimeter and planning the next moves was beyond frightening. He shouldn't have teamed up with this man, this weakling, at all. But what choice had he had?

"Ruso," Cordero mumbled in greeting. He'd never been

able to pronounce Rutskoi's name, calling him simply "the Russian." He fumbled to light a cigarette with trembling hands, inhaling deeply. "That didn't go well, did it? We'll have to try again in two weeks."

Rutskoi balled his fists to keep from smashing them into Cordero's stupid, degenerate face. It took a moment to level his voice out. "Forget it. That won't work again. We won't get another chance. He'll never go back to that alleyway, count on it. You had one chance and you fucked it up."

Cordero's eyes widened at Rutskoi's tone. He inhaled deeply on the cigarette, watching the tip flare red and scowled. "You can't talk that way to me, Ruso. We don't know exactly what happened. For all I know, my men were betrayed and Drake was waiting. His men sure came fast."

Rutskoi could feel a vein throbbing in his forehead. "His men came fast because he employs the best. They're fast and they're good." *Unlike your second-rate hoodlums.* "Right now he's wrapped up tighter than a virgin's ass and he's finding out who came after him, then he'll come after us. We're dead men walking."

Cordero's dark eyes gleamed. "Not if we get him first." He leaned over to stub out his cigarette in an overflowing ash-tray and almost lost his balance. He sat down heavily on the couch, leaning his head back and closing his eyes. "I say we go after him for real this time. Not to abduct him but to get rid of him."

Rutskoi sat down next to him, nostrils flaring at the smell of what seemed like half a bottle of expensive men's cologne, pungent cigarette smoke and the heavy musk of sex. "What do you mean?"

"You had some info, right? Someone on the inside willing to rat him out? Use him again."

"Telling me a small detail about Drake's schedule is a little different from setting him up for murder. The people who work for Drake have been vetted. And they're probably afraid of him, too."

Cordero waved that away. "No one's immune to money." He lowered his voice to a Marlon Brando-esque mumble, waggling his eyebrows. "Make him an offer he can't refuse." He burst out laughing at his own wit. The laugh turned into a hacking cough.

"Christ, Cordero."

"I mean it, Ruso. Throw money at the guy. Or better yet, find out if Drake employs women to clean his house and kidnap the family of one so she can plant a mike. Or a bomb. What the fuck. The idea is to get rid of the fucker once and for all. And then you and me, Ruso, we'll rule the world together."

You can't rule yourself, Rutskoi thought sourly. *How can you rule the world?*

Still . . . Rutskoi's mind raced. No one had ever had inside info on Drake. Could his informant be persuaded to put out once more? For the right price? Or even better, one of the cleaning staff. That was a good idea. He'd been at Drake's headquarters. There were multinationals with smaller offices than just the few spaces Drake had allowed him to see. That kind of space required a big staff, working seven days a week.

If his informant didn't come through, Rutskoi could kidnap the kids of one of the maids. He hoped it wouldn't come to that. He'd kill kids if he had to—in Chechnya, sparing them hadn't been an option, the fuckers were born with AK–47s in their hands—but he preferred not to.

Cordero's eyes were drifting over to the sideboard with its array of liquor. He was scooting forward on the couch trying to get up, but his balance was gone. The man was disgusting. What had Rutskoi been thinking of, teaming up with a miserable worm like this?

Rutskoi made a fast decision, like a soldier in battle would. "Give me ten million dollars," he said.

Cordero's head snapped around to him. *"¿Qué?"*

"You heard me. Give me ten million dollars and I'll do it. I'll get rid of Drake for you, forever. And I won't want to share in the business afterward. I'll leave it all to you. You can take over Drake's affairs, become the most powerful man in the business in one stroke, and I'll disappear forever. Ten million dollars is nothing. It's what Drake makes in a week. And even if you can't scoop up all his businesses, you won't have any rivals here. You'll be top dog forever. A man like Drake comes along once every couple of generations. You'll be rich and powerful, with no competition, for the rest of your life."

Cordero's eyes filled with a crafty light. Christ, Rutskoi could all but see the gears grinding away in his brain. Rutskoi had just put Cordero's secret dream right into his head. Drake gone, the business all his.

"Five." Cordero narrowed his eyes. A trickle of sweat fell from his coarse black hair down through the stubble on his cheek.

"Ten," Rutskoi said firmly. "And expenses. I'm going to need equipment and bribing money. I want you to give me a black credit card and some ID to go with the name. And I want ten million in my bank account in Switzerland. Up front. I promise you Drake will be gone, dead by my hand. I know him, know how he thinks. I've known him since he was twenty. I'm probably the only man alive who can do this."

"Ruso," Cordero said slowly. "How can I trust you? I give you ten million dollars and you disappear. How crazy do you think I am?"

"Drake isn't sure about you, but he *knows* I was involved in the attempt. My life isn't worth shit while he's alive, after this. He'll come after me, no question. So I need to get rid of him, in self-defense. I could maybe disappear, stay off his radar for a while, but you can't. Your business is here. He'll come after you, don't ever doubt that, and he knows exactly where to find you. You can't handle him. We saw that. Five of your men couldn't take him down. But I can. I know him, I know him well. We've worked together, we've even fought together. I know his ways and I have this inside informer. Give me enough money to do the job and I'll get rid of him for you. You stay put here for the next month, don't move, don't leave the compound, and I'll give you Drake's head on a plate. Not for you, but for me. And then I'll disappear forever."

Rutskoi could watch the greed dawning on Cordero's face. It was a win-win. Cordero could justify doing fuck-all for a month. He could spend it stoned, getting blow jobs every hour on the hour, while Rutskoi took care of taking Drake out. What was ten million to him? For access to Drake's kingdom or at least with Drake out of the way? Nothing.

"Okay," Cordero said, finally. He stuck his hand out. Rutskoi took it. "Deal."

Cordero's hand was soft, limp, humid; it was like touching a slug. Rutskoi barely managed to keep from wiping his hand on his trousers to get rid of the feel of it.

"Deal," he replied.

* * *

Grace felt the breath leave her lungs in a *whoosh*, making her light-headed, dizzy, completely disoriented.

It took her a second to understand. At first, she was overwhelmed by the magnificence of the room, which was like a small Versailles. The rest of the apartment was lush, hyper-comfortable in a very expensive sort of way, colorful and unique. This—this was lavish beyond anything she'd ever seen, the way royalty must live. Her eyes greedily drank in the jewel tones of the plush carpets, the enormous, brightly colored enameled vases with huge, thriving plants, a massive, highly polished desk that looked like the place where God would do his paperwork, if He had any.

And of course, as in every room in this unusual home, the magnificent nighttime skyline of Manhattan stretched like an immense diamond necklace outside, along one glass wall.

Then, a second later, what was on the remaining three walls popped out at her and she stared, unable to believe her eyes.

Dozens and dozens of paintings, drawings, watercolors, exquisitely framed and beautifully lit. The artwork fit into the room perfectly, the colors and shapes echoing the furniture, sculptures, vases. Seeing the artwork here, recognizing it, was so outlandish, it had literally taken a second to penetrate her mind, though every work of art was as familiar to her as her own heartbeat.

Hers.

Every single painting, every single drawing, gouache, watercolor—all hers. This magnificent room was like a Grace Larsen museum. She pivoted to the dark-eyed man watching her so carefully. She felt herself wobble and he steadied her.

"You," she whispered.

He bowed his head gravely. "Me," he confirmed.

Put it into words, pin it down. "You're the one who's been collecting my work for the past year."

"Yes."

Her head swam. "I think—I think I need to sit down."

"Absolutely." Drake's hand was once more on her elbow and it felt as if he were carrying her more than guiding her to the nearest couch. She sat down gratefully, not certain whether her legs would have held her one second longer. Drake sat next to her. The soft down cushions of the couch settled deeply under him, rolling her a little into him.

Here, too, a big fire was burning, framed by an intricately carved hearth of sandstone. She was grateful for the warmth.

Grace looked at the nearest wall, where two of her best oils flanked the fireplace. She remembered clearly all the emotions running through her as she painted them. The two big oils were meant to be shown as a pair. A Flemish-style still life of overblown roses in an earthenware vase, an open manuscript and a plate with grapes and apples on a wooden table. The other painting was a still life of a small topiary in a red terra-cotta designer vase, an open laptop and a box of Godiva chocolates on a transparent Philippe Starck table. The Flemish-style still life was a riot of colors and rotund, convoluted shapes. The modern still life was in cool tones of gray and beige, with hard edges and machined shapes.

She'd painted them more than a year ago, hoping that whoever bought them would buy them together and hang them together, the old and the new, but she hadn't been holding her breath. Artists never got any kind of say about who bought their work and how they displayed it.

These two had been bought together and they were displayed magnificently.

The far reaches of the room were in shadow, but she could see enough. A hand gleaming out of the darkness in one painting, the foam of the ocean in another. The walls were filled with her work.

"I—I don't know what to say, what to think. A whole year, I've been wondering who was buying up my work." Mind spinning, she turned her head to him. "Harold was disappointed that you hadn't organized a show. Most people who collect a lot of one person's work are planning a show to drive prices up. You were never going to, were you?"

He shook his head.

"I didn't really care, but Harold did. He felt he could have started pushing the prices even higher if you'd shown my work. Even though they were already going very high." She'd made a fortune off him.

Drake's jaws worked. "Mr. Feinstein could have quadrupled the prices and I would have paid. I would have paid ten times what he asked. I love your work. Your paintings have given me enormous pleasure over this past year. There's no price for that." His dark eyes held hers. "I'm sorry if I held your career back by not showing your art. I didn't want to—couldn't share it with others. I see now I made you suffer. I am deeply sorry."

Grace reached out with her hand to touch him, then stopped suddenly, her hand an inch above his. She looked down at their hands. At his, so sinewy and strong, with the tough yellow calluses on the sides. Not an artist's hand, not at all. It was an expression of sheer male power. Banked power.

He didn't move in any way, just watched her carefully. She was holding her hand above his for so long it was almost an insult, and yet he didn't act insulted at all. He merely waited for what she would do.

Her instincts told her he would accept whatever she did. Whether she slapped him or caressed him, he would accept it.

Her hand lowered over his and again she was shocked at the warmth emanating from his skin.

"It's okay," she said, hand curling over his. "Poor Harold got really exasperated with me because I wasn't as ambitious as he was. I mean, I am ambitious, but my real goal is simply to live from my art, not to be famous. I don't really do well in society, anyway. But he had this dream that I would be as famous as—I don't know—Andy Warhol, or even Picasso. Someone known even outside art circles. Like some kind of celebrity."

Grace couldn't suppress a shudder at the thought. She'd once been part of a collective show of ten artists, one of whom was a rich heiress, famous for a sex tape with a well-known movie star that had taken more than 10 million hits on the internet. The paparazzi outside the gallery had been like a swarm of angry bees, flashbulbs flashing aggressively in their faces. Grace could still feel the press of sweaty bodies, the anxiety and then panic she'd felt as she tried to push her way through. When she finally made it into her apartment, she'd been shaking and sweating, with a massive headache from the flashbulbs.

No, celebrity was not her thing.

"That's not for you," he said quietly. It wasn't a question.

"No. Definitely not. So I was more than happy to have someone buying all my stuff, even though it made Harold unhappy to have it hidden away. But I remember thinking . . . thinking that I'd like to talk to the person who was buying my work. Find out what he or she thought. What pieces they liked best. What worked, what didn't. Except the lawyer sort of hinted that his client lived abroad."

"That's exactly what my lawyer was told to say. And to tell you the truth, he doesn't know where I live. We communicate by e-mail and I send money from London."

He'd gone to such enormous trouble to remain anonymous. "So . . . you weren't ever going to stop by to have a chat, were you?"

His hand flexed under hers. "No."

"I—I see."

"No, I don't think you do. I'm in a dangerous business and I have dangerous enemies. Anything I care about would be considered a point of attack. If anyone knew I loved your work, they'd use that knowledge against me. So I bought them anonymously. I shouldn't have. But I did. Your work means a great deal to me and I simply couldn't renounce having it. I simply couldn't. Every painting, every drawing speaks to me. And I was selfish enough to want them for myself. And now, because of my weakness, I have placed you in jeopardy."

"You need to straighten this mess out," she said. She looked around her, at the magnificent room that managed to be exquisitely beautiful and amazingly comfortable at the same time. Something very few homes in New York ever managed. "I mean, it's nice here, but I can't stay here forever."

He shook his head, something weary beyond words in the gesture. "I can't make it go away, Grace," he said quietly. "Not immediately. And words cannot express how sorry I am about that."

He was. It was there, written in every harsh, exhausted line of that strong face. His face was so fascinating. She studied him openly and he let her. Grace was always curious about faces, about what they said of a person and what they hid. Particularly lived-in faces like his, which spoke of hardship and power and authority. Whoever he was, he'd lived through harsh times and prevailed.

"I'm not too sure you should be beating yourself up for something that you didn't do. I mean, you didn't invite those men to attack you, did you? It's not your fault."

"You're wrong." He closed his eyes wearily. "In a very real sense, it is my fault. I should have arranged for a discreet purchase of an oil or two, a drawing here and there." He opened them again suddenly, his gaze as direct and fierce as a falcon's. "But I was greedy, I wanted them all, everything you ever produced, would ever produce. And now you're paying the consequences."

The regret on his face, in his voice, pierced her. Most people evaded responsibility, even when it rested squarely on their shoulders. This man was clearly used to bearing heavy burdens and not foisting them off on anyone else.

He also looked utterly exhausted. Underneath his naturally olive complexion, he was pale, and it seemed to her that the grooves bracketing his mouth had carved themselves more deeply in the past few hours.

"Do you know, Drake—by the way, is that your first name or last name?"

"Neither. My name is Viktor Drakovich. But I'm known as Drake."

It was an odd way to phrase it. Most people would say *People call me Drake.* She tilted her head to study him some more. There was something so compelling about his face, with its high cheekbones, strong brow, sensuous mouth. Compelling and . . . and sort of familiar. Which was crazy, of course. She'd never seen him before in her life and she knew no one like him. Obviously, all these shocks had rattled her brain and that was the source of the déjà vu. Even his voice—incredibly deep and with a hint of an accent that she couldn't place—sank deep into her bones as if she'd heard him a thousand times before.

"Where are you from?"

He gave a frosty smile. "I have no idea." He held his hand up when she recoiled. "That's not—what would you call it? An answer that's not serious?" Deep grooves etched between his eyebrows. His accent was becoming stronger.

"A flip answer?" she suggested.

"Precisely. It's not a flip answer. I don't know where I was born. My first memory is of being a street rat in Odessa, running with a pack of what you'd call hoodlums there. But someone said something about me coming from Tajikistan." He shrugged. "I grew up speaking a mongrel mixture of Russian, Tajik and Ukrainian. Took me years to straighten the languages out."

He was trying to frighten her. No, not frighten. His body language was clearly protective, not aggressive. He was trying, for some reason, to put himself in a bad light.

"Well, Drake, let me tell you, I'm finding it really hard to be that angry with someone who made the mistake of loving my paintings too much."

A huge log crumbled into the fire with a crash and flurry of sparks. The fire was dying, consuming itself. She knew just how it felt. Before she could stop herself, a huge yawn bubbled its way to the surface.

"Sorry." Her eyes felt heavy. She could feel her neck muscles weighing on her shoulders. It took an effort to keep straight and upright.

Drake folded his hand around hers. "You're tired," he said. "You need rest after what you went through today. You need to sleep." In a lithe movement, he was standing and helping her to stand, too. He put a light hand to her back.

His hands were so amazing. Huge and hard and like heaters. The warmth of the hand at her back came through the silk of the gi as if it were a heating pad.

One hand holding hers, the other at her back. For a moment, it was as if she were in his embrace. Grace was utterly shocked that she was tempted to keep going, simply turn into him, feel those incredibly strong arms fold around her. The temptation was so strong that she had to freeze for a moment not to give in to it.

He misunderstood and dropped his hands to his side, stepping back sharply.

How crazy. She felt . . . bereft. Already missing his hands on her, the heat of them soaking into her, the feeling of being surrounded by his immense strength.

"Come," he said. "You must be exhausted." He turned and motioned toward the door. They walked silently down the immense corridor until he stopped outside the bedroom door, opening it and gesturing for her to enter. "I never have guests, so I am afraid there is just the one bed. I'll sleep on a couch."

Grace stiffened. "You most certainly will *not* sleep on a couch in your own home. If anyone sleeps on a couch, it will be me. I'd like to remind you that you've been shot, in case you've forgotten."

A wintry smile. "No, I haven't forgotten. But it is unthinkable that you sleep on a couch. I absolutely cannot permit it. You'll find a pair of pajamas on the bed and—"

"Drake." Grace stepped a little closer, looking up into his eyes. Dark-ringed, weary eyes. "Don't even think of it. I am not about to make a wounded man sleep on a couch, and that's final." She pointed at the bed, large enough to plant corn on. "If you insist, that bed is big enough for both of us, with a football team in the middle."

He sagged a little in relief, caught himself. His deep brown eyes turned almost liquid. "You—you trust me? I swear you'll be safe, I swear on my honor."

She believed him, utterly and completely. He'd done nothing but protect her since that horrible moment outside the gallery, when he'd been willing to disarm himself for her.

She looked at him, at the immense strength and power of him. They were in his home, which was essentially a fortress, surrounded by his men, who were obviously trained bodyguards and armed to boot. He had shown himself capable of violence. Violence so expert it was almost surgical in its precision. And yet Grace felt absolutely no fear. She felt shock and sadness and exhaustion, but no fear.

She wasn't stupid. A single woman living in the city learned fast how to read situations. She'd bought all the books, had taken self-defense courses—not that anything she could do could withstand the power of this man if she was wrong.

But her instincts were sound. She trusted them.

"I think that if you meant me any harm, Drake, I'd be hurt by now," she said softly.

"Oh God. Never." Swallowing heavily, he picked her hand up and brought it to his lips. "I can't bear the thought of you hurt or frightened. Today was a nightmare for me. Please, don't fear me or anyone who works for me. You're as safe as I can possibly make you. So put on those pajamas and have yourself a good night's rest."

Midnight-blue pajamas, brand new and of a heavy silk by the feel of them, lay at the foot of the bed. In the bathroom, Grace changed, turning up the sleeves and pants cuffs a couple of times. She switched off the bathroom light and, feeling shy, walked back into the bedroom, closing the door quietly behind her.

She walked toward the bed and then simply stopped, the artist in her rising up and crowding out the scared, exhausted, stressed woman.

The deep green curtains had been closed, shutting out the diamond-bright skyline. All the lights had been turned off, the only light a warm glow coming from the dying embers of the fire.

One side of the bed had been turned down, the smooth sheets unbearably inviting. True to his word, Drake lay on the other side of the bed, so close to the edge he would fall off if he turned in his sleep. There would be at least six feet between them. To reassure her further, he hadn't gotten between the sheets, but rather was lying on top of the emerald-green comforter, covered by a rich, thick fur blanket, looking like something out of a Russian novel.

No, that wasn't quite right.

He didn't look like a character in a novel, he looked like a *legend*. A warrior out of time. Tamerlane, perhaps, or Alexander, resting in his tent after conquering the known world.

He'd taken his shirt off. Massive naked shoulders rose above the soft fur blanket. The dying embers painted his face a dusky olive, highlighting the broad, high cheekbones and square jawline, leaving his eyes in shadow. The light threw his muscles in relief—the strong cords of the neck, the deep indentation between the pectorals, the bulge of his biceps.

A magnificent wounded warrior.

That's exactly the way she would paint him. The wounded warrior finally finding his rest in a tent, the glint of his bronze armor barely visible in the gloom, a soldier standing guard outside. The warrior's blood-flecked helmet, with a proud pennant and nosepiece, looking like a metal skull, on the table. A man who had commanded an army that day and been bloodied, and who would command it the next to victory.

Grace rarely had an entire painting come to her at once. Usually, the pieces of it, the order and balance, the shapes and the colors, came to her gradually. But this "Portrait of a Warrior" came to her complete, in one single vision, and she knew she wouldn't rest until her vision had become reality.

Drake's dark eyes tracked her as she made her way to the huge bed. She slipped between the sheets quietly. The bed was as comfortable as it looked, the sheets and silk comforter a delight to the touch. A faint scent of lavender rose from the bed.

She turned in bed to find him still watching her, face drawn with exhaustion and pain. She was exhausted herself, muscles sore, the scrapes still stinging.

A log fell with a hiss in the quiet of the night. She could feel herself drifting into the welcome arms of sleep.

"Good night, Drake," she said quietly.

"Sleep well." His deep voice came out of the gathering darkness.

It was the noise that woke her. A strangled sound of silenced pain. She came awake in a rush, heart pounding, in a strange bed full of unfamiliar textures.

There was the faintest possible glow from the fireplace. For a second, she couldn't place the cavernous room, the shadowy furniture, the plush bedding, until the memories exploded in a rush.

Drake's home.

Drake's bed.

There was that sound again. Coming from her left. She turned her head on the down pillow and saw him, lying on his back like a statue on a sarcophagus. He hadn't budged since falling asleep. Something about his stillness told her that he always slept in stillness, perhaps had learned to do so as a child on the streets.

The sound was of a man unconsciously stifling a groan of pain. The fact that he could do this in his sleep spoke volumes of the man, of the kind of life he'd led.

Grace knew it was insane to feel sorry for a man like this. He was clearly very rich, immensely strong. He commanded enormous resources, including what appeared to be an army of men and staff. There wasn't anything in the waking man that would make you feel sorry for him.

But the sleeping man, ah, that was a different story.

There was just enough light from the embers to see his face, its lines of pain drawn deep, jaws clenched to stifle any sounds. And yet, a soft noise sounded from deep in his throat, however he fought against it.

The anesthesia had long since worn off. Ben hadn't offered painkillers and Drake didn't seem to her to be the kind of man who would take them unless he absolutely had to. But right now, his body was contending with the minor surgery of the removal of a bullet and the stitches taken in his shoulder, without anything to dull the pain.

Had he sent himself to that place he'd gone to in the surgery? It seemed so. He looked utterly gone, eyes still behind the closed lids, body rigid. Feeling pain at some level but refusing to give in to it.

Grace listened to his labored breathing for another couple of minutes and then couldn't stand it any more. Moving softly, she slid across the enormous bed until she was close enough to touch him.

Another stifled moan. She touched his hand, intending to see if she could wake him up, ask him if he needed anything.

But when she touched him, amazingly, he stilled. The tense muscles went lax, the frown smoothed out, his breathing slowed. His hand grasped hers tightly, his grip warm and unbreakable.

He seemed to have found instant peace, the grooves in his face gone, breathing calm and shallow.

Quiet reigned in the room and as the last light from the fire waned, Grace felt the dark mantle of sleep fold over her once more.

Nine

November 18

Drake had often woken up after being wounded. Less often, he had woken up beside a woman, though he never liked it. Usually, he dismissed the woman after sex, preferring to sleep alone. But he'd never woken up next to a woman after being wounded.

Never fuck while vulnerable. One of Drake's hard-and-fast rules.

His women had no loyalty to him, and he had no reason to trust them while he was in a state of weakness. So when he woke up with the familiar feeling of having been wounded, he couldn't factor in the softness on his arm.

Even the way he came out of sleep was unusual. Drake was used to waking instantly, rising up out of sleep in a flash, combat-ready. It was the only way he could have survived his boyhood. Coming awake instantly was second nature, whether he was in a dangerous situation or not.

Yet now, he came up out of sleep in long, languorous swoops, aware of someone beside him who wasn't a threat. Aware of a certain warmth in the air and softness touching his skin. Rising, rising slowly until his eyes finally opened. His wounded shoulder ached, but that was nothing. What was astonishing was what was on his other shoulder. A mass of soft, reddish brown hair, pale skin showing from the too-large pajama top; long, lush eyelashes; a full mouth that begged for kisses.

Grace. Grace Larsen. Migrated, by some miracle, from her side of the bed.

No, not migrated. The nighttime memory came up from his subconscious like a cork bobbing up from a dark sea. He must have shown signs of distress in the night. The shoulder had been painful. Not the greatest pain he'd ever known, not by a long shot, but enough to pull him out of sleep. And she'd come to him, touched him, given him comfort.

He swallowed heavily, dry mouthed.

She had offered comfort.

He looked down at the beautiful woman whose head lay so trustingly on his shoulder, barely breathing so as not to disturb her.

He tried really hard to concentrate on his gratitude to her in order to take his mind off the erection that had sprung to life. What the Americans called a blue-steeler. If he needed any sign that he was going to live, it was right there, under his pajama pants, between his legs.

Having a hard-on was good, of course. He was going to have to seduce Grace to bind her to him. So fucking Grace was a really good next step—necessary even. And of course he'd have to have an erection for that; it went without saying.

Only . . . not quite such a *big* erection. He wasn't supposed to feel as if he'd die if he didn't enter her. This tightness throughout his body, culminating in his cock, stiff and straining to be in her, wasn't really necessary.

Drake kept his cool, always. Even under fire. He was always totally in control of himself in bed with a woman. He liked sex. He liked the release of tension, he liked the feel of the softness of a woman. He'd started young on the streets. Sex was a source of solace for the street rats he ran with, girls and boys.

As he grew in power and wealth, for a while sex with beautiful women was a way to keep count, to establish his place in the hierarchy, to get back at the world. A spectacularly beautiful woman on a man's arm was the perfect status symbol, and he'd had some real beauties in his day. It had pleased him to enter a room and have eyes widen at the sight of the eye candy on his arm.

It grew old quickly, of course. Drake soon realized that it was much better—certainly more efficient—to be feared than envied. So he made sure his revenge was public and his sex life private.

Sex was useful for releasing tension, pleasant for what it was, and nothing more.

But right now his entire body was drawn tight with anticipation. There was a huge band around his chest that had nothing to do with the bandages over his wound. As he reached out a hand to touch a lock of her hair that had spilled over his chest, Drake realized that his hand was trembling.

He hoped like hell it was a side effect of the bullet he'd taken yesterday, because if it wasn't, if his hand was trembling because of Grace, he was in a shitload of trouble. If he and Grace were to get out of this mess, he'd have to keep a cool head and a steady hand.

Since when had his hands trembled? Never. He'd been a sharpshooter since he was fourteen. He made his fucking *living* selling arms. He was expected to be a better shot than anyone he sold to, and he was. It went with the territory. The hands of a marksman didn't tremble. Not if the marksman wanted to live.

He touched the button next to the bed that opened the curtains. Judging by the light coming in through the windows, it must be around eight.

His finger touched her hair. The clear morning light picked out the highlights in her hair. Such an astonishing range of colors, from pale blonde to chestnut and everything in between. She was so right not to color her hair. There wasn't a salon in the world that could duplicate that range of colors, that sheen. He carefully fit his finger under the lock and lifted it. As if it were alive, it curled around his finger. He shifted, turning into her, watching her.

The cuts and scrapes and bruises only enhanced the delicacy of her skin. He winced at the round scab at her temple, knowing precisely what a bullet planted right there would have done.

It would have wiped this beautiful woman right off the face of the planet in a spray of brain and blood.

He'd have woken up all alone on his huge bed, aching and sore, with nothing to look forward to, save plans for revenge. Plans he'd made and executed many, many times before.

Instead, by some miracle, he had this woman next to him, bearing the gift of kindness and beauty. In her person and in her hands.

How much better to contemplate that lovely face rather than watch the walls in the rising light, listening to his own breathing. If she weren't here, he'd have been up at dawn, spreading his net to capture the fish of information.

And of course there was the business to run. He ran an empire, alone, and it required his constant attention, fourteen hours a day, seven days a week. Today, for example, there was a shipment to Yaounde to arrange, two new armorers to interview, the maintenance records of his helicopter fleet to check and the deputy premier of Montenegro to talk to on a secure video conference line.

None of these things held even a remote appeal. He let himself sink further into the bed, where he wanted to stay forever.

So be it. He wiped his mind of everything but the fascinating woman next to him.

He watched her face in sleep, the long lashes lying on her cheekbones. She was a quiet sleeper, the covers barely rising and falling with her breaths. He could stay here forever and simply watch her.

Grace's eyes opened suddenly, with no warning. She was fast asleep one moment, eyes wide open the next. She stared straight up at him, disoriented. He watched her take in their position, close to him. A faint rosy blush rose in her cheeks.

"You, ah, you were restless and in pain—"

"And you comforted me," he said softly. "Thank you. How are you feeling?"

"I don't really know," she confessed. "Better, I think. But sore." She stretched her muscles a bit, moving her head. She was brought up short by his hand in her hair. The stretching had brought her closer to him. Watching her eyes, he rolled in her direction. Inches separated them.

Her breathing had speeded up, the slight flush along her cheekbones grew deeper. The blush warmed her skin, puffing out her natural fragrance like a cloud.

If Drake didn't touch her, he would die. He finally gave in to temptation and ran the back of his finger over her cheekbone, marveling at the softness. She didn't blink, she didn't even breathe.

There was utter quiet, as if even the room were waiting for something.

This was the moment when Drake should start his seduction, that elegant dance between a man and a woman he was so familiar with. He knew all the moves, knew that he should touch her here and kiss her there.

But the music was off. Instead of a series of practiced moves, he found himself trembling with excitement, ready to burst out of his skin. He wanted to hold her so tightly her skin would be imprinted on his, he wanted to touch every inch of her, hold her breasts in his hands, suckle hard at her breasts, run his hand over her smooth, pale stomach. He wanted to roll on top of her, mount her, open her with his fingers and thrust inside, hard. Start fucking with all the strength of his body . . .

Whoa.

He was big and right now he was as excited as he'd ever been in his life. His size was a problem even for women who fucked constantly. The heated images in his head—holding her down with his hands while he fucked her as hard as he could—were crazy. He couldn't do that with Grace. He'd scare her, maybe hurt her. God.

Something of what he was feeling must have communicated itself to her. Her color rose, her beautiful blue-green eyes shiny, watchful.

He had to go slowly. Be careful. Be in control.

For a second the notion that he had to tell himself to be in control was so alien, he nearly snorted. He was nothing *but* control.

His finger moved down her cheek, over the delicate jawline, running along the vein pulsing in her neck. He lifted his eyes to hers, finger poised to go lower.

"I want to touch you," he whispered. "So badly."

"I know," she whispered back.

The finger hovered over her collarbone. He kept it steady only by applying the full force of his will, but the cost of that was that his entire body trembled, vibrated like a tuning fork.

He touched the soft silk of the pajama top. It was much too large for her and he could see pale skin bared where the material ballooned out. His eyes asked the question.

In answer, Grace arched, bringing her breasts close to his hand, baring that long, slender white neck.

Which to touch first? Both intriguing, impossible to resist.

Drake's mouth settled on her neck while his hand slipped under the soft silk to her even softer, silkier breast. Grace let out a long, shaky breath.

Drake would have, too, but he was too excited to breathe. Too excited to do anything but cup her breast as he licked her, feeling the pounding pulse of her blood on his tongue, speeding up when he circled her nipple with his thumb. Ah God. Giving into temptation, he scraped his teeth along that smooth, smooth skin, then gave a little nip, of excitement, of ownership.

Grace jumped.

He hadn't hurt her, but he lifted his head to check just the same. No, he hadn't hurt her, but he had excited her. Color bloomed in her cheeks, along her neck.

Down to her breasts? He had to know.

His hand hovered over her and touched the top button of her pajamas. Moving his arm hurt his shoulder a little and he welcomed the pain, the bite of it. It grounded him, just a little, helped to keep his excitement from raging out of control.

"I want to see you, Grace. Will you let me?"

She let out a little huff of air. "I—ah, I seem to be having some trouble in saying no to you."

He felt a slow smile well up from somewhere inside him, though he wasn't normally a smiler. "Well the answer to that is obvious. Don't say no."

"That could get a little dangerous."

"No, never." The smile disappeared. "I don't want you frightened of me, in any way. You can say no anytime you want, though I'm hoping you won't."

Grace shook her head, hair rasping on the pillow. "I mean dangerous in that you—you make me feel things I haven't felt before. I don't feel in control of myself."

That makes two of us, he thought.

He unbuttoned the top button. "Tell me," he urged. "Tell me what you're feeling."

To his astonishment, she did. Eyes wide, voice halting, she told him exactly what she was feeling, with an honesty that stole his breath.

"Where you touch me—I burn, Drake. Only burning isn't really the right word because it's not painful, not at all. It's pure pleasure."

The top button came undone, the second, the third . . . finally he had the pajama top open, revealing a strip of pale skin that was rapidly turning rosy. Drake wanted to watch her eyes, but he wanted to watch his hand touching her more. "And this?" he breathed as he folded back the heavy silk, revealing a pale, perfect breast. The back of his hand had touched her chest as he unbuttoned the top, but now he turned his hand to cup her. She fit in the palm of his hand, perfectly.

Perfect. She was just perfect. And real. What he was cupping was pure woman, not some artificial sac of liquid just under the skin. He hated that so much he ended up passing on the women who'd had their breasts enhanced surgically.

And why should she want to enhance something already perfect, anyway? His eyes greedily drank in every detail. The tender undercurve, the milky blue veins barely visible under the skin, the pale pink aureole, the nipples turning harder as he watched, a bright red cherry color.

"You're perfect here," he said, his thumb circling the nipple slowly.

"You certainly make me feel perfect. Ah . . ." She exhaled shakily as he gently pinched her.

"What else?" he asked urgently. "What else do I make you feel?"

"Warmth. No, heat. Your hand is hot on my skin. I noticed that yesterday. Even in the wet and cold, your skin emanates warmth. Only now . . ."

"Now, duschka?" he murmured. The endearment came from somewhere deep inside of him. Russian wasn't even his first language, though to tell the truth, he had no idea what his first language had been. He'd spoken a bastard medley until he was around eleven. But somewhere he'd heard this word murmured with love, man to woman, the tone unmistakeable, and the word came up out of him from somewhere deep in his chest, certainly not his head. "Now, what?"

"I feel the heat where you touch me, but I also feel it all over my skin. Oh!"

Drake had bent and taken a nipple in his mouth. The bud felt tender, velvety in his mouth. He pulled, as a child pulls at its mother's breast, only he pulled with a man's strength. Grace moaned, twisted, a hand coming up to cup the back of his head, the other his uninjured shoulder. He felt the small bite of her nails and would have smiled, except that the electricity he felt left no room for smiling.

"Oh God. When you do that, I feel it in my womb, with each tug."

Drake lifted his head, frowning, the unfamiliar word bouncing around his head while he tried to pin a meaning to it. Womb . . . wasn't that where pregnant women carried their babies? Then it struck him. She meant her cunt. She was feeling what he was doing in her cunt.

He had to breathe hard around his excitement. He pulled the covers off her, opened the jacket wide and, watching her eyes carefully, slipped the trousers down her legs. She swam in them; they came off easily.

Shaking, he pulled one long slender leg to one side and feasted his eyes on her. Narrow waist, round hips, smooth little belly. A puff of dark red hair between her thighs hiding a pale pink slit. He covered her with his hand. "Here, Grace?" he asked, his voice hoarse. "Do you feel it here?" He waggled his big hand a little and she widened her legs. His middle finger stroked her carefully.

She wet her lips, tried to say something, then finally nodded.

"Let me know," he insisted. "Let me hear your voice. Let me know everything you're feeling. I need to know if I'm pleasing you. I need that like I need air."

Another long, light caress along her slit. The muscles of her stomach contracted.

"I don't think—*ah!*" He'd bent his head again to her breast, suckling hard. He swirled his finger around her, thumb brushing her clitoris. She drew in a deep shuddering breath. "I don't think not pleasing me is a problem."

"That's very good," Drake murmured against her skin. God, touching her skin was like touching satin. Satin with the sheen of pearls. She didn't take the sun, her skin was unmarred by bathing-suit stripes. She was the same color all over—a pale pearl with a slight pink glow of healthy skin, healthy woman. He lifted his head, torn between closing his eyes to savor the taste of her breast, the touch of her soft woman's tissues, and wanting to see everything, every detail about her. All the soft little slicks and hollows, the unique set of muscles and angles that made up Grace. He wanted to watch her face as he touched her, watch the glow of arousal slowly blossom on her skin.

Grace smiled and Drake watched that lush mouth move.

It occurred to him that he hadn't kissed her yet. How could that be? How crazy of him to forget the rules of seduction, just toss them out the window. First you kiss, then you touch. Everything was upside down and inside out with Grace.

A smooth shift of his muscles and he brought his head up to hers, mouth aligned with hers. She was watching him carefully, smile completely gone.

His smile was gone, too.

They both knew that this wasn't going to be a casual kiss. Staring at her mouth, Drake actually hesitated a moment. He was at the edge of a precipice and should be windmilling his arms to get back to safety.

Instead, he lowered his head.

Ah, she tasted as delightful as he knew she would, though he tasted her briefly. A touch of his lips to hers, then a few molecules of air between them. A taste, no more. There was no hurry.

The room was quiet, as if they were the only two humans left alive on earth, which would suit him just fine. The walls were soundproof; rugs and tapestries absorbed any other possible noises. The only sounds were those of his mouth on hers. Another quick taste, lifting his mouth to angle for a better fit, his tongue meeting hers. At that first electric touch, they both exhaled shakily, then Drake finally just sank into her, tongue deep in her mouth, stroking.

One of her arms hooked around his neck and pulled, as if to bring him closer to her, when he was as close as her breath.

Drake was always hyper-aware of time. He wore an expensive Rolex because it really was nearly indestructible, but he rarely had to check it. There was a very accurate clock in his head that kept time for him.

The clock broke. He had no concept of time at all. Something broke loose in his head and drifted free.

The only time he recognized was the time it took to make her sigh, the time it took her hand to move from his biceps to his shoulder and back, the time it took for his skin to become so sensitive, it felt like she was touching raw nerve endings.

His tongue stroked hers again and he felt her little cunt muscles ripple. Oh God, yes! Moisture was welling up from inside her, as if he were licking her there instead of her mouth. They had a direct connection between their kiss and their genitals. With each sigh and each stroke, he could feel himself swelling, growing larger, longer, it seemed, with each beat of his heart, while she softened.

She was slippery. His hand moved with ease through the soft folds. He kept his touch light, delicate, trying to match strokes of his tongue with strokes of his thumb. The first time she nearly came off the bed, but he bore down with his mouth.

He lightened up. He was naturally dominant in bed, rarely letting the woman be on top, often holding her limbs down. He had to curb his nature with Grace, let her breathe, follow her lead.

Another slow journey around her labia, smiling inside at the light moan coming from the back of her throat.

Time to take the next step. She was wet. His finger was making slippery little noises as he explored the outside of her cunt. He opened his mouth wider over hers, and entered her with his finger.

Uh-oh.

Trouble.

Grace stiffened, then consciously relaxed her muscles, but Drake knew she wasn't in that dreamy, lax state she'd been in. His finger was hurting her. She was hiding it, but he could tell.

Fuck.

She was incredibly tight, much too tight.

He lifted his head and she gave an uneasy smile. She was trying to relax her muscles around his finger, trying to breathe her way through it.

He remembered an old movie line. "Houston, we have a problem."

That earned him a laugh.

"Sorry, I'm—"

He lay a finger across her lips. "Shhh. God, no apologies." He slid his finger out a little, then back in. Tight little muscles clenched around him. "But if I make love to you now, I'll hurt you, and I don't want to do that. When was the last time you had a man . . . here?" He thrust his finger a little more deeply.

"Not . . . for a long time." Her narrow rib cage was rising and falling rapidly.

Drake stilled, astounded. "Are American men blind, then? Or crazy?"

Grace laughed, her hands kneading his shoulder muscles. "Actually, I think American men think *I'm* crazy. Or eccentric beyond their comfort zone. I guess I actually stopped thinking about sex a couple of years ago." Small frown lines appeared between ash brown eyebrows. "Is this really going to be a problem?"

Yes, but he would get around it.

Drake took her hand, lifted it to his mouth, then brought it under the drawstring of his pajama pants to fold around his cock. His breath blew out in a hiss at the feel of her hand around him. "You tell me if we have a problem."

"God," she whispered, her face showing shock. "I'm not—I can't." She sucked in a breath, her hand flexing around his cock. Experimentally, she ran it up over the head, feeling it weeping, then pulling her fist down to the base. She had to open her hand up to do it. Her touch electrified him. "What do you suggest we—"

The words were drowned in his mouth. The kiss was deeper, harder, more possessive than before, and it reverberated in both their bodies. He could feel how the kiss affected her. She clenched tightly around his finger, growing slicker by the second. And Grace could feel how his cock surged in her hand, echoing her inner muscles. She was growing wetter and so was he, the tip of his cock weeping so hard he could feel the cool air. It wasn't all he was feeling. As he shifted so that his chest covered hers without breaking the kiss, a hot electric line raced along his spine. His balls tightened painfully. He could move his finger with ease now, in and out of her slick folds. His thumb passed over her clitoris again and she passed her own thumb over the slit at the tip of his cock that was weeping to be in her.

He felt it with every cell in his body.

"I will have my cock in you here, soon," he breathed into her mouth, finger sliding into her deeply, so slick and hot. "But only when you are ready."

Her hand speeded up. So did his. "I might . . . be ready now," she panted.

She wasn't ready for his cock but she was definitely ready to come.

"First you come for me," Drake murmured against her mouth, setting up a rhythm of penetration and retreat echoed by her hand fisting his cock.

Grace gave out a little cry, almost of surprise, the walls of her cunt clenching hard, over and over as her legs shook. It pushed him right over the edge as every muscle tensed and the base of his spine exploded. He bit the pillow next to her head as he came in long, rhythmic spurts, in time with her contractions. She kept her hand around him, hot and tight, milking him as they both shook and moaned.

Finally, Drake's muscles relaxed, felt like water as he lay half over her, one hand cupping her mound, one hand cupping her head. She released his cock finally.

Their breathing slowed, evened out.

"Well, that worked," she finally whispered.

Drake could barely lift his head.

He rarely felt wiped out after sex. If anything, it energized him. But right now, lifting his head to give her a quick kiss seemed to be the most he could hope for. God help him when they could finally make love. It would probably kill him.

Ah, well. You had to go some time.

They lay like that, not asleep, not awake, as the room slowly filled with late-morning light. It was the first time Drake could ever remember when he hadn't started the day early, with specific business plans. His big plan right now was to keep Grace in bed with him, making sure she got used to being naked with him, until her skin smelled of his.

He'd try again to fuck her, just as soon as he could move.

See if she loosened up a little, so he wouldn't panic at the thought of hurting her when he entered her. It would happen, he just didn't know when.

His head had come to rest against hers on the pillow, his lips close to the skin of her neck. Much too beautiful to resist. He moved forward the inch necessary to kiss her, breathing in deeply. He could smell her skin and his. The scent of their sex was unlike any other he'd smelled.

Grace's hand dropped from his shoulder, making a faint plop sound as it fell to the mattress. "Drake, I think real sex is going to be too much for me. I'm not too sure I can handle it."

He breathed in and out, slowly. Every single muscle felt

lax, like water. His mind was completely empty, no thoughts at all. Only sensations, all connected with her. the feel of her silky skin under his fingertips. The scent of her skin, the sound of her breathing.

He'd traveled the world, racking up more air miles than any pilot possibly could. He'd lived in eight countries, was intimately familiar with fifteen more.

This was an entirely new country for him, a new, completely unfamiliar landscape.

He didn't know if he could handle sex with her, either, but he was willing to try. His cock, ten minutes after an explosive orgasm, twitched at the thought. His fingers knew how she felt inside and now his cock was jealous.

You'll get your turn, Drake wanted to tell it—and then thought that he was going crazy, talking to his own penis.

He wanted to lift his head, reassure her, but he didn't have the energy. It was the oddest lassitude. Not the frightening weakness of being wounded. He'd been weak from blood loss only a few times and it was terrifying. When he was weak, he was instant prey.

No, this was different. His muscles weren't weak, they were . . . relaxed.

How odd a feeling.

Grace's stomach growled, loudly. Drake laughed into her neck. "I guess I know what you want. And right now, it appears that sex isn't it."

He could feel the slight shift in the air as she smiled. "To tell you the truth, breakfast sounds good right about now."

He'd already ordered it. Trays would be waiting on a trolley outside the bedroom door.

Drake lifted his head. "Something tells me it's ready. Stay right where you are."

The weakness disappeared instantly. Grace needed food. Just the thought of her being uncomfortable—God, *hungry*—in his home, was enough to energize him. He rolled out of bed naked, making for the door, then heard a soft noise behind him.

Drake turned. She was up on one elbow, staring, mouth slightly open. Her hair was tousled, falling in soft locks over her shoulders. One lock, delightfully, had fallen to encircle one nipple, now not cherry red and diamond hard but soft and pale.

An enchantress that had been tumbled and would be tumbled again.

Her eyes widened and he didn't have to look down to see what was shocking her. He could feel it. His cock rising, lengthening, thickening. Color rose in her cheeks and her nipples turned a deeper pink. His cock rose higher on a thick pulse of blood at the sight. A vein pounded in her neck, bringing the blood that now flushed brightly down to her breasts. Breasts he'd touched, kissed. At the memory, his balls tightened, drew up while his cock burned.

They were seducing each other across ten feet of space.

Her stomach growled again. "Food," she said weakly.

"Food," he agreed, turning back around.

Ten

Fifty thousand dollars. So much, for so little. Andrew Peters, born Andrei Petrov, continued peeling potatoes while thinking it through.

Peeling potatoes as the kitchen *commis* was not where he wanted to be, in his tenth year out of cooking school. By rights, he should have been the chef, or at least the sous-chef, in a decent restaurant, socking money aside for his own place.

And he knew exactly what he wanted. He'd had his eye on the place for a while. A small place, a thousand square feet, in Chelsea. It would be decorated like the dining room in Tolstoy's town mansion, serving pre-Revolutionary Franco-Russian haute cuisine, what the czars and barons ate before the Soviet monsters came and ransacked Mother Russia.

The Petrovs had been aristocracy in St. Petersburg, the family fortune and nearly all the family members wiped out by Stalin.

But books and photographs had somehow survived the

monsters, ah yes, and had come down to the last Petrov. Andrei had an entrée into the lives of his forebears. Though he read the books and pored over the photographs in a small room with plyboard walls which hid nothing his drunken neighbors said or did, though he lived in a small, cramped fourth-floor walk-up in Brighton Beach, that wasn't his life. His life was in another place and another time. In his imagination, Andrei was Prince Petrov, a grandee in nineteenth-century St. Petersburg.

He lived on Nevsky Prospekt in a palatial Italianate mansion, which had been his great-great-grandfather's town house. As a young boy, before his parents emigrated, he used to stand in the street, small hands clutching the bars of the elaborate wrought-iron fence guarding the building, and imagine that the building now housing the state archives was still his. The mansion of Prince Petrov.

He knew every detail of his great-great-grandfather's life. The number of servants, the coaches and the horses, each horse with its own groom. The social calendar filled with balls and concerts and parties. The elaborate meals with fifty guests eating off the one-thousand-piece gold-trimmed set of Limoges china.

And the food! He'd come across a set of menus for meals during the Christmas season of 1904 and his boy's mind swam with the grandeur of it all. Borscht and *kvass*, *kholodets*, *pelmeny*, twenty different types of *pirozhki*, kebabs from woodland game hunted on Petrov land, *sudak* fished from the well-stocked ponds of the country *dascha*. Fruits and berries collected by the serfs, an enormous *Sharlotka* carried in on a two-foot-long silver serving tray borne by four servants. Washed down by the finest imported French champagne. Fifty guests, one hundred servants.

Andrei's young heart thrilled at the images. Russia's finest, at the Petrov table by candlelight, a quartet playing Mozart on the balcony overlooking the immense mirrored dining hall, an army of servants in livery, quietly serving the *ton*.

His parents applied to emigrate to *Amerika* when he was eleven, and he thought yes, perhaps *Amerika* would be the place where he would make his money and return in triumph to Russia, where the Petrovs would take their rightful place amongst the rich and mighty.

It didn't turn out that way. Andrei's father, an engineer, could only find work as a cab driver, working fourteen hours a day for a company that paid him a pittance. Andrei's mother developed breast cancer and the two Petrov men watched helplessly as she died a fast, painful death.

When they buried her, his father died, too, except his body. He could barely work with his grief. So it was all on him—on Andrei, now Andrew. His shoulders had to bear the burden of the Petrovs.

He'd had such huge dreams of returning to the motherland, dreams with the solid feel of destiny to them. A Petrov picking up after seventy years of the barbarity of the Soviets. Yet with each passing year, as he grew taller, the plans grew smaller, shrinking steadily, until he was reduced to applying for aid to enroll in a second-rate cooking school.

It might have been his way out. A quick rise through the ranks, a few years at the top. Celebrity chefs could pull in hundreds of thousands of dollars a year in salary and millions in sponsorships. But not him.

He'd been interviewing for the lowly job of *garde manger*, the fucking *pantry supervisor*, in a third-rate restaurant in Rockaway, when he'd heard of a job opening for a Russian speaker. In Manhattan, the heart of fine cuisine. And it paid three times the going salary.

It was a good job, in a superbly well-equipped kitchen, but his talents went unnoticed. Well, what could he expect? He was cooking for Russian *thugs*. Men who knew the best gun to use in a firefight, but who had no clue how to judge the fineness of crepes or the smooth consistency of a good béchamel. Or even appreciate the fine porcelain they ate on or the heavy crystal of the glasses they drank out of.

Andrei wouldn't have cared one way or the other, except that they spoke the language he worshipped. The language of his forefathers. The language of Pushkin and Tolstoy and Yevteshenko.

Only this wasn't the Russian he'd been taught by his parents. The language the thugs spoke was rough, ungrammatical, provincial, the Russian of illiterate goons. Gutter Russian, fit only for guttersnipes.

Yet the money was so good, he was forced to stay, even though every day was an assault on his senses, another day amongst the barbarians. He considered it a form of indentured servitude, the exorbitant salary he could never hope to duplicate elsewhere, like a noose around his neck, slowly choking him.

He studied his surroundings, seeking a way out. He was a prince among swine. It went without saying that he could outwit them all.

The kitchen fed forty-five men twice daily, like a small restaurant. It was also open whenever necessary, as men came and went at all hours of the day and the night. The food was copious, fresh and good, without any attempt at sophistication. After a week in the kitchen, Andrei realized that any decent housewife could do what he did. Only it had to be in Russian, since almost the entire staff was Russian or Ukrainian.

He worked for a mystery man everyone called Drake. Andrei knew very little about him and no one talked, ever. The closest Andrei could come to information on Drake was a friendship with the butler, a Russian-Ukrainian called Shota. Shota was fanatically faithful to Drake, though Andrei couldn't understand why. The mystery man kept to himself on the top story of the building, rarely interacting with the staff except through intercom messages.

It wasn't until Andrei had spent a couple of months working for Drake that he understood that he was working for an international criminal, one of the most powerful men in the world. A frisson had run up his spine. Surely there would be a way to use this information. An enemy to sell information to.

It wasn't easy, because this Drake was mysterious as hell. It was an impregnable fortress up above, the domain of a powerful, untouchable ruler. Very few people knew Drake's comings and goings. The man was like smoke—impossible to grasp, impossible to pin down.

And then Andrei had two strokes of good luck. Fabulous luck, actually. Shota developed a crush on him, and a Russian came to Drake as a friend and left as an enemy.

Shota was easy to lead on. He was a romantic, and was deliriously happy with soulful looks and stolen kisses in the pantry. Andrei had no interest whatsoever in fucking Shota, but he did want to string him along as much as possible. It was through Shota that he learned that Drake disappeared two Tuesday afternoons a month. It was through Shota that he learned that Drake was buying the entire production of an artist called Grace Larsen. Finding the gallery that sold Grace

Larsen had been a snap. He waited in a coffee shop across the street on the right Tuesday afternoons and—*voilà!*—the mysterious Drake, slinking in an alley.

Hard info on a billionaire running a crime empire was worth money, big money, but you had to find a buyer for it. Then he overheard that a Russian was offering fifty thousand dollars for information on Drake. None of Drake's men was willing to cross their dangerous boss for half a year's salary. But then none of Drake's men had any ambitions, other than to be a thug for hire.

Andrei did.

There was a Hotmail account. It had all been so easy.

If you want information on Drake, transfer $50,000 to this bank account.

The response, and the fifty-thousand-dollar payment, had come fast. Someone wanted the information badly. Andrei had sent the information and the money went into his savings account.

For a sweaty couple of hours after the attempt on Drake's life, Andrei expected a tap on the shoulder and—well, fuck, Drake was a mobster, after all—two bullets through the back of the head, Soviet style. But as the hours ticked by, Andrei's hands steadied and the sweat along his spine dried. His exquisitely sensitive antenna told him that no one suspected him. He was a sous-chef, a kitchen servant, off everyone's radar.

The BlackBerry in his chef's pants vibrated. Andrei took a bathroom break and checked the screen.

$100,000 for further information.

Andrei's breathing speeded up, his heart raced. One hundred thousand dollars—100K per pop. Oh yes, this was it, his moment. In a day, maybe two, he could accumulate more money than in a lifetime of working hard in shit jobs in other people's kitchens.

He was smart. He could feed the information in tiny incremental bits, string this Rutskoi along. In a couple of days, Andrei could have five hundred thousand dollars. Maybe more.

Five hundred thousand dollars would allow his father to retire, would allow Andrei to open up Troika with enough style to guarantee its success. This was opportunity knocking at the door, what everyone said would happen in *Amerika*. All he had to do was answer.

OK, he typed into the tiny keyboard. He combed his long blond hair, dabbed some Hugo Boss cologne on his pulse points and went off looking for Shota.

Though Grace was starving and though her stomach was making embarrassing noises, it was hard to keep her mind on food with Drake walking naked across a room.

The man was simply magnificent. There were no words to describe him. Luckily, Grace didn't need words. Her artist's eye told her everything she needed to know.

She'd studied human anatomy all her life. During art school, she'd drawn literally thousands of human backs, but had never seen anything like the musculature of Drake's back. It was immensely broad, rippling with muscle, tapering to a lean waist. There wasn't an ounce of fat on him. It almost looked as though he didn't have any skin, either, the muscles underlying it were so prominent. Clothed, he was impressive. Naked, he looked lethal. The pristine white bandage over the enormous ball of his left shoulder looked almost like a decoration. It was impossible to think that he'd taken a bullet only the day before. He looked completely fit and moved with utter ease, like a huge panther.

It was hard to imagine what kind of exercises he put himself through to maintain a body like that. Bodybuilding exercises pumped muscles up, made them rise. These weren't built muscles: they looked . . . forged. Out of iron and steel.

He didn't move like a bodybuilder, either, with that muscle-bound waddle they developed. No, he moved like water, smoothly flowing across the floor, like a force of nature.

She remembered the feel of him in her arms. Amazing. Like holding a warm, perfectly proportioned rock. No, that wasn't the right analogy. Though he'd been hard as stone, what had come through her fingertips had been *life*. As if the man had a greater proportion of life force in him than others. She'd felt her fingers sizzle with electricity when she touched him, a connection to something almost superhuman.

Everything about him was outsize. His physique, his fighting ability, his . . . wow. Yeah, that was outsize, too. Grace didn't have that much experience with male members, but even so, she understood that she'd just held a champ in her hand.

It wasn't that she didn't like sex, it was just that sex involved men, and a goodly portion of them turned out to be unlikeable jerks. She'd tried, she really had. Done her best to relax, go with the flow, all the other clichés, but she never quite managed it.

With Drake relaxation hadn't been a problem. Her muscles had turned to mush. All he had to do was touch her, and her entire body softened for him.

Drake opened the door and walked back to her, pushing

an enormous trolley carrying covered plates, cups, cutlery, a
Thermos. She could smell the rich aroma of coffee, buttery
croissants and juicy meat from across the room.

Grace sat up against the headboard cross-legged, pulling the sheet up under her arms, covering her chest. Drake
parked the trolley next to the bed and poured two cups of
steaming coffee from the Thermos.

He held a cup out to her, while the other hand tugged
down the sheet. "Don't cover yourself up," he said softly.
"You're much too beautiful."

She could have put up a fight, but of course it would have
been ridiculous, thinking she could win a tussle against Drake.
She was naturally modest. Even in the locker room, the few
times she made it to the gym, she preferred dressing in the
toilet cubicles. Not out of prudery, but out of shyness.

Which, clearly, had taken a hike, because she let him tug
down the sheet without a murmur. It might have been the
molten heat in his eyes that convinced her to just let go of the
sheet instead of clutching it to her. No one had ever looked at
her like that, like he wanted to eat her up and was restraining
himself with difficulty.

Once the sheet was down to her lap, he handed her the
cup and curled his hand around her breast, his thumb lazily
twirling around her nipple. Grace could barely hold on to the
coffee. What he was doing made her shake, made her muscles lax, made her vagina contract so hard, even her stomach
muscles clenched.

Drake was watching her closely. He understood exactly the
effect he was having on her. She chanced a glance at his lap.
Well, it was mutual. He was fully aroused again, his penis
flat against his stomach, thick and dark, with ropy veins running up the column.

His dark eyes were hot.

"Drink the coffee," he growled.

Coffee. Right. She had to hold the cup with both hands, otherwise she'd spill the hot coffee all over herself and all over this beautiful bed. She tipped her head back against the headboard and sipped.

God, it was delicious. Sharp, yet with a smooth smoky taste. Some outrageously expensive blend, no doubt. She took another sip. Perfect.

His hand continued stroking her breast, movements lazy. "Good?" he asked.

"Wonderful."

"Give me a taste," he said suddenly, stretching over to cover her mouth with his. Oh lord, she could simply sink into his kisses. This one was long, languid, the strokes of his hand on her breast echoed by his tongue in her mouth. He lifted his head for a second, then moved in more closely, tongue deeper in her mouth. He lifted his head again and smiled down at her. "It *is* delicious."

"Mmm." Grace was too shaken to talk. It was the first time she'd seen a full-fledged smile from him. She'd made a study of faces and knew by the lines in his that he rarely smiled. Perhaps it was for the best, because he became frighteningly attractive when he did. She drew in a deep breath to steady her nerves. His hand was caressing her left breast, and she was certain he could feel her heart thumping away, as if she'd been running.

Drake's hand left her breast to run down her side. He frowned as he felt along her rib cage. "But you must eat. You are too thin. I'll take care of that."

He sounded like an imperious third-world dictator and she had to work to suppress a nervous laugh. "Ah, Drake, I hate to break this to you, but I am not considered too thin here. If anything, I've been told I could stand to lose some weight."

The frown deepened. "Fools, such fools here in America. American men like their women with their ribs sticking out. They have never known hunger, known women whose ribs are visible because they are starving, otherwise they wouldn't be so foolish. Healthy flesh is a blessing and relatively rare in this world. So here, open wide."

He was perfectly right. Grace obediently opened her mouth then moaned. She closed her eyes and tipped her head back. Oh God, there was a little explosion of pastry softer than an angel's wing, butter and sugar on her tongue. The faintest hint of vanilla and cinnamon. Heaven.

"Again." Drake's imperious voice.

She opened wide and the second bite was even better. She washed it down with some more of that ambrosial coffee. Drake didn't give her any relief. The instant she swallowed a bite of the pastry, he had another piece ready for her, watching carefully. As if she were fool enough to spit out the best pastry she'd ever eaten in her life.

His mouth was on hers again, tongue licking deep in her mouth, his taste better than that of the pastry.

After that, it was two perfect soft-boiled eggs, brown-shelled, with the rich yellow yolk of very fresh eggs. Whole wheat toast with salted, freshly churned butter and home-made black-currant jam.

"Open," Drake said, again and again. And she did.

More was opening than just her mouth. It was like being a pampered princess, sitting naked, cross-legged on a fur blanket, fed from the fingers of a man who looked like a conquering warrior from some primeval steppe.

Every time her lips closed over his fingers, he stared directly into her eyes, the gaze hot and direct. Pure, unadulterated sex. And then when she swallowed, he'd allow that small smile to crease his face.

"And now," he announced, whipping the silver cover off a huge porcelain plate, "*voilà!*" Slices of cooked ham and lean grilled sausage. "*Le petit dèjeuner à l'anglaise.* Enjoy."

Grace propped her chin on her fist and observed him. "How many languages do you speak, Drake?" To her ears, admittedly not expert, the short French phrase had sounded perfect.

"A few. Some better than others. My business dealings are with the world, and I've learned at my expense not to depend on interpreters."

She imagined that he spoke them perfectly. His English was nearly perfect, with only a faint accent. He looked like the kind of man who did things well or didn't do them at all.

"I've always wanted to see Paris," she said dreamily, opening her mouth for a bite of the sausage. It was delicious, with fennel seed and pepper. She waved away another bite.

"Have you now?" Drake narrowed his eyes. "Open up." Sighing, she took in another bite of pure, lip-smacking cholesterol.

"Mm-mm. But my real dream is to see Rome. The Caravaggios, the Titians. The Sistine Chapel." She watched his face as she recited the sights she'd always dreamed of seeing. "But you know Rome, don't you? You've been there."

"I know Rome very well, yes. Another bite, that's a good girl. I lived in Rome very briefly some years back. But the Rome I know has nothing whatsoever to do with Titian or the Vatican. So why haven't you been to Rome? It's only about a six-hour flight."

"I know." She sighed. "It's my fault. It never seemed to be the right time. And I only finished paying off the last of my college debts two years ago. And of course, over the past year I've been busy working hard for a patron who never seemed to have enough of my work and never gave me any respite."

Drake's hard mouth lifted in a half smile. Her heart skipped a beat. God, he was attractive when he lost that hard, harsh look.

"I had no idea I was keeping you from your dreams."

"No, no, you don't understand." This was serious. Grace put her hand on his arm and dropped the teasing note. "You weren't keeping me from anything, Drake. You were . . . you were saving my life. I'd tried so hard to earn my living from my art, but it wasn't working. So I tried everything else. Waitressing, temping. None of it worked. I'd do my damndest, but somehow I always came up short. I don't seem to be programmed for the world, only for painting. So the fact that you were buying me up meant that I could do the one thing in the world I loved."

He dipped his head. "Delighted to be of service."

Speaking of service . . . "You need to eat, too. You've done nothing but feed me. Now it's my turn. In the meantime, drink your coffee."

"Yes, ma'am." He sipped obediently, watching her carefully out of dark eyes.

She clambered over him to get a croissant, trying to ignore the large hand that briefly cupped her bottom. The warmth of his hand jolted her. Somehow, once she was perched on the side of the bed, she was in his embrace, one long arm around her waist, a big hand resting at her hip.

The embrace brought her close to him, so close her breasts touched his chest. There was absolutely no need for the pajamas, his body emanated as much heat as a blanket. He took another sip of coffee. "Aren't you curious?" he asked, voice low.

"Curious about what?"

"Whether the coffee tastes just as good from my mouth. Why don't you try it?"

Curious wasn't quite the word. *Fascinated* was. Everything about the man was fascinating, mysterious. Enticing.

Another long sip and he put the coffee cup on the tray, bringing her closer to him with one huge hand to the back of her head.

Grace had been on literally hundreds of dates in her lifetime. She was pretty, she got asked out on a lot of first dates. Not so many second dates. There was always something wrong. Sometimes something big, like a total inability to relate to any of the man's interests, sometimes something small, like being made to feel she was a raging eccentric because there was a music group she hadn't heard of or a TV show she didn't watch.

Most of the time, there was a great deal of physical incompatibility. The man made all the wrong moves, touched her wrong, at times hurt her. More times than she could count she wished she were a lesbian, because at least then she might be able to work up some kind of a love life. But no, darn it, she wasn't a lesbian. She liked men. In theory anyway.

There wasn't anything uncomfortable or awkward about touching Drake. Or kissing him. She moved her head until she was close enough to smell the coffee on his breath, and as naturally as breathing, their lips met.

His lips were warm, surprisingly soft for such a hard man. They moved together perfectly, Drake tilting his head just so to gather a deeper draft of her.

She was the one who had kissed him, but he'd taken control of it immediately, one arm holding her tightly to him, the hand at the back of her head holding her steady for his kiss. Her breasts were crushed against his chest, the wiry hairs faintly tickling. His erect penis was a warm, hard column of heat against her stomach. It pulsed every time their tongues met. Her sheath answered with a long, hard pull of her internal muscles.

It was almost too intense, too deep.

She broke the kiss to move back an inch and take a deep, shaky breath.

"So?" he asked, eyes gleaming. "How was it?"

She blinked, barely able to understand his words. *How was what?*

A long finger flicked her chin, the calluses scraping her skin. "The coffee, little one." He bent forward for another kiss, a light one this time, just a light touch of his tongue. "Does it taste good from my mouth?"

The taste of him was hot and dark. It might have been the coffee. It was probably just him.

"Delicious," she breathed.

"Relax against me," he murmured. His long fingers massaged her scalp. "You're so tense. You're not frightened of me, are you?"

Grace *was* tense. Just the touch of his hands fired her skin, made her pulse pound. And yet being in his arms calmed her, calmed something deep inside her. It was frightening.

"Grace." His deep voice had lost all humor. He shook her a little. "Tell me you're not afraid of me."

She lifted her head to look at him, at his sober dark eyes, hard face looking as if it had never smiled in his life.

"No," she answered softly, truthfully. "I'm not afraid of you. Not in any way."

His face didn't clear. There was still a deep furrow between his eyebrows. She touched it, lightly, with her fingertip. A furrow of doubt. But there were also lines in his face that had been caused by pain and suffering.

Her gaze drifted to the large gauze pad taped over his shoulder. Was it hurting him? It was impossible to tell.

"How's your shoulder?" she whispered.

"What shoulder?" he whispered back.

Right. What shoulder? The violence yesterday seemed distant, another time, another place. She could hardly think of it. Drake filled her entire vision; every inch of her skin touched either Drake or soft fur. Decadent and dangerous, but oh, so enticing.

She leaned forward, watching his eyes, closing hers only in the moment her lips touched his. Her torso lay on his. She tried to ease up on his wounded shoulder but he was having nothing of that. His arms held her tightly to him, so she felt every dip and hollow of his strong frame, unyielding flesh as hard as steel.

Their mouths met again, clung, the kiss so long she was breathing through him. Each stroke of his tongue had her heart pounding, made her hands shake, her entire lower body clench.

The hand at her back slid around her waist, drifted over her belly, touched her between her legs. An electric touch. She was supersensitive from the orgasm, but somehow he knew not to saw at her as some men did, thinking that the harder they touched, the harder the orgasm. They were often the kind of man who thought women loved having their nipples pinched.

Those men vanished from her head. *Poof!* As if they had never been. It seemed unthinkable to Grace that any man other than Drake could ever touch her again, this immensely strong man who only touched her gently, softly.

Like right now, finger slowly circling over her clitoris. She was still soft and wet from the orgasm. Her hips began an unstoppable rotation in time with his finger, completely involuntary.

He liked that. She could feel his lips turning up in a smile. Yeah, he liked it. Well, so did she.

His touch still light, he stroked her labia, gently, circling around her opening. His calluses were rough, lending a little bite to his touch. When he'd made a full circle she let out her breath in a little huff. He released her mouth, scooting up a little in bed, watching her eyes carefully. His finger speeded up, moving gently around her, at times in her.

He was watching her so carefully for her reactions, but her body was telling him everything he needed to know.

"I want to kiss you here." His voice was deep and dark, as delicious as the coffee she'd drunk from his mouth. "Right here, a long kiss, over and over, my tongue in you."

The vision blossomed in her head—she was spread-eagled on his fur blanket, legs wide open, his dark head buried between them. It was such a lascivious, erotic picture, her vagina rippled with excitement.

He felt it. He didn't smile; if anything, his face grew harsher, the muscles along his jaw jumping as he gritted his back teeth. His hand was moving more quickly and her hips were writhing around it. He knew exactly where to touch, and how. The muscles in her thighs pulled tight and her stomach muscles knotted.

"Come for me." That deep voice was used to command. She had to obey.

As soon as he said the words, her body tipped over the edge and with a cry she started convulsing.

"Now," Drake said, his voice guttural. In a second he was sheathed in a condom. He opened her completely with two fingers, holding her open for him as he thrust inside, the movement slow, strong. He thrust to the hilt, so embedded in her she could feel his pubic hairs against the soft tissue of her sheath.

Oh God, she was clenching now around the strong, thick column, tight clenches of her muscles in sharp electric pulses. They watched each other, deep grooves bracketing his mouth, his breath coming fast. Just as the contractions were dying down, Drake started moving, slowly at first. A gentle circling with his hips, as if stretching her, then sharp little thrusts upward.

Oh God, he managed to reach some spot in her she'd never known about, because each thrust set off sparks of sensation—sharp, almost painful. His movements prolonged her contractions.

"That's right," he grunted, "keep going. Don't stop."

She couldn't. With each passing second, the sensations intensified until her heart was hammering, her entire body throbbing. Drake's strokes were sharp and hard, big hands holding her hips still for him.

It went on and on until the contractions were almost painful in their intensity. Grace cried out, shaking. It was simply too intense to bear.

Drake stopped under her abruptly, and she fell forward onto him, exhausted and sweaty, wrung out. Who knew her body contained all that erotic energy? She was totally spent with the force of her orgasms, her mind a complete blank.

It took long minutes before she could take stock, her senses firing up once more, like a spent machine sputtering back to life.

Sensations came back slowly. The feel of him under her, hard muscles tense as steel. His breaths so deep her legs were stretched as far as they could go to accommodate his chest.

His penis inside her, still hot and hard.

Oh God, she couldn't. There was nothing more in her.

She shifted slightly, feeling him surge inside her.

"You haven't, um . . ."

His mouth was against her shoulder and she could feel his lips moving in a smile.

"No," he said, his voice so deep she could feel the vibrations in his chest against her breasts. "But I will, count on it."

Eleven

Rutskoi looked up at the skyscraper right across the street from Drake's building.

Most of the building was made up of offices for everything ranging from import-export to dental studios. There were a few apartments, scattered here and there throughout the building. Most of the apartments were rented by companies on short-term leases. Two he suspected were used by high-class sex professionals for by-appointment-only sex.

Rutskoi was tempted . . . but no. Not until the job was finished. But afterward, hell. He'd have 10 million dollars. There wasn't a woman in the world he couldn't buy, for the rest of his life, or at least until his dick gave out. And even then, there was always Viagra.

Bless the Americans and their inventions.

By a fluke, there were two apartments on the thirtieth floor facing Drake's quarters, both in the middle, across from where Drake's living room was. A corner apartment or office wouldn't do any good, because Rutskoi needed a straight shot from the center of the building into the room at the center of the building across the street.

Drake's windows were treated with polycarbonate, probably lots of it, knowing Drake. His windows would be as bullet-resistant as you could get. Bullet*proof* didn't really exist—not even armored cars were entirely bulletproof—but Drake's would come close. Even a bullet fired from the most powerful weapon—and Rutskoi had the best, a Barrett 95—wouldn't penetrate the treated glass at a sharp angle with any degree of accuracy. If it did penetrate, he couldn't be sure of a kill shot.

He had to be sure. Absolutely positive.

So he needed to be in a place with a direct line of sight straight into Drake's living room. It was the only room Rutskoi had been in and he'd counted the doors. Fifth from the south end.

The plans of Drake's building were nowhere to be found, not even in the municipal zoning offices. Rutskoi had found the name of the architect's studio that had designed the building and there, too, the plans were gone. Disappeared, like a puff of smoke.

Well, Drake was smart but he wasn't God, all-knowing and almighty. The plans of the building across from his were right there where they should be, both in the city zoning office and the architect's offices, and Rutskoi studied them carefully. Then he hacked into the building administrator's office.

The thirtieth floor held the offices of an interior decorator, an ad agency, a graphic designer, the New York offices of a Chinese manufacturing company, a ballet school and two small apartments.

Apartment 3033 belonged to one Christopher Wright,

low-level broker and sometimes day trader. Which meant he did a lot of work from home. Wright was thirty-four, married to a freelance designer who did a lot of volunteer work. They had a child.

While Rutskoi was perfectly prepared to take a family out so he could establish his sniper's nest, there could be consequences. Wright and his wife seemed to be plugged into the world. The child went to school. A family like that couldn't just disappear. Inside of twenty-four hours, forty-eight max, someone would call and, not getting an answer, would show up.

Rutskoi needed to hole up for as long as it took, or as long as the situation let him.

Apartment 3034 looked better. It was owned by one of the advertising agencies and used as a residential hotel for visiting clients. Rutskoi took a look at the schedule and saw that he had a stroke of luck. The next occupancy was one Oscar Melim from Florianopolis, Brazil and he wasn't due until December 2. Until then, Rutskoi was free to arrange his nest. He would have liked an open-ended availability but it was unrealistic to hope that the perfect spot would remain eternally empty. Still, fourteen days wasn't bad.

About time things started breaking his way.

"Come on, get up." Drake tugged at Grace's hand, the only thing visible under his fur blanket besides a swirl of shiny, reddish-brown hair.

Grace waggled her index finger. *No.*

"Come on," he wheedled, "I've got something to show you. You'll like it, I promise you."

The finger wheeled. *Later.*

"Presents," he said slyly. "Lots of presents, for you."

The hand flapped up and down. *Bye-bye*.

The sex had exhausted her, but not him. He was thirty-four years old and he had no idea sex could do that to him. Make him feel relaxed and on top of the world, while forgetting all about the world.

He didn't even mind that he hadn't come. Just watching her, that beautiful face flushed with pleasure, feeling her soft little cunt milking him, feeling her shudders, ah—it had been worth it.

He bent down and kissed the tip of her shoulder, the only piece of skin showing besides her hand. A pretty little shoulder it was, too. He kissed it again. A sigh came out from under the blanket. "Not fair." Her voice was muffled.

He loved the English saying *All's fair in love and war.* "Not fair" was a concept for losers. He kissed her again and she rolled over, looking at him out of mutinous eyes.

"I was just falling asleep. Someone exhausted me. You might be Iron Man, but I'm not."

"I think a bullet hole pretty much proves I'm not Iron Man. And you can sleep later, I promise. But right now you need to get up, love. There are some things I have to show you."

There was nothing more he would love to do than to slip back into bed beside her, hold her tightly while she slept. And when he felt her begin the slow rise toward wakefulness, he would slide his hand downward, gently caress her soft little sheath until he felt the dampness begin, and enter her with his fingers. He wanted her to awaken on an orgasm, her own body's pleasure the gentlest of alarm clocks. He would turn her until he was flush against her back, lift her leg and slip inside. She would be tight. But a little less tight than last time. She would soon stretch to accommodate him. Over

time, her cunt would slowly become branded as his, shaped
to receive his cock, and his only.

They'd make love very, very gently, half asleep, coming
slowly awake in a haze of pleasure. Afterward, they'd snug-
gle in bed until late afternoon, when Drake would ring for
more food. He'd have fun feeding her again, watching that
luscious mouth open for his fingers, stroking her breasts. He
wouldn't let her get dressed. Clothes were for civilians.

Quiet time, for two lovers just discovering each other. The
most natural thing in the world.

Of course, that was all on an alternate planet, in another
universe, where Drake was free to love whom he wanted,
without fear that his woman would get her brains blown out,
or her skin flayed off, or raped for days as payback.

Wasn't going to happen. They weren't going to get her. Not
while he drew a breath.

He needed to start on a long and treacherous path today,
if he was to be able to guide them to safety, and he needed
to start now.

"Grace," he said, putting the bite of command into his
voice. "I'd like for you to get up now, please."

It worked. She turned over, sat up, startled. "Sure."

Throwing back the blanket, she stood up in one graceful move. She took in his work clothes—a black turtleneck
sweater and black jeans—and reached for his gi. Drake
nearly sighed as he watched her pull up the pants almost to
her breasts so she wouldn't trip on them and wrap the top
around herself almost twice.

On this other planet, Drake would simply keep her naked.
Make it easier.

It pained him to see her in his ugly gi, but luckily, he had
an answer for that. In boxes in the study.

He stepped close to her and kissed her on the neck. "Sorry to disturb your rest, love, but there are some things I have to show you."

Any other woman would have berated him for making her get up. But Grace took one look at his face and merely nodded. Good girl.

Now that he was in work mode, the relaxation he'd felt when they were rolling around on the bed like puppies was gone, as if it had never been. He'd clawed a few hours out of the face of the rock for them, but now it was time to start putting things into action. One misstep and they were gone. He knew his face reflected that.

"Come with me." They walked into the study, where it looked like Shota had outdone himself. There were two piles of boxes plus a folded easel leaning against the wall. One pile was of plain brown cardboard boxes with the logo of the art supply shop; the other pile was of elegant boxes in every color of the rainbow, with enormous ribbons and bows. He was amused to see that her attention went immediately to the art supplies.

Sitting on the arm of a chair, he brought her to stand between his legs. She looped her arms around his shoulders. Taking her cue from him, her face was sober as she looked down at him.

His hands spanned her narrow back. He could feel the delicate rib cage, the sharp indentation of her waist. Against the stark black of his gi, her skin was pale, fine-grained. She was so damned . . . vulnerable. In every way. The world isn't kind to the vulnerable, not even to artists with the gift of the gods in their hands.

It was a miracle she'd survived the firefight outside Feinstein's. It was by no means certain that she would survive the next. And there would be one. If it was Rutskoi teamed up with Cordero, Cordero was too stupid to quit and Rutskoi knew Drake, knew that he wouldn't rest until Rutskoi was down, so he'd have to go on the attack. This wasn't going to go away.

And if Drake survived their next attack, there would be the next one and the one after that to deal with. They'd never gotten him, up until now. They never would, as long as he was alone. But now there was Grace and they would get her, oh yes. No question of that.

There was nothing in Grace's beautiful head that would help her defend herself. No survival instincts at all. There was kindness, a unique way of looking at the world to discern its shapes and colors, a constant striving to reinterpret the world in her work. But she had no strategy for survival, no idea of the treachery of the world and how to combat it. To a certain kind of man, Grace had *target* written on her forehead.

With her to worry about, he'd be off balance. He already was. Just the thought that Rutskoi and Cordero might be planning her kidnapping right now, and with some inside help, too, drove him a little crazy.

He tapped the small dent in her chin and breathed her in. "I knew you'd probably go nuts without being able to paint or draw, so I got you as many art supplies as I could. If anything's missing, or if you want more, all you have to do is ask. The other pile over there is clothing. Again, just let me know what you need and it's yours.

"For a while, you're going to have to stay here, so I want you to be as comfortable as possible. I have books, music, movies. Anything you want that I don't have, ask me, or press the intercom and you'll get it within the hour."

"Drake . . ."

He grabbed a quick kiss. "Yes?"

She looked troubled and he tried to wipe away the small frown between her eyebrows with his thumb, wishing he could wipe away the threat as easily.

"How long do you think I'll have to stay here?"

Forever. Or until we disappear.

"Let me worry about that. I'm going to start work on that right now. You just relax." He stood, because if he stayed, he'd walk her straight back to the bedroom, and he couldn't indulge, not with all that he had to do this morning.

Reluctantly, he stood, breaking her hold, and walked across the room, hating it that he had to leave her. He stopped at the door, then turned. She hadn't moved. He pointed to the brightly colored pile of boxes. "There are several boxes of underwear there. But Grace?"

Her face was a pale oval, eyes glittering. "Yes?"

"Don't wear any."

Rutskoi had had a mistress many years ago. An actress. Though she'd been beautiful beyond compare, she'd been a lousy lay. Much too preoccupied with herself to think of pleasing him. Rutskoi had kept her well past her sell-by date because of her beauty, thinking that sooner or later things would warm up in bed, but they never did.

He could barely remember her name now and he considered the three months she'd lived with him a failure. But one good thing came out of all that sexual frustration. She'd given him a professional course in the fine art of disguise.

He'd watched, fascinated, as she made up for the theater, explaining all the tricks of the trade as she did. How to change skin color and the shape of the nose, the cheekbones. How a change in hair color—whether by dyeing or a wig—and hair length altered perceptions. How to call attention away from identifying characteristics by emphasizing other traits. How to appear taller, shorter, fatter, thinner. He'd watch, fascinated, as she dropped a decade, aged twenty years, became a nun, a streetwalker, a peasant woman.

So the doorman didn't blink twice at the handyman who announced his presence at ten A.M. A leak on the twenty-first floor, causing electrical shortages and blowing out the computers of a travel agency.

The doorman saw a man of medium height, dark brown hair, dark brown eyes, light brown skin, wearing stained workmen's overalls and carrying a big aluminum case. The man spoke with an accent, but then most repairmen did these days.

The doorman pointed out the elevator and turned back to look out the huge ground-floor windows in time to see the first snowflakes fall.

Rutskoi was certain the doorman had already forgotten his existence by the time he swiveled back to his monitors.

He went up to the fifteenth floor, got out and took the stairs to the thirtieth. He knew what sniping was, what it entailed. It was perfectly possible that he'd have to wait, prone, unmoving, for days. He welcomed the tiny toll fifteen flights of stairs at a run took on his muscles.

Never get soft, he reminded himself.

He drifted along the corridor of the thirtieth floor, head down, big-billed cap hiding his features. The lock took only a few seconds more than if he'd had a key. A few movements hidden by his back, and he was in.

It was a studio apartment, some 80 square meters, with two bedrooms and a modern kitchenette in the corner.

Carpeting, which was nice. He'd spent more hours of his life than he could count lying on the hard, stony ground, waiting for a shot.

Working quickly while there was still daylight, Rutskoi pulled on latex gloves, then opened his case and took out the pieces of the broken-down Barrett from their foam cutouts. *Snap snap snap.* His hands assembled the pieces without any conscious thought, performing the task automatically, perfectly, the fruit of thousands and thousands of repetitions. The tripod was next. Several efficient twists and snaps and there it was—the stable platform for his rifle.

He placed a plastic tarp on the carpet and carefully smoothed it down. A wrinkle could feel like a mountain after a couple of days. That tarp was going to be his home for however long it took.

He was going to get one chance at this, *one*. He had to do it right. He had to wait until the opportunity arrived, then use it. He couldn't afford the least distraction.

This was like any military op, he reminded himself, only better paid. He had an enemy to observe and then take out. All the military rules for urban sniping held here, too. In Manhattan, as in Grozny, the principles were the same, only this time he wasn't holing up in the rubble of a building destroyed by tanks, or behind an abandoned vehicle or on the rooftop of the tallest building around, but in a comfortable studio apartment with heating.

Everything else was the same. The sniper's cool ability to wait out the prey. Planned routes in and out. A stable platform. And—above all—the right equipment.

He lay it all out beside him on the tarp on the floor.

Thermography infrared scope and night-vision scope with

germanium lenses. Plenty of ammo. Once he had Drake in his sights, he would lay down withering fire. Two weeks' worth of energy bars, bottles of Evian he'd found in the pantry and four empty water bottles for when it came back out again. BlackBerry.

He looked around and dragged the sofa cushion seats onto the tarp, blessing the decorator who'd opted for the cheapest solution. Down-filled cushions would have been impossible to use as a platform—too soft. The hard, flat foam-rubber rectangles covered with fabric were perfect.

The distance to the window was crucial. The outside windows were lightly reflective. Not as much as Drake's windows—which were basically mirrors and showed absolutely nothing of what was inside—but enough so that he didn't have to position himself at the back of the room in trapped shadow, as he had in Chechnya. In one ruin of a building in Grozny with a southern exposure, he'd had to position himself a room away from the window and bore an aperture through an internal wall for the rifle muzzle. It wouldn't be necessary here. Even looking straight out, Drake wouldn't see anything. He would also be used to seeing the drapes of this apartment open, since it was rarely inhabited.

Shooting through glass was always a problem. It was best to shoot in a straight line. The glass in this apartment was only laminated. The powerful bullets would sail through without deflection. Drake's windows would be a bitch to shoot through, but with the thermal imager to give away position, and his .50-cal bullets, there was no doubt in Rutskoi's mind that one of his bullets would catch Drake.

One bullet was enough.

He had boxes of ammo, including incendiary rounds,

enough to fucking blow up the room if he had to. Once he started, he wasn't going to let Drake out of the room and he wasn't going to stop until Drake was dead.

Rutskoi settled onto the tarp, slightly to the left of his line of fire, bracing himself over the tripod, letting bone, not muscle, take the weight of his body. His cheek found the familiar position against the exact same point on the stock weld, as always. He was prepared to wait in this position for as long as it took.

As he assumed the position that would give him maximum comfort over what might be a long period of time, while at the same time assuring maximum accuracy, he felt himself disappear, sinking and floating at the same time, cut off from the world, his entire being narrowed down to his finger on the trigger and eye on the scope.

It was the closest thing he knew to happiness.

This is where he belonged, he realized in a sudden rush of insight. This is what he was born for—the hunt. And what greater, more exciting hunt, than that of man?

How wrong he had been to want to go into business with Drake. Rutskoi wasn't a businessman, not even close. Drake knew his guns but his real genius was in moneymaking. Drake would have made a fortune from whatever it was he decided to sell. Cars, real estate, stocks. It just happened that he'd started business in a godforsaken part of the world where weapons were the main commodity.

What the hell had Rutskoi been thinking? He'd been so eager to get out of the Russian army and out of Russia, he'd somehow convinced himself he was a businessman. Wrong. He was a hunter. That was his nature.

And—he finally understood—that was his future.

A 10-million-dollar contract would never come again, because there would never again be a target like Drake, not in this lifetime. Drake was an outlier, a black swan. Like Tamerlane or Alexander or Napoleon. His like would not come again for another hundred years.

But the world was full of targets. Thousands of them. Millions. Men standing in your way, blocking the path upward, men with knowledge that could hurt you, men who betrayed you, men who'd killed and needed killing in turn. The world was full of them and full of their enemies.

The world was *not* full of men with Rutskoi's skill set. He was a genius with a rifle, and was one of the few military snipers who could take his skills out of the armed forces and not go insane. Hired killers were often unbalanced, a step shy of madness, highly unreliable, blunt tools.

Not Rutskoi. He was as sane as could be. Not a coldhearted killer, but a technician with a highly prized skill, which he was going to start selling very dearly to the highest bidder.

Once he took Drake down, Rutskoi would invest part of his 10 million dollars in a new identity and a luxurious home base, far from prying eyes, and send out the word that he was available, for a fee. Success and discretion guaranteed.

As his body settled on the carpet, his entire being settled into this new plan. It felt utterly right, as right as the rifle in his hands, his cheek at the spot weld, his eye on the scope. This was his destiny; he just hadn't realized it before.

His sights settled on the mirrored surface of the floor-to-ceiling window of Drake's living room, where they would remain until the end.

Once Drake stepped foot into his living room, he wasn't leaving it alive.

Grace set up in the library. God knows there was enough room for her.

The light streaming in through a whole wall of floor-to-ceiling windows put her own small skylight to shame. Drake's home was an environment she found conducive to work. Some invisible hand always lit a fire for her. The room was beautiful and utterly quiet. No one disturbed her. When she remembered to eat, there was always a trolley outside the door with delicious food.

She worked like a woman possessed. The violence of the attack at Harold's gallery, the burning flare of sexual heat between her and Drake, the blossoming of tender feelings for him—all these things made their way from her soul through her fingers and onto canvas.

She lost herself totally in her work, at times stopping when she noticed her back aching, to discover she'd been painting for eight solid hours.

Drake secluded himself in his study all day, doing whatever mysterious things he did.

The day before, an elderly man had come and with quiet efficiency set up a makeshift yet highly professional photographic studio where she was working. He had a selection of wigs and glasses and was very adept at makeup. He must have taken a hundred photographs of her, in every possible permutation, some in which she barely recognized herself. Blonde Grace, brunette Grace, old Grace, studious Grace, slutty Grace . . .

Drake sat watching, impassive, as she changed personas,

then quietly walked out the door with the man and didn't come back to her until nightfall.

Each evening, he apologized for spending time away from her until she finally had to put her finger over his mouth and tell him to hush.

The truth was, she didn't mind spending time alone. She was used to it, used to being able to dedicate herself whole-heartedly to her painting without distractions. And Drake was a huge distraction, in every way.

When he came to her, he filled her entire mental horizon. Everything was forgotten in his presence, as if he were this huge magnet that pulled everything in her to him.

The sex was almost frighteningly intense. She'd dreamed about someday finding a man she could be with, but in her daydreams, sex wasn't that much a part of it. Truth was, the daydreams were puerile, like toothpaste ads, two people running in slow motion toward each other in a sunny field. Nothing like the dark, powerful, frightening, almost visceral tug between her and Drake. The sex in her fantasy—like those movie trailers for all ages—was bland and pleasant. Utterly unlike the mind-altering experience it was with Drake. Something that turned her inside out, turned her into a woman she barely recognized.

As if her thoughts of him had conjured him up out of thin air, there was a sharp knock on the door, and Drake looked in.

She put her brush in a solvent can and wiped her hands on a cloth, realizing that the palms had turned damp the instant she saw him. "Hi," she said softly.

He didn't answer, just walked to her. No, that wasn't quite true. He didn't walk, he *flowed*.

Grace, strength, power, it was all there in the strides. And it was totally subconscious. She had no doubt that when he wanted to intimidate, he'd be a master at it. His body—his entire being—exuded power and an ability to erupt into devastating violence at a split second's notice.

But he wasn't trying to intimidate her in any way. His walk to her was simply the walk of a powerful animal in its prime, moving toward something it wanted.

Her.

It was right there in the gleam in his dark eyes that never once looked away from her face, in his ground-eating strides, the intensity that surrounded him like an almost visible aura. He was even smiling as he took her elbow and sat them down on the couch in front of the fireplace, lifting her hand to his mouth. He meant the smile, but it somehow looked unnatural on that hard, somber face.

He kissed the palm of her hand and curled her hand in his fist. "I have some things to see to, but I don't want to stay away from you too long. Will you wait here for me? I love the thought of coming back to you here, right here, surrounded by your paintings. As a matter of fact, I thought maybe we could eat lunch in here."

As if she could refuse him anything. That strength wasn't just physical. His will was like a force field around him, almost shimmering in its intensity.

"Yes. Yes, of course I'll wait here for you, if it pleases you." She reached out with her hand to touch his wounded shoulder. "You're not overdoing it? You shouldn't be resting?"

Just like that, like throwing a switch, his aura changed. Became pure, animal sex. Those dark eyes gleamed, thin nostrils flared. She felt it on her skin, as if an electrical charge had washed over it, striking sparks where he touched her.

He leaned forward to kiss her on the neck, lips warm, breath hot. As he spoke, she could feel his lips moving. "My beautiful Grace. I am fine. Please do not worry about me. I do not need rest, I need something else. When I come back, I'll show you exactly what I need. In the meantime . . ." He nipped her earlobe and a shudder went through her body. He took her hand and lay it over his groin.

My God. He was huge, so hot the warmth punched through even the tough fabric of his jeans. He slowly licked her ear and her breath came out in a shaky rush.

This must be life's payback for having been so indifferent to sex all her life. She'd been like a locked door and it turned out that only this one man had the key. His mouth on her neck gave her goose bumps, made her back arch, giving him access to more of her.

As he licked her, dragging his teeth over her skin, her hand tightened around his penis. She wasn't the only one affected by his mouth on her. Impossibly, as she ran her hand up the amazing length, his penis moved, thickened, lengthened even more. When she cupped her hand around the bulbous tip, discernible even through the jeans, his breath came out in an explosive rush of air that ruffled her hair.

"God," he breathed. His big hand covered hers, trapping her hand over him. It wasn't actually trapped, though. Her hand was more than happy to stay right where it was, feeling him moving beneath her. It was like touching a primeval source of energy. Strength, power, male potency. Her hand burned as the surges of blood rushed through him.

Each jump in her hand was met with a clenching of her internal muscles, an elaborate sexual dance she did only with Drake.

He licked her ear again, breathing slow and hard. His deep

voice was low. "I need to go right now, or I won't go at all. I wouldn't leave you if I didn't have to. But when I come back, I want you to remember what you're feeling now."

As if she could forget.

"Okay," she whispered. She'd closed her eyes to concentrate on the feel of him in her hand and on what was happening with her body. She opened her hand and felt his lift from hers. He moved so silently she heard nothing. It was only when she heard the big door close that she realized he was gone.

Grace tipped her head back, eyes still closed, and simply concentrated on her senses. She'd ended up following Drake's order and hadn't put on any of the amazing collection of underwear she'd found in those boxes. The clothes she'd found had been exquisite, exactly the kinds of clothes she would buy for herself if she had the money.

The underwear, on the other hand . . . Well, wow. She'd never have had the nerve to buy what she found in those fancy boxes.

Bought on a tight budget, her underwear was plain, comfortable, white, stretchy cotton. A world away from the frothy silk and lace confections she'd found, incredibly sexy and revealing.

She'd pulled the lingerie from the boxes like Gatsby pulling out his shirts. No plain white cotton in these elaborately wrapped packages. None. Instead, all the colors of the rainbow.

Pink, lilac, pale yellow, taupe, teal, mint . . . the colors were simply exquisite. Every frothy piece looked delectable enough to eat. Bras, panties, teddies, silk-jersey tank tops, camis and tap pants and tee shirts and . . . slips! Whoever had done the shopping had old-fashioned tastes, because there were *slips* included. Grace had never worn a slip in her life. Her mother had never worn a slip. Slips were things people wore long ago, in movies. While carrying long cigarette holders and exchanging witty dialogue with someone like Cary Grant in a huge white bedroom.

She was tempted, though, fingering the fine satin slips with the lace bodices.

In the end, while choosing between a teal La Perla bra and panty set with lace insets and a gorgeous satin cami and tap pant duo, his words had came back to her. *Don't wear underwear.* The silk, satin and lace just slipped from her nerveless fingers as she remembered him touching her. Remembered the feel of his hands on her. And suddenly another layer of clothes felt stifling and constricting.

So she'd gone without these past days. Her nakedness wasn't visible of course, under the cashmere sweaters and soft wool pants. But she knew, and so did he. She felt everything so keenly against her skin.

Grace concentrated on what her senses were telling her, right now.

The softness of the sweater was a caress against her breasts. She was slightly wet between her thighs from fondling Drake. Without panties on, the wetness was as tangible against the sensitive skin as a kiss of cool air.

It was hard to feel the danger lurking just outside, because against all the odds, right now she felt so very safe and warm. Not just because she was in a fortress guarded by a small army of men, but also because there was . . . Drake.

He was the reason she was in danger. He was the reason no one would harm her.

Sitting on that magnificently comfortable couch, head tilted back, eyes closed, listening to the roar and crackle of the fire, Grace pondered her situation.

It had been clear to her from childhood that there were forces loose in the world much more powerful than she was. Forces that were indifferent at best, and at times even hostile to her. She wasn't a child anymore, and could to a certain degree defend herself, or at least take precautions. But by the same token she also knew she was not a powerful person, able to cut a swathe through life.

All she had wanted was to be left alone to paint; she asked for nothing more. And if that meant a life that was a little lonely, so be it. It was all she had asked for.

Even that, now, was taken away from her, in that same whirlwind that had blown her into Drake's arms. She wasn't powerful but he certainly was, in every way there was.

Denying it was stupid, fighting it wouldn't help. She was in Drake's hands. Completely and utterly.

It was a good thing those hands looked so huge and strong. And it was an even better thing that they were protecting her.

There was absolutely nothing she could do about any of it.

It was like a little surrender, there on the comfortable couch.

Twelve

A huge, complex mechanism was being set in motion.

There was some pain. Less than Drake would have thought, but still. After all, he was destroying a lifetime of work, everything he had built since he was a homeless boy on the streets of Odessa.

Drake had spent the past twenty-five years becoming stronger, faster, bigger and more powerful than anyone else. He'd sweated for his empire, bled for it, killed for it. And now it was going to crumble like sand and disappear down a hole.

Drake had turned it over and over in his mind, wondering whether what he was doing was too drastic, but in the end it came down to a stark truth. He could keep his life as it was, or he could keep Grace, but not both.

As long as he headed his empire, there would be men wanting to kill him. Once word got out that he had a weak spot, Grace's days were over. It wouldn't even be a quick kill, oh no.

It was the most terrifying thought in the world.

Long ago, Drake had made his peace with the thought of his own violent death. It seemed to him to be the only way he could die. The only question was when. To a certain extent, the thought didn't even bother him that much, he'd been used to it since childhood.

But the thought of Grace in the hands of mobsters who would use her to exact revenge against him—it drove him insane. He could scarcely stay in the same place as the thought. It hurt him constantly, a painful jolt to the chest, as bad as a bullet wound.

Most of his enemies had grown up in places where women were treated like cattle.

The images came to him in sharp, slicing flashes that were physically painful. Grace—tied to a chair while they pulled her fingernails out. Grace—hanging from her arms while they cut her to ribbons. Grace—bound to a table, gang-raped for weeks, dispatched with a knife across the throat.

As far as he knew, Drake didn't have a neurotic bone in his body. He was a cold realist, through and through. Those weren't hallucinations. Those images in his head terrified him so much because they were a possible reality. They weren't horror images from some nightmare you wake up from, but images from this world, *his* world, one mistake away.

What stood between these images of a broken and bleeding Grace and a healthy, laughing Grace was him. His strength and power. If he did this right, Grace would live. If he did it wrong, she'd die a screaming death, begging for it.

Entering the library silently in late afternoon, Drake stopped. Grace was resting on the couch, eyes closed, perhaps asleep. She'd been working nonstop these past days, producing remarkable work. Every once in a while she'd catnap on the couch in the library.

Coming in and seeing her on his couch made a sharp pain pierce his chest. For one terrifying moment, it felt like his chest was splitting open.

She was just so damned beautiful. All the other beautiful women he'd known and fucked—they vanished from his head like a cloud dispersing in a high wind.

Just look at her, he thought. Curled up on the couch, eyes closed, head tilted back.

The leaping fire loved her face. It washed the pearly skin with a pink glow, highlighted the high cheekbones, outlined the lush, full mouth. In the open vee of the sweater, the delicate collarbones cast tiny horizontal slashes of shadow. Her hair came alive in the glow from the hearth, the fire finding licks of flame in the shiny depths.

Everything about her was so delicate, even fragile. Those narrow, elegant artist's hands were folded calmly on her lap.

Drake had once seen an Afghan warlord take a hammer to the small hands of a female servant who had spilled a little hot lamb stew, *qorma*, on his lap. Drake had been unable to stop him since they were in a room full of the warlord's armed guards.

Later, it had been Drake's distinct pleasure to find that warlord's gross, misshapen head between the clean crosshairs of his rifle and gently pull the trigger.

He sat next to Grace, carefully, not wanting to disturb her slumber.

She wasn't sleeping. She turned her head toward him, then

opened her eyes. They gleamed like fragments of the sea in the penumbra.

He touched her face lightly. "Did I disturb you? I didn't mean to."

"No." Her lips curved slightly. "I wasn't asleep. I was just— thinking."

His heart gave another painful hammer blow in his chest, only this time not with longing.

"What—" His voice was slightly hoarse. At some point, she was going to come to the realization that he had ruined her life. "What were you thinking about?"

"About the situation," she said softly. Her eyes never left his. "I guess we'll be here for some time, won't we? I mean, this situation isn't going to resolve itself anytime soon, is it?"

Never, Drake thought.

"I'm sorry," he said, wanting to say more, but nothing came out. Sorry was a ridiculous word for what she'd lost. A nothing word, totally unable to cover the damage he'd done to this beautiful woman. He'd put her life in danger, deprived her of her home; because of him a good friend of hers had died.

Sorry was nothing, but it was the only word he had.

She nodded gravely, as if understanding everything that the word conveyed. There was no censure in her gaze, no anger, no rage.

Indeed, there was something there that angered him almost as much as the sons of bitches who had attacked them.

Resignation. That was what he saw. Resignation. Sadness. Acceptance.

It made him angry. Beyond angry.

This woman was magic. How could it be that there was

no man in her life, protecting her from the shit that was all around? What the fuck was *wrong* with the men in Manhattan?

Well, she had a man in her life now, by God. Him. And he would sure as hell make certain she was kept safe and happy.

Grace lifted her hand, that long, graceful artist's hand, and cupped his jaw. Her fingers were right on where the long scar had been. If she probed with her sensitive fingertips, she'd feel where the underlying tissue was still rent. Her hand traced where the scar had been as she watched him, frowning.

"What—" she began, but he covered her mouth with his. Ah, she tasted so good. Sweet and fresh. In a moment, her mouth opened to his. When he lifted his mouth for a second, she took in a deep shaky breath.

He tilted his head slightly and she did, too. The fit was perfect. So incredibly perfect. The heat of her mouth, the way she curved into him, the way his arm fit around her narrow back, the way her hair fell in a warm wash over his hand cupping her head, cascading over his arm.

Without breaking the kiss, he lifted her until she was on his lap, arms clinging to his neck.

Drake moved his mouth to her neck, to the sensitive place behind her ear that made her shiver.

His hand slid under the sweater, wide palm covering her stomach. Every time his mouth moved, her stomach muscles contracted.

He kept his hand on her belly and moved his mouth to her ear.

"Are you still obeying my orders, hmmm?" he whispered.

He loved it that she'd left all that expensive underwear in

the boxes, so that his hands were only one layer of material away from her skin.

It excited him to see her in clothes he'd bought, looking so elegant and classy, and knowing that underneath she was bare because he'd asked her to be. He could barely keep his hands off her. Even when they weren't making love, it was so luscious to slip a hand under her sweater and briefly stroke her breasts, just long enough to tighten her nipples. Know that he could easily touch her in that secret soft spot between her legs, feeling her growing instantly damp for him.

Each time he touched her, it took less time for her body to get ready for him. Now at times it only took the briefest of touches. Of course, the downside was that in her presence he was almost always semi-erect, just thinking of her naked beneath the clothes.

Like now. Only it wasn't a semi-erection, it was the real thing, hard and aching.

Goose bumps broke out on her forearms when he licked her ear and she shivered. Thank God her body was on his side. No matter what her head might be telling her, her body was clear on what it wanted. "No underwear?" He prodded. "Hmm?"

Her eyes, heavy lidded, opened, blue-green slivers glowing in the darkness. "No underwear," she whispered.

"Ah." His hand moved up over the flat planes of her belly and cupped a breast. He had to be so careful here. His hands were strong, he didn't want to hurt her in any way. Right now the biggest crime in the world would be causing her any pain at all. So he kept his touch softer than air, just a bare grazing of the satiny skin with his forefinger, around and around. When the back of his finger brushed over her nipple, she jumped. He nipped at her earlobe, loving the soft jolt. She was so incredibly responsive.

His finger ran over the nipple again, just a little harder. "Do you like that?" he whispered in her ear.

He could almost hear her smile. "If I said no, you'd know I was lying, wouldn't you? You can feel what my body is telling you."

Oh yeah, her body was shouting. The nipple under his finger had turned from a soft bud into a small, hard point.

His hand moved to her left breast, where he could feel the fast beating of her heart under his fingertips.

"Yes, your body is talking to me, Grace. I can hear it, feel it in my hands." Another gentle rasp of his thumb over her nipple, followed immediately by a little shudder. "You like that. You like my hand on your breasts." He pulled back, looking her in the face, hand gently cupping her breast.

She was flushed, the blood rising to her skin, warming it, puffing out a rich aroma of his soap and her woman-scent. Wonderful. It was all he could do to keep from putting his nose to her skin and sniffing like a dog.

"I like everything you do to me, Drake," she replied simply.

Her mouth was flushed red, lips swollen and wet. When she spoke, he didn't even hear her at first, he was following the movements of those lush lips so closely, fantasizing about them closing over his cock.

He felt an almost violent need to crush her to him.

Careful now, he told himself and nearly laughed. The fact that he had to tell himself to be careful was so alien it was as if he were talking to someone else.

Drake was always careful, always. He never got carried away, never got out of control, never had to worry about hurting anyone unless he wanted them hurt.

He never hurt women, though, ever. It wasn't in him.

He was always controlled during sex, always made sure the woman was wet enough to take him, always made sure his strong hands never bruised.

It had never been difficult. He'd learned to control his emotions and his body at an age so young he didn't remember learning the lesson. Control was as deeply ingrained in him as his bones or blood. A part of him for as long as he could remember.

That control was now simply . . . gone.

He just looked at Grace, perhaps the most beautiful woman he'd ever had in his arms. And not just beautiful—an immensely talented artist. So gifted he couldn't even imagine now having a home where her paintings wouldn't have pride of place. So gifted, the little peace he'd had in the past year had been thanks to her. Amazingly, too, this woman with the gift of the gods in her hands had a good heart, as well. Was gentle and kind, instinctively so.

This was a woman in a million. He should treat her like porcelain, like glass that would shatter at his touch. He should get down on the floor on his knees as if before an angel.

Instead, crazily, his predator's blood was up. He had to clench his teeth against a growl rising in his throat, a growl of possession, almost violent, like a war cry. His hands itched to grab her, hold her so tightly his fingers would be imprinted on her skin.

He wanted to rip those clothes off her right now, not even take the trouble to slide them off, but simply hook his finger in the collar of the sweater and pull. Put his hands on the pants and rip them off her. It would be ridiculously easy to do. He could kill a man with one blow of his hands; ripping material was nothing.

He could picture it, rending her clothes with a snarl of impatience, pulling her down on the rug in front of the fire, pulling her legs apart and up and slamming into her, whether she was ready or not.

He'd fuck her as hard as he'd ever fucked anyone, like a mindless beast, with the full strength of his body, pounding into her. He was so aroused, he would never stop at the first climax. He'd spurt into her, happy that it would make her wet, and then just continue slamming into her, for hours.

Oh God, he could feel that, taste it. He shook with the images that blossomed in his head. He'd fuck her until she was sore, then fuck her some more. Every cell in his body was screaming to have at her, with all the strength of his body, for as long as he could.

He'd hurt her.

If he did what he was shaking to do, he'd fucking *hurt* her. Hurt Grace.

It didn't bear thinking of.

He'd controlled himself with hundreds of women who didn't mean a thing to him. It had been easy, ingrained. This one woman, who meant everything, tested his control.

Drake threw his head back and breathed the desire back down. Such a strange, unusual feeling, this grappling for control with his arms full of warm woman. She shifted, moving her hip right over his erection and froze, like a deer in the hunter's sights. Her eyes met his, wide open and startled, as if she'd never felt a man's erection before.

A log fell heavily in the hearth and she jumped a little in his arms.

Her nervousness made him force himself into a little calm. They'd made love several times in the night, and this morning. He had to learn how to be with her without tipping over into mindless lust.

He leaned back and relaxed, content even with just the warm feel of her skin next to his.

When she realized he was relaxing, she did, too, leaning forward to rest against him with a soft sigh, one finger idly stroking his jaw, lips close enough to his neck to kiss him softly. His body relaxed further and so did hers, until they almost melted into each other. As the minutes ticked into an hour, they started breathing in unison, as if they were one creature, with two heads, four arms, but only one heart.

There was the sound of the fire, their breaths, and nothing else. Drake felt his mind drifting.

He was hard as stone, but there was just something about the moment that felt right exactly as it was, something fine and rare. He couldn't quite pin it down, until he realized it wasn't something, it was a *lack* of something.

His mind was quiet and still, a deep pool, so deep it could not be fathomed.

Remarkable.

Drake was used to the continual background hum of calculations in his head, there since before he could remember. When he was a homeless child on the streets, the noise was a constant lookout for food and shelter, while avoiding the many men who preyed on the helpless youngsters infesting the streets of Odessa like rats. His mind had been like a lighthouse beacon, constantly surveying surroundings in a 360-degree sweep. He'd taught himself to remain alert even while sleeping, when he wasn't in secure surroundings, which had been always, until he started earning good money.

Drake had lived like this his entire life, constantly alert, calculating the odds, working to make sure they were always in his favor.

True, his concerns now were not finding food and shelter, and they hadn't been for a long time. Now he ran an empire, single-handedly. He kept vast amounts of information in his head at all times, an enormous array of data that kept shifting and recombining. In his world, things moved fast and so did he.

Nothing like that, now. Now his head was filled with peace, a still, golden, calm pond of it, a welcome silence that allowed him to savor this moment, a moment so rare as to be almost incomprehensible. No busy buzz of business, harsh hum of calculations, whirr of thoughts. Just silence and warmth.

He looked down. Grace was watching him with calm blue-green eyes, lips slightly uptilted at the corners. As if wanting to smile, but uncertain of his mood.

His mood was great. He smiled down at her, feeling unused muscles moving in his face, delighted to see her smile fully in return.

He'd never had this before—this slow calm moment, skin to skin, heart to heart. If he held a woman in his arms, he was fucking her. The other moments were undressing or dressing. He rarely lingered after sex.

Why not? Why had he always been in such a rush? There was something so delicious about this, calm yet exciting at the same time. Not better than sex, not worse, just . . . different. And good.

She wiggled slightly, right over his enormous hard-on. "You, um, you seem to be—"

"Yes, I am." His smile broadened. It felt so *odd* to be smiling. "But it's okay. We'll make love soon, you can count on it." She turned pink. Such a pretty color, like a rosy dawn over a white mountaintop. He leaned down to kiss her jawline, then put his lips against her ear. "Once I get in you, I'm not going to stop for a long, long time."

She was stoplight red now.

He shifted her gently so she could lie against him more comfortably, pleased when she moved with him, into him. She rested her head on his uninjured shoulder and looped an arm around his neck, careful of the wound. Every time she touched him, she was careful, he'd noted.

What an odd sensation, a woman looking after him.

Drake tucked a lock of bronze hair behind her ear and bent until his mouth touched her ear. "Are you cold, love? Do you want a blanket?"

He could feel her lips curve up. "No, you're a furnace. And the fire is still burning high, so no, I don't feel cold at all." She sighed. "Drake . . . how long is this going to last?"

He didn't have to ask what "this" was. Men gunning for him, the danger spilling over onto her.

The rest of our lives. That was how long this was going to last. But she wasn't ready to hear it yet.

His arms tightened. "Are you so very eager to get away from here, then? Are you not comfortable? Is there anything you need?"

Silence. He looked down at her, expecting . . . he didn't know what he was expecting. Anger, maybe. Impatience. Sorrow. But she only looked thoughtful.

"I'm fine, Drake. And thanks to your generosity, I have everything I need and more."

He waved away the thanks, watching her carefully. "But?"

Her narrow shoulders lifted on a sigh. "But . . . however

huge your home is, however comfortable, we can't stay holed up here forever, can we? When do you think we can venture out? If only to get some fresh air."

He was tempted to say that he'd take her up on the roof if she wanted fresh air. Maybe tomorrow, if he could get rid of the helo. His pilots had been making noises lately about taking the helo away for a day of maintenance. Maybe tomorrow would be a good day. If he took Grace up on the rooftop, she might not be ready to know he kept an evacuation helicopter at the ready at all times.

But the rooftop wouldn't be enough. She was asking when she could walk the streets freely.

The answer was *never*. Not the streets of Manhattan, anyway. She wasn't ready for that info yet.

"As soon as I have a handle on the situation, I promise I'll find a way out. You'll be free to walk around at some point. You have my word." She'd be free to walk around, just not in New York. And not in the United States.

For the moment, Drake wasn't setting foot outside this building—and more important, wasn't going to let her set foot outside—until he had finalized his plans and knew where they were going and how.

Grace watched his eyes carefully. "And you always keep your word, don't you?" she asked quietly. "That's important to you, to be a man of your word."

She could read him so well. It was frightening.

It was true, he was a man of his word. Even in the business he was in, his word was his bond. There'd been a goodly chunk of his life in which the only thing he had in this world was his personal dignity. His word. He'd die before he let that go.

"Yes, I keep my promises. So you'll see the day again. And when you do, where do you want to go? What do you want to do?"

"Take a walk in Central Park," she said promptly. "Go down to the farmers' market. See some new galleries."

Shit, how tied was she to Manhattan? Was she going to suffer if she never saw it again? The thought lay there, heavy in his chest.

"What about outside New York? What do you want to see outside the city?"

She looked up at him. "The world," she said simply. "I've always wanted to travel. I told you, my dream is to see Rome. Paris, London. And the East. I love reading travel guides and imagining myself in a Tibetan temple or a Hindu *mandir*. I never had the money before."

"I hate to say it, but I'm glad you didn't take off this past year." He nodded his head at the overspill of her paintings from his study, simply glowing on the library's walls. Just like she glowed in his arms. He ran the back of his fingers down the side of her face, slowly, just enjoying the feel of her. "I'm the richer for it."

She moved into his hand, smiling. "I hate to contradict you, but *I'm* the richer for it. You paid me an almost obscene amount of money. I made more last year, thanks to you, than I did in the last ten years."

"Worth it," he said.

"Do you know, you could have had my paintings for half of what you paid?"

"Worth it," he repeated.

She turned in his arms, smiling, then settled with her face against his neck, breasts brushing full against his chest.

His cock pulsed hopefully. Maybe now . . .

"I'm glad you—" she began, then her eyes opened, fixed on something over his shoulder. "Oh! Just look at that!"

Drake stiffened, ready to push her to the floor and whirl to face a new danger, when he saw her face. Relaxed. Smiling. Whatever it was she was seeing, it wasn't a danger to them. He followed her gaze, turning his head.

Snow.

Night had fallen while he'd held her in his arms. He hadn't thought to pull the curtains and the entire wall showed a nighttime Manhattan skyline softened by falling snow.

He factored that into the equation of how to make the next few days work. Snow made everything slower. People arrived later for work, some didn't arrive at all. His master forger, Yannick Zigo, was scheduled to deliver new passports tomorrow, together with backup documents. He traveled from Upstate New York. If there was a big snowstorm, he wouldn't venture out. He often complained that his bones were too brittle for bad weather.

Grace rolled off Drake's lap and walked toward the windows, keeping well back from the glass itself. Drake watched her every step of the way, admiring the look of her back, the slim line of her glowing in the penumbra, that glorious multicolored hair that fell past her shoulders swaying gently with each step. She'd only just left him and his hands already missed her, missed the soft skin, the deep indentation of her waist, missed cupping her breasts and touching her where she was soft and wet, just for him.

He stood up and followed, like a chunk of iron to a lodestone.

She'd stopped halfway to the window, watching, a half smile on her face.

Drake put his arm around her waist.

"You can go right up to the window, you know. The outside is coated with a strong, reflective surface." Not to mention a thick polycarbonate film. "There is absolutely no chance of anyone seeing you. None."

"No one can see me?" Her head whipped up to him so fast a fall of hair lashed across his chest. She blinked. "Are you sure?"

"Come with me." He tucked a lock of shiny hair behind her ear and walked forward, his arm around her waist. After a second's hesitation, she followed his lead.

He walked her right up to the window, inches from the pane. The lights behind them were low, the ambient light outside brighter. They had all Manhattan before them.

Drake placed himself right behind her, left hand holding her breast, the other arm angled downward, cupping her. He felt her tremble once as his fingers touched the soft labia, then settle against him.

"Look out across the street. What do you see?"

"A—a building," she said hesitantly. He could feel her heartbeat against his hand, quickening at his touch. "A few stories taller than this one."

"Uh-huh. Now look carefully at the windows of that building. They're reflective, too."

She nestled the back of her head against his shoulder. "I don't see what you—"

And then she saw it.

The entire building across the street had slightly reflective windows. Drake's building didn't, except for the top floor. Mirrored across the street, he could see a number of offices still open in his building, people moving around, a cleaning crew in one, a late evening meeting in another, twenty people around a long oval desk. The traffic of a busy commercial building.

Except on the top floor, his. Nothing was visible of what was inside. The top floor was like one long mirror. You couldn't even see if the lights were on or off.

"See?" he said softly into her ear. "You're completely invisible."

They were so close to the floor-to-ceiling window that he could feel the cold coming off it. "Are you cold?" he asked.

She shook her hair, soft, warm waves of it swishing across his chest. "No, how can I be cold with you at my back? You're like a furnace. And it's sort of . . . exciting to look out over the city through a window like this and know that no one can see me."

"Except me," he growled in her ear.

It was true. They were lightly reflected against the window, the merest ghosts of themselves. She was like a slim line against his breadth, pale skin glowing against his darker tones.

In the window, she smiled, eyes on his. "Except you," she agreed warmly. Then her gaze shifted to the scene outside.

The snow was still relatively light, just small icy flakes so light the wind sometimes blew them up. Every once in a while the snow fell in soft drifts. Drake had no idea what the weather forecast was, which was just one more sign of how out of synch his life was at the moment. He *always* knew the weather forecast. It was an integral part of him, to know what the weather would be, what the Dow Jones was doing, to be one of the first to know of any shifts in the geopolitical situation, to know where his men were at all times. To be taken by surprise by snow was unheard of.

Many a time his life had depended on whether it would rain or snow.

Grace's eyes were tracking the light drifts. "So beautiful," she murmured.

"Hmm." He'd buried his face in her hair, nose next to the soft skin behind her ear. Why look outside when he could watch her in the dark glass? It was just snow, for fuck's sake. He'd once nearly died from exposure in a snowstorm when he was still living on the streets. Snow was cold and wet.

Better to be warm and dry.

She shook his arm a little. "Look, Drake. Look out." He reluctantly dragged his ghost eyes from her ghost eyes to focus on the scene outside.

She held her hands out, as if to encompass the entire scene. "I want to paint it, just like this. All silver and midnight black, the buildings gleaming mysteriously in the darkness. Look down, Drake. See the fog rising? It makes the buildings look like islands in the sky, doesn't it? I'll paint it with the contrast between the billowing fog and the slanting snow with a monochrome palette. You'll love it, I promise."

Drake froze.

For a second, something terrifying happened. All those hours over the past year simply staring at her paintings caused a shift in his perception. For a second, he saw the scene through *her* eyes. Not merely snow, which he hated and considered a nuisance at best, even life-threatening at times. He'd seen past his hatred of snow to the landscape beyond.

It was magical, this landscape, seen through her eyes. A rich fantasyland of silvery darkness. Her eyes were tracking the snow and he followed her gaze in the reflection of the dark glass. She was imprinting what she was seeing, and sometime in the future—maybe tomorrow or next month or next year—a masterpiece would form beneath her clever hands and he would look at it forever. Only this time, he would look at it and remember the exact instant she got the inspiration.

By some mysterious alchemy, she was changing him. Opening his heart to the beauty of the world. It was frightening and he wasn't altogether certain he liked the thought, but there it was.

He was looking at the black and silver shapes, the misty fog, the slanting snow and finding them fascinating instead of calculating how much the bad weather would impact his business.

The world was vastly more mysterious and beautiful than even he knew.

For the past fifteen years, he'd lived in locked-down conditions in his homes, traveling only under the tightest security he could devise, from car to plane to hotel and back. His life was work and sleep, with little in between; he lived in sterile and controlled surroundings. His world had narrowed to walls, whether of a hotel room or a car or a plane didn't make any difference. The outside world had become an abstraction, a mere construct to include in his calculations.

She met his eyes again in the glass, a small smile on her lips, as if she understood what she'd done to him.

She'd fucking changed him, that's what she'd done.

This woman had reached down inside him, with her art and her beauty and her kindness, and pulled him inside out. He didn't much like it, but he couldn't deny it. He was changing, feeling the ground beneath him shifting in a terrifying and exhilarating dance.

His hands moved fast and in a moment she was naked.

"Lean forward," he said, his voice suddenly guttural. "Brace yourself against the window."

Startled, Grace watched him in the window as she leaned forward. He felt her narrow rib cage arch as she placed both hands on the pane. He put a foot between hers and forced her to open her legs, fitting himself more snugly against her.

He'd been erect the whole time, but now she could feel him surging against her, his cock swelling as he pulled her tightly against him.

He couldn't wait one second more. She was in his head. He had to be in her body.

He watched her carefully in the window. She was pressed against the pane. Her breasts would be cold, but he was keeping her warm from behind. And his cock would warm her up.

He undid his loose cargo pants, grabbed a condom from a side pocket, then kicked them away when they fell to the floor. He whipped his sweater up and off, eyes never leaving hers in the reflection.

"Open your legs more, Grace," he whispered.

She obeyed immediately, kicking his excitement up, making his blood flow hot and thick through his veins.

It was going to be rough.

Oh God. It was going to be rough.

Grace watched her lover's face in the dark window, the image more ghostly than if it were a mirror, as if he were insubstantial. Yet Drake wasn't insubstantial at all. He was male power and male muscle, treading this earth more heavily than most.

She could feel him hot and heavy at her back, his hands

holding her tightly. He opened her legs with his and fitted himself against her.

Each time they made love, there was this startled moment when she realized just how big he was, long and thick and as hard as steel. In the beginning he had been so careful with her, entering her slowly, by degrees.

Lately, though, he let his excitement get the better of him, understanding that her arousal grew each time they made love.

His control was paper-thin now. Grace knew this moment was coming, but now that it was here, fear tempered her excitement. Up until now, though he'd brought her to orgasm over and over again, Drake had been in utter control of himself.

Now the reflection in the window showed a man straining for control. The cords in his strong neck stood out, his jaw was tight with tension, muscles bunching along the jawline.

His power struck her anew. Though he didn't tower over her, his shoulders were almost twice the width of hers. Looking down at his hand cupping her, she saw the taut, thick, sinewy muscles of his forearm, wildly erotic against her belly. He slid his hand further, fingers stroking her labia, his hand rocking back and forth in a silent request for better access.

Of course. She didn't even think twice, merely widened her legs further. Whatever Drake wanted, she'd give him.

He fit himself to her, big, blunt, hot. She braced herself because that first entry was always slightly painful, no matter how aroused she was.

He was watching her face carefully in the dark glass. He must have seen her slight wince. He didn't move forward as she expected he would. He merely waited, poised at the mouth of her sheath, breathing so heavily against her that she could see her hair sway in the dark pane.

His jaw muscles worked. "Not yet," he muttered, watching her eyes. "Press up against the window."

Grace could barely understand his guttural tones. "What?"

"Lean against the window. Now."

His voice was low, utter male command. She obeyed instinctively.

She sharply drew in a breath as the entire front of her body met the cold window, hands splayed, breasts, hips, legs meeting the icy pane. He crowded right behind her, like a huge hairy man-furnace. The two extremes of temperature somehow excited her, her nipples puckering with the cold.

Shockingly, he reached down and opened her with his fingers, nudging her forward with his hips. His fingers had exposed her clitoris, which was pressed against the freezing window. She registered the chill against her sensitive flesh in exactly the same second as he entered her, his penis a huge, hot column heating her up from the inside out. Her entire body went into overdrive.

She gave a cry as he started moving, hot and hard inside her, pressing her against the freezing window, a raging furnace at her back and inside her. His movements were hard, almost harsh, on the edge of being painful but . . . not.

She lifted her eyes to look at their reflection, his face grim as he moved in and out of her, the thrusts fast and hard. Their eyes met and she was shocked at her expression, eyes unfocused, mouth open, throat arching back against him. The very picture of a woman in sexual ecstasy, reduced to her animal nature.

A keening sound filled the room and it took her seconds to recognize it as her own voice. It was unlike any sound she'd ever heard herself make, an animal cry. She wasn't even feeling the cold of the window any more, her entire body was suffused with heat, she was burning up alive.

With a thrust that drove her to her toes, Drake grunted and started coming, swelling even larger, his thrusts irregular and fast as his breath huffed in and out. It felt like he wanted to punch her right through the window. She looked down at the shops and people and cars, the busy street of a great metropolis.

Grace came with a cry, every hair on her body standing up, shaking with pleasure. Suddenly, her senses expanded. As she looked down, it was as if the window had disappeared and she had become one with the people she could see hurrying along the streets, one with the snow drifting down from the sky, one with the energy of the city, pulsing in her fingertips.

She was no longer Grace Larsen, separate and alone and somehow always apart. In one electric pulse, she became one with everything around her, as her body convulsed and shook.

Across the seventy-five feet of a Manhattan street and slightly to the north, giving him an oblique shot, Rutskoi watched the two figures through his thermal scope.

Drake and the woman. It could only be them. One slender, the other not much taller but much broader.

Naked.

Fucking.

He watched the fiery red-and-blue bodies writhing in the small circle of his scope, completely unmoved.

Rutskoi liked sex just as much as the next man, maybe more. He'd blown half his first paycheck as a newly minted lieutenant on whores in Grozny, celebrating staying alive for one whole month by staying drunk and with his dick in a prostitute for days at a time. But on the job, it all went away. He felt nothing on the job—not lust, nor hunger nor thirst nor exhaustion. All he felt now was the deep sniper's calm, a oneness with the ground and the rifle and the scope.

The woman was now flattened against the window by the weight of Drake's body and Rutskoi's finger tightened slightly. Christ, she was in his sights. Right there, in the crosshairs.

A 4-kilogram pull on the trigger, double the pull on a beer can, and his .50 caliber bullet would travel at 2500 kilometers per hour toward the red and green and yellow outlines shimmering through the thermal imager.

But he had no way of knowing how thick Drake's windows were and at this angle of inflection, he had no guarantee that it would penetrate or, if it penetrated, whether it would pass through the woman to Drake.

So he watched the fiery figures writhe and told himself to hold his fire, watched the woman's hands outstretched on the glass like five-fingered flames as Drake fucked her from behind.

They would be in his sights at a straighter angle soon enough.

He could wait.

For 10 million dollars, he could wait for as long as it took.

November 24
Early morning

Blood. Blood and the bleak darkness of violence. Blood was everywhere. It came up to her ankles, deep red, glistening in the darkness. So dense it dragged at her feet.

Her heart beat fast, like a trapped animal's. Danger was close, she could feel it, she could almost smell it. In the distance was a faint light. Not the white light of hope, but merely a slight lifting of the penumbral gloom. She could barely see. The darkness was oppressive, close and dank.

Her skin prickled in animal warning. Something was there. Something alive, something ferocious. There was cruelty here, vast cruelty and a love of death. Death was a thick pall in the air.

She looked down at where she was walking. Under the lake of blood, her feet bumped against obstacles, odd shapes. It was hard to keep her balance, though she knew she had to move quickly. The menace was close, coming closer. Her muscles screamed at her to run, but she couldn't, it was like walking over stones barefoot. She tripped and almost fell. At her feet something rose to the surface, bobbing. As it rose, small pale points appeared, like a mountain rising up from the primordial mud. A white tip, then smooth waxen surfaces that resolved themselves in nose, lips, cheeks, eyes. Black blood-streaked hair flowed from the smooth pale forehead.

A severed woman's head, bobbing in the red blood.

She tried to scream, but there was no breath in her lungs, no air to be found in this airless, soulless place.

He was coming. She didn't know who he was, but she knew what he was. He was cruelty, he was death, with a vast gaping hole where his heart should be. And he was coming for her.

The blood at her feet stirred, started moving like a sluggish river. Whatever was coming was big—big enough to sweep everything before it.

There was no place to hide. The lake of blood stretched

out to infinity. Now she could see broken bits of bodies rising to the surface. A hand, outstretched, as if asking for help for a body that was no longer there. A foot, still clad in a shoe. Another head, popping up like a balloon, then subsiding.

She was walking through a bloody river of death.

The blood was flowing faster now. Darkness fell suddenly, as if something behind her was covering the feeble light on the horizon. Whatever was coming for her was huge.

She tried to hurry, but kept tripping over parts of people, like offal in a slaughterhouse. The faster she tried to move, it seemed, the denser the parts became, until there was an interlocked puzzle of human pieces blocking her path.

She chanced a look backward, breathing fast. There was something there, huge and dark on the horizon, dressed in a long coat. Moving forward in giant strides, unperturbed by the bodies.

She could hear a faint crackling that grew louder. The cracking of human bones as the monster carelessly stepped on them. She turned her head forward, blindly seeking a hiding place, and tripped. Her hand fell out to break her fall and she pushed a head down under the surface. Snatching her hand away, the head bobbed back up. A child's head, small features looking puzzled.

Oh God, oh God, coming closer . . .

A frigid wind rose at her back. What was coming for her was cold, with no human warmth at all. Something grazed her back. His huge hand. He'd almost caught her.

Faster! Faster! Sobbing, she bent to push the cadavers away so she could run faster. A cold wind came and went, the monster breathing.

She was tiring and he was tireless. He would never waver, never renounce. It wasn't in his nature.

She tripped, then tripped again. Oh God, he was almost upon her!

A head rose to the surface just before her. It took her exhausted, terrified mind a second to realize that the head was rising vertically, up up up. Broad, naked shoulders emerged, dripping red. A man, a hugely strong man. He lifted his hands, muscles rippling with tension and strength. Huge hands held a sword, glinting in the uneven light. He lifted the sword to his shoulder, ready for the cutting blow.

He had fully emerged now, an immensely powerful man standing on the blood, sword at the ready. He lifted one hand from the sword and beckoned to her, fingers curled in a universal message.

Come to me.

He was aware of her but wasn't looking at her. He was looking behind her, at the danger close on her heels.

Safety. He was safety and protection. Every line of his strong body was a wall she could hide behind if only she could reach him. But it was so hard to move, as she tripped and slipped in the blood, stumbling over the bones of men and women and children, terrified of the icy cold at her back.

She cried out as something cut across her back in a fiery line of pain. The creature had claws, fully out, and slashed her again across her back. She was bleeding, her blood mingling with that of the uncounted dead.

The pain was unbearable, the creature had slashed across muscle, down to bone. She slipped, fell to one knee. The creature's claws snapped over her head.

The man with the sword was striding forward, eyes still fixed on the monster behind her, face hard, determined. He'd been caught by the monster, too, some time ago. A broad white scar ran down the side of his face, gleaming in the gathering darkness.

Leathery ropes wrapped around her torso, squeezing so tightly she could barely breathe. She was lifted from the earth, her body dripping blood.

They weren't leathery ropes, they were fingers, their grip tightening so hard she felt a rib crack. She looked up, into blood red eyes, a cruel mouth with sharp teeth. The mouth was smiling.

He had her. It was over. This was how her life would end—in pieces at the bottom of a lake of blood, dying cold and alone.

She turned for a last look at the last human she'd see. The man with the sword was running, slashing at the monster's legs.

The monster laughed. She struggled desperately in his cruel grip, trying to free herself.

"Grace!" The man screamed. "Grace!"

She tried to call to him but there was no breath in her, the world was fading . . .

"Grace!"

She couldn't breathe . . .

"Grace, wake up!"

She came awake on a shuddering gasp, trembling and shaking, flailing madly, as if she'd been underwater and crested the surface an instant before drowning.

Two strong arms were around her, pinning her. Oh God! He was going to kill her! She struggled, twisting wildly, but there was nothing she could do against this kind of strength. She was going to die . . .

"Grace, Grace, love, look at me."

That deep voice. Not cruel, not insane. A voice she knew . . .

Her eyes opened and she stilled, panting, staring into steady brown eyes. A soft brush of lips across her forehead. "It's all right. You're safe. You had a nightmare."

Only one word penetrated. *Safe.* She was safe. No drowning in blood, no horrible monster with claws gripping her. No dead bodies.

She blinked, tears springing to her eyes.

Except, of course, there *was* a dead body. Harold's. It all came back, rushing in like a river whose dam had broken. The four men gunning for Drake, using her as bait. Harold's head exploding off his shoulders, what was left of his body falling loosely to the ground like an empty sack, all the goodness and humor in him, vanished like a light being snuffed.

The monster in her dreams wasn't real, but the monsters loose in the world were, something her unconscious had recognized. One of those monsters had killed her friend, a man known, even in the art world—a cutthroat business if ever there was one—for his gentleness and generosity. A man who had truly loved art, who had never harmed anyone, had been wiped off the face of the earth by one of the monsters who inhabited it.

She'd been strong and had tucked her grief away, shoving it into a dark corner, but now it all came rushing back. The nightmare had robbed her of her usual resilience, sapping her strength. Grief welled up, fierce and unstoppable.

She turned her head into Drake's shoulder, inhaling his scent, sensing his strength around her like a coat of armor, clinging to it desperately. She shuddered with her sadness and pain at the loss of Harold. Her horror of the violence at the gallery. The loss of her own life, cut off abruptly; the loss of her home. It all came tumbling out in an upwelling of sorrow that she tried to breathe down, heart pounding, trembling.

"Let it out, duschka," a deep voice said in her ear. "Cry. I'm here to catch you."

It was all she needed. With a wild moan, she buried her head against him and let go. She wept out her grief and her rage, her sorrow and her desperation. She wept for Harold, for the violence that was still stalking her, for the loss of her freedom. While she was at it, she wept for her mother's immense sadness at being abandoned by her father, and for her own inability to find a place in the world that felt right. She wept for sorrows past, present and future.

She wept until there were no more tears, until she ran out of breath, until her throat ached with sadness. And then she wept some more. Grace had no idea so many tears were in her, and it was only when no more came that she subsided against Drake's wet, bare shoulder, eyes closed, dazed with the force of the tempest that had passed through her.

He'd held her all through it, without moving a muscle except for the slow beat of his heart, giving her the animal comfort of his body. She lay against him, spent, listening to his strong, steady heartbeat, feeling his even breath ruffle the hair on the top of her head. One huge hand covered the back of her head and one arm was around her waist, holding her just tightly enough to give comfort, without making her feel restrained.

Her eyes were swollen, her throat ached. She lay heavily against him, as if her skin could melt into his.

"I'm so sorry," she whispered in a soggy voice.

His hands tightened briefly. "Don't apologize, duschka." She had no idea what *duschka* meant, but the tone made it unmistakably an endearment. "You can cry all you want. It is a world made for crying. You lost your friend."

She rolled her forehead against his shoulder. It was like rubbing it against a warm rock. "Yes," she said simply. "I lost Harold. I miss him so much."

"I know you do." He nodded. "And you lost your paintings in your home. Your beautiful paintings in the gallery. They'll be gone by now."

It was what she'd suspected. "Yes."

"And you lost even more than your friend and your paintings. It is no wonder you cry."

They were both silent, because the last thing she'd lost was her life, the life she'd known.

Grace was held so tightly against Drake, felt so surrounded by him, by his utter physicality in the here and now, that her old life felt far away.

Her entire system had quietened, the crying jag like a violent tropical storm that then moved on, leaving behind silence and calm. Her breathing slowed, quieted. During the jag, she'd focused on the hot ball of grief and sadness in her chest, but now outside sensations seeped in.

The warmth of his body, like a huge heater under the covers, the feeling of being utterly surrounded by strength, the slow thud of his heart against her breast. She shifted slightly, and her hip came up against his erection, huge and ready, as always.

An electric current swept through her body at the feel of him as he surged against her at her lightest touch. She'd just cried her heart out, and yet her body was already preparing for him, softening, becoming wetter . . .

She lifted her head to look at him. Drake's face was so solemn, strong features still as he watched her. As always, he made no effort to charm her. He never used words to seduce her. He was a man of action and he showed what he felt by actions, not words.

Each feature was fascinating. The dark, hooded eyes that seemed to see so much. The full, sensual mouth. The high cheekbones and beard-roughened jawline. Features becoming so dear, so . . .

So familiar?

Grace cocked her head, blinking. How could . . . ? She stopped breathing for a moment, overwhelmed.

"Oh my God," she whispered, cupping his face with her hand. How had she missed it? Why hadn't she recognized him? She felt her eyes go wide.

He brushed his lips across the ball of her shoulder. "What is it, duschka?" he murmured.

"It—it's you." Grace ran her finger over his features, tracing the dark wings of his eyebrows, the slight lines fanning out from his eyes, easing down the straight bridge of his nose. Why hadn't she seen this before?

"You're the man of my dreams," she whispered, then stopped, heat rushing to her face. "I mean—I dream about you, Drake. I've been dreaming about you for over a year now. They're more nightmares than dreams, actually. Danger and violence, always. And always safety provided by a man. I've tried to paint his face but I've never come closer than a generic look because I never remember his face when I wake up from the nightmares. But . . . he's *you*. Somehow, Drake, he is you. The man who saves me. Now that I can see it, it's so clear. I have been dreaming of you." She ran the back of a knuckle down the left side of his face. "Except . . . in my dreams, the man who saves me always has a big white scar here. As you must know, because you've bought five of those portraits." She frowned. "I haven't seen them hung in your study, though."

"No." Drake shook his head slowly. "They were too . . . personal. They're in a vault, where only I can see them. Because I recognized myself right away."

Grace shook her head, amazed. "How could you? How could you recognize yourself when I didn't? I only now realized that I was painting and drawing variations on you. Each portrait was different, because I never saw your features clearly. The only things they had in common were dark hair and dark eyes and a—a strong look. But each portrait was different."

He took her hand and placed it against his left cheek. "How could I not recognize myself? Each portrait was the same," he protested. "Each man in the paintings had a long white scar on the left side of his face."

He pressed her index finger into the flesh of his left cheek. "Feel, duschka. Feel what is underneath the skin." At first Grace didn't know what he was talking about, but then she could feel it—a line underneath the skin, following the scar of her dream saviour. "I had the best plastic surgeon in the world, but even the best plastic surgery only heals the skin. My scar ran deep and the surgeon couldn't repair all the tissues underneath."

She watched him, fingers on his skin, running the pad of her index finger up and down his face. The hidden scar was there, from his temple down to his chin, exactly as in her dreams.

"This is impossible," she whispered.

"Yes, it is," he said simply. "And yet, impossible or not, it is so."

Grace's head swam. She was such a . . . a *prosaic* person. She didn't do shrinks or self-help books or group therapy. She didn't believe in ghosts or past lives or angels. She led a quiet life, painting and reading, mainly in her own apartment, almost always alone. All she'd ever wanted was to paint and be left alone.

She'd never had a feeling of destiny or of great things in store for her. Fate had never been a factor in her life.

But here it was. Inexplicable and otherworldly.

She'd dreamed, over and over again, of this man. A man she'd never met, never even thought to meet. Somehow she'd known him, known that they were fated to be together.

Goose pimples ran up her forearms and the hair on the nape of her neck rose. She felt an inner trembling, as if she were in a frozen wasteland instead of in a warm, comfortable bed with a fire blazing in the hearth.

The chill went deep, to her core. Her icy hands shook.

She'd been touched by something she had no words for. She knew only that it was big, tapping into something that she now realized was the energy that ran the world.

At that moment, in an act of total surrender, Grace gave herself over to her destiny. She was somehow meant to be with this man.

Drake. Drake was her destiny.

"It was you," she whispered. "Always you."

"Yes, duschka," he said quietly, face sober. "We are somehow linked. I don't know how and I don't know why, but I knew there was a connection the first time I saw your portrait of a man I recognized as myself." He ran his hands along her side, as if shaping her. His eyes searched hers. "I knew you were important to me, but I stayed away from you for a full year. I knew I couldn't share my life with a woman, it was much too dangerous. So I stayed away. But I couldn't stay away completely. I was there every time you came to the gallery."

His head shook slowly, eyes never leaving hers. He shifted her until she was on top of him, opening her legs with his until her knees flanked his sides. He was hugely erect, hard and hot. With a soft touch, he reached down to open her until the lips of her sex rode him.

The deep voice grew even more deep, the timbre rougher, the accent stronger.

"It was like you were giving me life, duschka. Your paintings, the way you talked, moved. Your very existence. There was no way I could do without seeing you, after that first time."

He was moving his hips under her, a slow surge up and down, rubbing his penis along the oh-so-sensitive lips of her sex. Her tissues were so sensitive she could feel everything about him—the large, bulbous tip, the smooth, thick column, the dark wiry hairs at the base. She felt it all as he moved himself slowly along her. A ball of heat rose from between her legs, banishing the chill she'd felt, banishing even the *thought* of cold.

His eyes were so dark, so deep. She couldn't look away from them. She was trapped by those dark eyes, those strong hands holding her hips, the powerful body moving sensuously beneath her. She was trapped, with no desire to escape.

"The first time I saw your work, I was in a car. I couldn't believe what I was seeing. I got out and doubled back to the gallery, thinking to buy a few paintings, not having any idea who the artist was and not caring. And then—and then you walked in. You brought in sunlight and beauty, duschka. I could barely keep my eyes off you, but I knew I had to, for your sake."

His voice was tuning in and out, she was finding it hard to follow him through the blossoming heat and wetness between her legs.

She looked down, mesmerized by the sight of his penis emerging from between her thighs. The enormous head, a dark plum color, already weeping at the tip, appeared, followed by the massive shaft. The semen showed how excited he was, though there was no sense of him losing control. His movements were regular, calculated for maximum stimulation. Oh God, he'd positioned himself so that each stroke rubbed against her clitoris in a long, slow, lingering slide that made her skin prickle and her vagina clench. They weren't even technically making love and she was a hair's breadth from a climax.

Those dark eyes were burning. "Bend down to me," he growled. "Give me your breast."

It didn't occur to her to do anything but obey. She didn't even have to exert any effort, those huge hands on her sides just brought her to him, held her still for him.

His mouth on her burned. He nibbled at her breast for a moment, then opened his mouth to suckle at her nipple in long, liquid pulls. She felt the pulls down to her loins, clenching in time to his mouth.

She drew in a shuddering breath, completely concentrating on what was happening between her legs, held up by his hands because her muscles had turned to water.

He suckled hard and her inner muscles clamped down on his penis. She was so wet and slick his back and forth movements made little sucking noises in the quiet of the room. He swelled even larger under her. Grace braced herself on his iron biceps, head down, hair forming a little curtain of privacy around them as she shook.

His movements speeded up, not so controlled now, his hands pulling her down on him. The sensations magnified, ballooning with heat and friction, Drake moving so fast the huge bed beat hard against the wall.

Grace began that long freefall into orgasm, like jumping out of an airplane, stomach swooping with the absence of gravity. Usually, it lasted only a second before she climaxed, but there was something about this that prolonged it, kept her hovering on the edge for long minutes, as she hung above him, shaking, barely breathing . . .

Her entire body went ballistic, shaking, shuddering as an electric line of pleasure ran from the top of her head to her toes, centering on her loins, where she clenched strongly around Drake's penis.

It set him off, too. With a low moan, he bucked strongly under her, swelled, and started spurting all over his stomach, a hard shudder accompanying each spurt. His teeth were clenched, hands hard at her hips, groaning as his hips moved wildly under her, completely out of control.

He was sweating all over, the short dark hair turning black with sweat. His head fell back against the pillows, strong neck arched, eyes slitted with pleasure, jaw muscles bunching. He looked in pain, but if he felt anything like what Grace had felt, it wasn't pain. It was pleasure on an almost unimaginable scale.

Grace collapsed onto Drake's chest, panting, wiped out, still shaking with the force of the orgasm. They lay there a moment, breathing heavily, eyes closed, creatures of their bodies.

After a moment, Drake's arms went around her, one big hand cradling the back of her head, the other wrapped around her waist, the way he always held her. She was surrounded by hard man, utterly safe.

Feeling safe was a mistake. Intellectually, she knew that. There was nothing safe about the situation at all. Hard men were gunning for Drake and, by extension, for her. Drake himself was an extremely dangerous man, not at all the kind of man you thought of as "safe."

And yet she'd never felt safer in her life than right now, because she knew beyond a shadow of doubt that he would fight to the death for her.

There had never been anyone to defend her, ever. Her father had skipped out with all the family's money when she was nine years old, and even before that, he hadn't been much of a father. Her mother had been wrapped up in her father and, after his abandonment, in her own misery, with no time or thought to her daughter. There had been no aunts or uncles or cousins to form a loving layer of protection around her.

Grace had never had a protective boyfriend. Her lovers had been few and far between and the affairs never lasted more than a couple of weeks, often less. She'd been a passing fancy in their lives. By some twisted turn of fate or maybe by some twist in her psyche, the men she'd been with had been obsessed with their careers or their bank accounts, or often, both. Grace Larsen never figured very highly in their lives. She was there and then she wasn't, and they didn't much notice the difference.

The closest she'd felt to being special to someone had been with Harold. It had been a lovely feeling, but knowing that this charming, elderly man had her best interests at heart in the art world wasn't the same as having someone as strong as Drake solidly on her side in all things.

Like now.

Grace let herself lay on Drake, draped over him, knowing in some deep recess of her mind that, somehow, she was precious to him. That he felt something strong for her and that it was real.

The sharp smell of sex was in the air, a compound of her arousal and the semen that had jetted all over his stomach and that now glued her to him. Her head had fallen to his hard shoulder, nose against his neck. She barely had the energy to open her eyes. Through slitted eyes, she could see about four square inches of his skin, even this small patch of him beautiful and intriguing.

Golden-brown skin, corded muscles so pronounced they cast shadows, even here sleek and strong. With her nose so close to her skin she could smell the essence of him above the keen smell of sex—a dark, fragrant spicy scent, redolent of musk, unlike anything she had ever smelled before in her life.

In a dark, crowded room full of men, she would be able to pick him out blindfolded, by scent alone.

And certainly by touch. No other man she'd ever seen had his deeply muscled physique. One brush of her fingers and she'd know him. No other man on earth could feel like that.

He reached over and punched a button. With a gentle whir, the curtains started sliding open.

It took her a minute to find the strength to turn her head toward the window. By the time she did, the curtains had opened all the way, letting the morning and New York come into the bedroom.

It was still snowing. Not a storm like last night, just gentle flakes hovering in the air more than falling out of the sky. Clouds hung so low over the city they hid the tops of many of the skyscrapers. This high up, it looked like the sky was close enough to touch.

"It's still snowing," she said dreamily, turning her head back into his neck, one hand over his heart.

Drake sighed, the huge deep chest filling with air, lifting her up. "Yes, love. Everything becomes more difficult in the snow."

True, but the world wasn't made for ease. "And everything becomes more beautiful in the snow."

She could actually hear his smile. "Yes, duschka. Very beautiful. I never noticed that before you."

She smiled against his neck, happy to have given him something, if only an appreciation of the beauty of snow.

She drifted, thinking of nothing at all, feeling warm and safe in his arms. She was beginning the luscious slide back into sleep when Drake said quietly, "Duschka."

"Mm." If he wanted to talk, he was going to have to do it to a semi-comatose woman, because she was way too comfortable to pay attention to whatever he wanted to say. Something serious, from the sound of it.

No, she didn't want to talk about anything serious, not right now. Now was her time out of time.

Another enormous sigh as Drake's big hands shifted to cup her shoulders. He lifted her torso slightly so he could look her in the eyes. "I need to tell you something, something you won't want to hear. It is time for you to know, because we need to be making plans."

It *was* serious. Any hint of a smile had gone, and his face was drawn in tight lines, as if in pain. Grace dropped the smile. Whatever it was, it had him worried, so it worried her.

She folded her hands on his chest and rested her chin on them. Whatever the bad news was, she wanted to be touching as much of him as possible while hearing it. "All right," she said quietly. "Shoot. I'm ready."

He shut his eyes briefly, then opened them, gaze fierce as an eagle's. "These . . . problems we're having. They're not going away. Ever."

She said nothing, just watched him.

"The people who are after me are not going to quit, love." His hands on her back clenched lightly, as if reasserting ownership. "Particularly not now, not when they have you as a bargaining chip and when they know what you mean to me."

She spoke through a suddenly tight throat. "And just what do I mean to you, Drake?"

"Everything," he said promptly, eyes never leaving hers. "You're everything to me."

He lifted himself slightly to her, hard stomach muscles clenching, so strong they actually lifted her up as he brought his mouth to hers for a hot, biting kiss that went on and on. She'd just climaxed but her body started waking up, bit by bit, each time his tongue touched hers.

His body was already awake. His penis had only softened a little after his climax, but with the kiss he surged into a full erection, lengthening and hardening in powerful pulses that sent shivers through her.

Grace melted.

Drake broke the kiss, easing back down. The pupils of his eyes had expanded so much the irises looked black. A deep flush rode his high cheekbones and his jaw muscles bunched.

"Later," he growled. "We'll have all the time we want later. But now we need to make plans. I told you my enemies aren't going to give up and I will not give you up."

Grace's heart gave a huge thump in her chest. Something big, something dangerous was coming. "So—what's the answer?"

"We disappear," he said simply, his eyes never leaving hers.

At first Grace didn't understand. The words garbled in her head. *Dis a tear?* Or was it *we'd appear?* Appear where?

And then it struck her.

She frowned. "You mean—go away for a while? Hide out in some sunny resort until the situation resolves itself?"

"No, love." Drake fingered a lock of her hair, brought it to his nose, then gently tucked it back behind her ear. "I mean disappear completely. Disappear forever. Leave our lives behind and make new ones far away where no one can ever find us."

Grace blinked. "You mean—just walk away? Forever?" Wow. It was almost impossible to even contemplate the thought. It was one thing to hole up somewhere for a while. It could even be . . . well, if not fun, then certainly interesting, as long as Drake was with her. A little time out of time. But he wasn't talking about that. He was talking about a new life, a new identity, like those people in the Witness Protection Program. And even then, as far as she knew, when the danger was over, the people went back to their lives.

He was searching for something in her face. "Yes," he said simply. "Forever. Stop being Grace Larsen and Viktor Drakovich and become someone else, far away. And stay that someone else for the rest of our lives."

Grace let out a slow breath, mind whirling.

"And we're going to have to be really clever about disappearing, too, because if my enemies find us, we're dead. There will be no statute of limitations on this, Grace. No going back, ever. You'll never be Grace Larsen again, never see New York again. Never see the United States again. Everything you have and are will have to go."

"I—is that possible? I thought only governments can do that kind of thing."

He allowed himself a small smile. "It is indeed possible, and I can do that kind of thing much better than a government can, if I have the time to plan it right. The question is—are you all right with this? Can you stand the thought of leaving everything and everyone behind? Because it will make my task difficult if not impossible to create new lives for us if you can't let go. If you contact any of your old friends, if you resubscribe to a favorite magazine, if you get in touch with old clients, that would be a huge door for my enemies to walk through, Grace. It could get us killed. You must be able to walk away and never look back. I know how much I'm asking of you and I know this is all my fault. But there is no way to undo what is done, and now I must ask you—can you do it?"

She thought it was typical of him that he wasn't wheedling or coaxing her. He wasn't even seducing her, though he must realize by now that sex was his most potent weapon. If he started kissing her, making love to her, she would melt and acquiesce to anything he said. Disappear to the North Pole or to darkest Africa? Yes, of course, darling Drake. Kiss me again.

No, he wasn't using any weapons at his disposal. His body under hers was very still. He wasn't trying to smile or charm her in any way. He'd made his apology and she imagined it would be the last. Drake was a realist above all, and this was now their new reality. It wasn't really his fault and it certainly wasn't hers, it just was.

She was at a crossroads, and the decision she took right now, in this very instant, would color the rest of her days. She looked down at him, at this man who, in a storm of violence, had someone become more dear to her than any other human on earth.

It would be easy to say that she had bad taste in men, but she knew it wasn't true. The lovers she'd had had been vain children, wanting in important ways. She'd known that and she'd been with them anyway, because at times she'd just been so damned *lonely*. So she'd closed her eyes to their defects, trying to pretend that this time, this relationship would work, all the while knowing it wouldn't. All the while knowing that they didn't really care for *her*, Grace Larsen. They wanted some eye candy on their arm, and the fact that she was an artist made for fun cocktail party conversation until they got bored with it, and with her.

Nothing had ever worked out and with the kind of men she met, nothing ever would. She'd resigned herself to being alone.

Fine, upstanding, successful American men—and they had all been morally weak, even fragile, inside. Take away their money and their jobs and their status, and they were nothing.

Drake was the opposite. He'd had a hard life. She could feel the strength of him down to his core. She was important to him, she could see it, she could feel it. Every cell in her body told her this.

This was such an important moment. She had to get it just right.

Grace leaned down slightly, right hand resting lightly over his heart. She could feel the faint rasp of his chest hairs against her breasts, his nipple centered against her palm, the steely muscles under her hand striated with muscle and deep down, the solid, regular, calm beats of his heart.

She bent her head until her nose almost touched his, her

hair a curtain around them, as if shielding them from a world that meant them terrible harm.

He kept his hands light, barely touching her.

He was now highly aroused, she could feel him, hard and hot, between the lips of her sex. Each time she moved, it seemed to trigger a surge of blood through him, and he thickened and lengthened. Each movement of his penis was mirrored by an answering movement of her inner muscles, which he felt, too. She was growing wetter by the second.

But what she wanted to say had to be said without sex clouding the issue.

She looked him straight in the eyes, his question still echoing in the room.

Can you do it?

"I can do it," she said softly. "I know you think I'm giving up a lot, but really, I'm not. I don't have that many friends and their lives will go on without me. I have no family. My connection with the working world was exclusively through Harold and that is now severed. And I've been painting only for you for the past year, anyway. But there's one more reason why I can do it."

She paused, breathed slowly, trying to find a way to say words she had never said to another human being in her life.

"I can do it for another reason, not just because I'm not leaving much behind. I don't know how and I don't know why, Drake, but there is a connection between us. I have been dreaming of you for a long time, without even knowing you existed. I hardly know you . . . and yet I know you down to your soul. To an outside person, I probably sound insane, but Drake—I'll follow you to the ends of the earth . . . because I love you."

He stiffened under her, his eyes slitted, muscles clenched. A sound escaped him, a hissing moan, almost as if in pain. He brought her to his mouth again, big hands cupping her head, and kissed her deeply, wildly, as if he would never get a chance to kiss again in this lifetime. It called up an answering wildness in her as she opened everything wide to him—mouth, sex, heart.

His hips beneath her began pumping up and down, sliding along her. She was so wet, his penis slid easily between the lips of her sex, as exciting as if he had penetrated. Clinging to Drake's shoulders to keep her balance, Grace kissed him as if she would die if they were separated. His movements were fast and rough, creating a hot friction against her vulva, her breasts rubbing against the hard planes of his chest. Heat blossomed, welling up fast, and it was impossible to resist. With a wild cry, she began coming, clenching against him, feeling the surge of blood in his penis with each contraction.

He wasn't slowing down. He was keeping her climax going for what felt like forever, while another orgasm, riding hard on the waves of the first, caught her by surprise.

He was close, muscles bunched hard, movements jerky, uncontrolled. He gave a deep moan in her mouth and with one last upward thrust started coming again in hot spurts that covered his stomach and hers.

Oh God, it was so intense.

Grace felt like she was leaking emotions that came out of her as moisture. Somehow her eyes were full of tears, though she wasn't crying. It was as if the emotion in her simply had to find a way out and had opted for her eyes. She was sweating from every pore, shaking and trembling, holding on

tightly to Drake, as if she'd drifted far out to sea and he was
a lifeline.

They lay together holding each other tightly for a long
time, long enough for the sky outside to turn a light shade
of pewter. Her trembling muscles slowly relaxed and their
breathing evened out.

Grace was sliding into sleep when Drake turned his head to
kiss her ear, then whispered into it, "I love you, too, Grace."

It jolted her awake. She lifted her head to look at him, at
this man who had become her lover. Who had become her
beloved. Each feature of his face was exotic, fascinating, new
yet familiar.

Who knew? She didn't believe in past lives, but there had
to be something that could explain the deep, intense and immediate connection with this man.

She meant what she'd said and so did he. Neither of them
took love lightly.

"There's so much to say." Grace ran a finger over his eyebrows, down that high, broad cheekbone, over his full mouth.
"I don't know where to start."

His head dipped in agreement. "Yes, there is much to say,
my love, but we have the rest of our lives to say it. And if we
want the rest of our lives to be more than a day or two, we
must plan carefully. A man will be coming with new documents for you. He will be here by noon, unless all this . . .
beautiful snow—" his hard mouth quirked upward in a smile,
"slows his progress."

On a long sigh, Grace rolled out of bed and stretched,
naked. She lifted her arms to the ceiling and rose on her
toes. She felt so . . . *good.*

"Where will this meeting be, Drake?"

"Good question, dushka." One hand reached out from under the covers to stroke her hip. Grace smiled at his touch. "Not my study. That is too . . . personal, with all your paintings there. No, I think we will meet in the living room."

Thirteen

I have news . . .

The message came over Rutskoi's BlackBerry, which he'd parked in full sight. He ground his teeth together. When this was all over, he was going to comb Drake's personnel files and find the fucker who was fucking with him.

Whatever the news was, the man, or woman—nothing like a woman for betrayal, in his experience—wasn't talking until the next installment was transferred. And Rutskoi had to take it on faith that the news was going to be worth a hundred thousand dollars.

Rutskoi took his eye off the scope and texted his Caribbean bank. His Caribbean bank lived for this. The transfer was made immediately. A quarter of an hour later, his informant texted:

Target will be in living room at noon. Living room is five rooms from southern end, tenth and eleventh windows. He ordered food and might stay in the room for a while.

Yes! Drake finally in the living room, in a straight line from his Barrett, staying there for a while—if Rutskoi didn't make this shot, he might as well hang up his rifle.

All of a sudden, Rutskoi could feel a huge surge of power running through his body. He had only catnapped over the past days, but suddenly the fatigue disappeared as if it had never been. He felt alert, refreshed. Ready. This would work, he could feel it in his bones. He was going to get Drake, and become rich and, in the right circles, famous.

He settled back over his rifle, feeling a preternatural clarity. His destiny was awaiting him.

Drake would go down and he would go up.

It was the way of the world.

They had a leisurely breakfast, left outside the door by the phalanx of good fairies that apparently ran Drake's household. The fairies were excellent at what they did. Strong Indian tea, homemade yogurt, homemade croissants, fresh blueberries.

Drake said he would offer a light lunch to the mystery man coming at noon, so she ate sparingly.

The atmosphere between them had changed, sharpened. Grace no longer felt any shyness at all around Drake. They spoke naturally, as a couple, making their plans. He asked her where she wanted to end up and she said far away, in a place with palm trees.

He'd been quiet for a long moment, then nodded.

"It will take a few steps, duschka," he said, "but so be it."

Grace caught his hand and brought it to her face. "Together, though." She kissed his hand lightly. "We will do it together."

He turned his hand to run the back of his forefinger down her cheek. "Oh yes, my love, we will do it together. It will be difficult and even dangerous. You will have to learn to inhabit a new life in a new place, and possibly learn a new language. Nothing will be easy and nothing will be familiar, but I will be with you every step of the way."

Drake stood, keeping his hand on her face. "We have much to do today, my love, so it would be a good idea for you to get ready. I'll let you shower and prepare yourself and we will meet in the living room at noon."

He was out of the room quickly. Odd how so large a man could move so quickly and so quietly. He was there and then . . . not there.

Grace stood and walked to the windows, placing both hands against the cold glass. The snow had intensified, swirling spirals of white in the updrafts between buildings. The clouds had lowered, turned darker. It was entirely possible that a big snowstorm was coming.

Would it be the last snowstorm she'd ever see?

How odd, to think of it. How odd to think that her life was turning such a sharp corner into something else. She might never see snow again. And she would certainly never see New York again.

Grace positioned her hands so that they formed a frame and moved her hands over the huge window, capturing scenes of New York and committing them to memory. They would be stored in her subconscious, processed, and would come out at some unexpected moment.

She went into Drake's insanely luxurious bathroom, trying to choose between the whirlpool and the perfumed shower—finally opting for the shower—and dressed in one of the outrageously expensive and beautiful outfits he'd bought her.

She knew, instinctively, that it pleased him to buy her expensive things. She didn't much care. She'd done without all her life and would have happily dressed from Gap and Target for the rest of her days. But the clothes were beautiful and she appreciated beauty, so she washed and dressed with care.

Today, she and Drake had united their lives. It felt so strange, not to be alone. They would disappear together, spend the rest of their lives together.

It was such a delicious thought, one she'd never thought to have.

A clock on the huge mantelpiece chimed. Eleven o'clock. As in all the rooms, there was a huge fire going. Drake must have suffered greatly from the cold growing up, he made such a point of being warm. Maybe a sunny place, with no bad memories, would be good for him, too.

Walking across the enormous room, Grace smiled as she thought of the new life they would start planning in the living room.

Three rooms down, a woman lingered at the window, hands up against the glass. She stayed there for a time, in the same position, as if drinking in the view of the snow. The snow didn't make any difference to Rutskoi; he was seeing a clear green and red outline, with no interference.

Rutskoi's trigger finger tightened. The angle was such that a kill was a real possibility. It was Drake's woman. Rutskoi would bet everything he owned on it.

The crosshairs were right on her heart.

One pull and she would be dead.

Oh, what a temptation. Losing his woman would make Drake insane. Poetic justice.

But Drake had to be his first target. If Rutskoi let his emotions rule, he would be useless in his future profession. Drake, then the woman. That was the way it had to be.

Rutskoi watched the woman through the thermal imager as she gazed down at the snowy scene below and then moved away.

His finger eased off the trigger.

Not yet. But soon.

He glanced at his watch. Eleven o'clock. Another hour to go.

In the study, Drake shuffled some of his passports together. He would need a couple of identities that tallied with those that would be created for Grace.

Design mavens were wrong. Less wasn't more. More was more.

He had seven deeply embedded identities from five different nations, with credit cards and birth certificates and data going back years. And a couple of shallow identities, to be used in emergencies, as one-offs.

He wasn't going to have time to establish deep identities for Grace, so what they did create was going to have to be perfect. Luckily, he had the perfect man for the job.

A large trolley suitcase containing two million dollars in hundred dollar bills was waiting in the living room for that man, together with lunch and two bottles of wine.

In half an hour it would start. Drake allowed himself a few minutes to contemplate the huge twist life had thrown at him. He was going to spend the rest of his life with a woman. They'd go to a remote island in the Pacific, a part of the world where he had never had business dealings, and he'd build or buy them a beautiful home open to the sun and air. Grace would paint and he would buy up the local airline company and shipping company. These were businesses he knew down to the ground, and that way he could keep track of everyone who came to the island and would have a good cover for his money.

His lips curved. Running a legitimate business. Could be interesting.

Most magical of all, Grace was coming with him. Grace was *happy* to come with him.

Grace loved him.

He'd never been loved. He'd been hated and feared and envied, even admired, but never loved.

Grace loved him.

He would never grow tired of that thought.

He could leave behind the wealth and the power because they had started to weigh heavily on him, like a huge burden he'd carried far too long. He'd never thought to put down his shield and sword, but life had handed him exactly that opportunity.

Not that he intended relaxing his vigilance, particularly with Grace to protect. But violence and power would no longer define his life. They would simply be the means to protect his life. His life with Grace.

He was so taken with the idea that he wasn't even pursuing the traitor in his midst. Soon, they would be gone. Whoever had betrayed him would end up with ashes.

A light knock on the door and he smiled. His heart rate actually picked up. Drake's heartbeat stayed as steady as his hands, no matter what. Cornered, under fire, surrounded by enemies, he kept his cool. Grace changed all that.

"Enter," he called to his new love.

He would get over this stage. Probably. Maybe. But while he was in it, it was a delight. To be so attuned to another human being you could feel her thoughts, to be uppermost in her mind, to *matter* . . . these were all such rare joys, it was as if he'd been visited by a unicorn.

No, not a unicorn, even better.

Grace. That she loved him seemed like such a miracle. And yet he recognized in her the same deep loneliness that afflicted his own life. How men could stay away from such a gentle beauty was a stone-cold mystery to him, and yet no one knew better than Drake how irredeemably stupid and dull-witted most men were. Grace was indeed a rare beauty, but she seemed to have been born without the heavy armor most beautiful women are born with. She was open, vulnerable, incapable of playing games.

It was what endeared her to him, but he understood full well what it made her. Prey.

Well, she was no longer prey, and never would be again. She would be fiercely protected by him, for the rest of their lives.

A fall of shiny bronze hair, long white fingers clutching the edge of the door and half a face peeking in.

"Drake?" she said softly. "It's early, I know. I thought I'd go wait in the living room for this man." She walked over to his desk.

"Good idea," he said. "While you're there, open a bottle of wine and pour three glasses. I'll be right there."

She gave a slight smile. "So I guess we're starting our new life right now, huh?"

God, that sounded good. "Yes, duschka," he replied softly, reaching up to stroke her cheek. She rubbed her face into his hand. He loved the way she reacted every time he touched her, his touch pleasing to her. "It starts now. In the living room."

* * *

Someone entered the living room.

Rutskoi had been in a constant state of alert, but now adrenaline rushed through his body, heightening his senses even more. He loved this. He was born for this.

It was time. He felt it in every cell of his body. It was happening *now*.

The fiery red, gold and green figure walking into the room was slender, narrow-shouldered, with shoulder length hair. The woman.

His trigger finger loosened slightly.

Rutskoi breathed evenly, in and out, letting the adrenaline settle throughout his body. Enough to sharpen him, not enough to make his hands tremble.

Perfect.

The woman walked to the center of the room and picked something up . . . it was hard to tell what she was doing as her back was turned. Ah. It looked like she had opened a bottle of wine and was pouring. Knowing Drake, the bottle was undoubtedly excellent, rare and expensive.

He'd never live to drink it.

The woman's head turned and she walked to the door. Rutskoi tracked her through his thermal scope. A man walked into the room. Not overly tall but with immensely broad shoulders. Drake.

The woman was kissing him.

It made for a bad shot. A doable shot, of course. A .50 caliber bullet could go through the woman, through Drake and through the door behind them and the wall beyond that.

But he didn't like the angle and the odds. He waited, patiently, observing them kissing, detached and cold.

Okay. The woman was backing away, holding Drake's

hand, leading him toward the center of the room, toward the large hearth. The intense heat from the fire distorted the picture. Drake's body heat would be lost in the greater heat of the fire. Rutskoi had to shoot before Drake walked in front of it.

The woman's heat signature disappeared as she moved in front of the fire, her hand outstretched, holding on to Drake's. He was walking toward the fire, in profile.

Shit. The best shot would be frontal. Rutskoi had to make a split-second decision. To aim for a profile requiring millimeter precision, dealing with the distorting effect of the thermal signature through a dense glass that could deflect the bullet, or to wait for Drake to turn and present a full-frontal target.

Every ounce of training and experience said *wait*.

Rutskoi lay, alert but not tense, focused but not overwhelmed, right leg slightly bent for stability as was the Russian sniping style, and waited.

Drake had one hand on the mantelpiece. Rutskoi remembered that mantel—a huge monolith of white and gray marble—just as he remembered everything about the room. He remembered the luxurious sofas covered with cashmere throw rugs, the deep carpets, the antiques. Drake lived like a prince. Goddammit, Rutskoi wanted to live like a prince, too.

Ah! Drake was turning, the woman was walking back toward him carrying something. A glass. He was reaching out for it with one hand, the other still perched on the mantelpiece.

Turning, turning . . .

Yes!

Rutskoi took a breath, breathed half of it out, waited until he was between heartbeats, and pulled the trigger.

Fourteen

Drake was smiling at Grace, reaching for the glass of wine she held out to him, when she tripped on a rug. Instinctively, he moved fast to catch her before she fell.

And the world exploded.

He went down on his hands and knees, head hanging low, watching a slow dripping of something thick and red, not understanding what. Nothing moved, his vision dimmed, sound had deserted the world.

And then vision, hearing and understanding came back in a sick rush and he realized they were under attack.

Shards of marble were flying off the mantelpiece as bullets gouged enormous holes. One, two, three.

Someone was firing at where he'd been a second ago, firing .50 caliber bullets, judging from the size of the holes and the fact that they penetrated his bullet-resistant windows. If Grace hadn't tripped, three .50 cals would have turned him into human hamburger in an instant.

Grace!

The shots kept coming, at a steady pace, set to single-shot fire, shot by a man who knew what he was doing but who couldn't see what was happening.

Drake fast crawled to where Grace was crouching in front of the sofa and threw himself on top of her.

"Stay down!" he shouted, wishing he could somehow crush her down below the ground so she wouldn't in any way be a target.

His movements were clumsy, slow. He wasn't clumsy and he wasn't slow. His slow reflexes told him he was concussed, and he swore. He needed all his wits about him to get them out of here, but he could barely think.

"—invisible?" Grace said. She was still under him, head turned to take instructions from him, eyes wide with fear.

Another bullet smashed a large Ming vase. Drake curved over Grace, trying to shield her as much as he could, sharp shards piercing his back.

Drake shook his head, trying to say he didn't understand her, but no words came out. He scanned the room, trying to figure a way to the door, but his vision was blurred and he saw double.

Another thunderous shot exploded above them, and another.

Whoever the sniper was, he'd have plenty of ammo. This was a planned hit.

Drake had to get them out of the room fast, because sooner or later, one of the bullets would strike its target. Even a shoulder- or thigh-shot from a .50 caliber bullet would prove fatal in seconds. There would be no way to staunch the blood—they'd simply bleed out fast.

Grace was shouting something over the noise. Something about—

The clouds in his head parted for a second and meaning rushed in.

He put his mouth close to her ear. "He's using a thermal imager. It doesn't matter that he can't see through the windows. He's seeing our heat signature."

Another bullet crashed into the floor two feet from them, gouging a hole inches deep, then another a foot away.

The shooter was laying down withering fire, getting off a round every five seconds.

Though his muscles had lost most of their strength and coordination, Drake gritted his teeth and rolled off Grace. "Crawl!" he shouted. "Crawl to the edge of the fire!"

He thought he was shouting but his voice came out frighteningly weak. He coughed and wiped his mouth. His hand came away red.

Oh God, no. Jesus no. Had he been lung shot? If he had, he had only minutes to live, and he was leaving Grace to die alone. He refused even the idea of it.

Drake tried desperately to take in a deep breath, while trying to stop the room from spinning. He breathed in hard. There was no sucking sound. He hadn't been shot through the lung, thank God, but he was badly concussed.

"Drake!" Grace put her face right next to his and he realized she'd been shouting at him and he hadn't responded. She looked terrified. Another shot went straight through the sofa and into the wall, inches from them. "Drake, answer me!"

Drake coughed again and tried to lift his head. It felt as if he had lead weights in it. "Get—" He coughed again, desperately trying to pull in air. "Get close to the fire. Heat . . . distorts."

A series of shots in quick succession, but off the mark, burying themselves into the wall over the fireplace.

The room filled with the deafening sound of a fusillade of bullets.

Grace looked confused, glancing back at the window. Drake narrowed his eyes, trying to focus. The shooter was concentrating fire to punch a hole through the window.

Drake reached out and took Grace's face in his hand. He turned her to face him, desperately trying to make her understand. "Thermal . . . imager," he gasped. "He sees our heat." He wheezed heavily, trying to gulp in air. "You need to stay close to the fire . . ."

They needed to blend their image with the fire's image. The shooter wouldn't see human shapes then, only a wall of fire. Somehow Grace understood. She nodded and started pulling him toward the fire.

"No!" he choked. "Get to the fire." She was wasting time trying to pull him.

Suddenly, Grace looked at the trolley containing lunch and then back at him. "He can't see through heat?" she asked.

Drake nodded, trying to coordinate hands and knees to crawl to the hearth. Another round embedded itself in the wall and he watched as a big chunk of laminated window fell to the floor.

Grace let go of him and, crouching, made her way back to the trolley.

"Come back! Come—" Drake's vision darkened, his head pulsed and he gritted his teeth to stay conscious. Damn his reflexes!

But Grace was already at the trolley, moving fast. She picked up both bottles of wine and threw them at the windows.

Drake's thoughts were slow, dull. He wanted to tell Grace

that, brave as she was, throwing bottles at a sniper across the street wouldn't help anything, but he couldn't articulate the words, could barely think them.

She was by his side again, shaking his shoulder. "Drake—is there a way out of the building?"

He nodded slowly, painfully.

"Good." She left his side and reached into the fire. Drake watched, gritting his teeth against the pain and the encroaching darkness. What was she doing?

It wasn't until he saw her pick up a log that was burning on only one end and throw it at the window that he understood. The curtains burst into flame, fueled by the alcohol. The flames spread along the hardwood floor, following the line of the spilled wine.

Grace picked up a bottle of cognac and whiskey and threw them into the flames. The fire blossomed, covering almost the entire wall.

The sniper was now blind.

"Drake—get us out of here! Darling, we need to run!" She tried to help him stand, forcing a shoulder under his arm. He did his best, but he fell heavily to one knee. The room was spinning. She'd bought them some time, but it wasn't going to help them if he simply passed out.

The sniper was firing wildly now, blindly, shot after shot, in a deadly fusillade. It was only a question of time before he hit them.

"Go." Drake wanted to caress her face, but his hand wouldn't coordinate. All he did was leave a streak of blood down her cheek. "Go. Get to the end of the corridor. Under the print on the wall is a keypad. The code is—"

"No, absolutely not." Grace's voice was sharp, the voice a

soldier would use to a wounded comrade. "We're going to-gether. You must get up, my darling. I can't carry you and I won't leave you, so you need to get up."

A round came so close he felt the air displacement. They had to get out *now*.

Grace put her shoulder under his arm again and stood, shakily, bearing a good portion of his weight. She slipped on his blood getting him upright and he could feel her effort.

"Go," Drake gasped, trying to push her away. They flinched as a series of shots flung needle-sharp shards of marble from the mantelpiece. One stuck in her cheek and she simply reached up and pulled it out. Goddamn it, they were going to die here, right now. "Get out of here," he whispered.

Her jaws clenched. "Not without you. Forget about it. We live together or we die together, it's your choice, Drake. Do you understand?" She waited a moment to allow him to gather what little strength he had, then nodded. "Now, let's go."

She lurched forward, right arm around his waist, left hand holding on to his hand dangling over her shoulder. Drake straightened, ignoring the pain from his chest and back, grit-ting his teeth hard against the blackness that threatened to overwhelm him.

They were supposed to run for the door, but instead they shuffled. The burning curtains provided a good screen, but Drake had no way of knowing where the sniper was positioned across the street. They couldn't be certain that they weren't in his sights right now, the sniper preparing in this very instant to blow Grace's beautiful head off her shoulders.

He stiffened his knees. He couldn't fail her.

He heard her heavy panting as they made their way to the door. She could have saved herself by now, been long gone, but she'd made it clear she wasn't leaving without him.

He wasn't going to be the cause of her death. No way.

A lifetime of discipline asserted itself. He wasn't going to slow Grace down. Fuck it if he could barely stand, barely see, barely think. She needed him.

Grace left him, rushed to the trolley and poured a bottle of grappa over the couch and threw a burning log into the cushions. It caught fire with a roar. Smart woman. The sniper wouldn't be able to see anything within a radius of at least a few feet around the burning sofa. She had bought them another precious few seconds.

They had to move fast.

"Wait." He stopped, swaying, then turned around. It was a sign of his mental confusion that he had walked right by the trolley.

"Where are you going?" Grace gasped. She was panting, face dripping with sweat from the exertion of holding him up and the heat of the burning room.

Drake shuffled forward. "Trolley." He didn't have the breath to explain.

In his study, his vault contained at least twenty million dollars in diamonds, credit cards on accounts with hefty sums in them, and cash in a number of currencies. They couldn't stop to empty his vault. They had to make it out as fast as possible, via a route no one knew about, not even his bodyguards.

"Stay here, I'll get it." Grace took a deep breath and plunged toward the burning sofa. She grabbed the trolley's handle and was by his side in an instant, putting her shoulder back under his arm and urging him forward, all in one smooth move.

The sniper had shifted tactics, deciding to sweep the room starting from the north end. The shots were badly distorted, ricocheting, but they still had more than enough punch to kill. They were coming at a steady pace, heading straight for them.

Grace was trembling badly, trying to bear his weight. He straightened, moved away from her, shuffled as fast as he could toward the door and all but shoved her through it, then fell forward.

They landed in a heap on the other side, Drake toppling on top of Grace. For a second, he was stunned, fighting hard not to black out, holding ferociously onto consciousness. Under him, he felt Grace's narrow rib cage moving as she fought to pull in air. She was pale and sweating. Drake rolled off her and gathered his energy to kick the door closed.

Now the sniper had a fire and another thick wall to see through. It was entirely possible that they had become invisible.

There was pounding on the steel door that led into the vestibule, shouts ringing out. His men, having heard the shots, trying to get to him. Smoke sensors would also have sounded an alarm.

For an instant, Drake was tempted to simply punch in the code that would open the door from the inside and let his men take over. Right now, he was in no shape to lead Grace to safety. There was something wrong with him. He was probably badly concussed and if his brain was swelling or if there was subdural hemorrhaging all the willpower in the world wouldn't keep him on his feet.

His men were handpicked for loyalty, but even the remote

possibility that one or more of his men were traitors was too big a risk to take. He would be handing Grace over to his enemies.

Unthinkable.

He was used to risk taking, though not on behalf of someone he loved. It was terrifying, yet it had to be done. He'd rather go down fighting, trying to shield Grace, than hand her over like a lamb to slaughter.

He made for the end of the corridor, for what looked like a blank wall but was a secret passageway to a hidden elevator in the building only he had access to.

The wall was only fifty feet away. It looked miles away, at the end of an endless tunnel surrounded by gray fog.

He talked quickly, hoping to get it all out before he lost consciousness, gulping in air, shaking his head in an effort to keep conscious.

"Grace, there's a keypad on the wall at the end of this corridor, under the flower print. Code . . ." He sucked in air, coughed. "Code 9076. Punch it in, door will open . . ." The gray was turning to black at the edges of his vision. "Elevator," he gasped. "To basement. SUV in slot 58." With a fumbling hand, he dug into his pants pocket. He always carried the key to a getaway car no one knew about, a secret cell phone and several credit cards. He'd spent his life ready to run at a second's notice. "Key." It dangled from his nerveless fingers.

They'd been shuffling forward as he talked, Grace bearing almost his entire weight, pulling the trolley behind them.

Finally, after what felt like a century, they were at the wall and Grace punched in the code. The pounding at the door to his quarters grew fiercer, the shouts louder. They would be debating amongst themselves whether to break down the

door. They could try. It was built to bank-vault specifications. If and when they finally managed it, they would open
the door to the charred remains of what had once been his
home.

The sniper was still shooting at a steady pace, but had
started to shoot into other rooms, hoping for a random hit.

A section of the wall slid open and Grace helped him into
the elevator, still dragging the trolley. He found it almost
impossible to pick up his feet and if it hadn't been for Grace's
arm around his waist, he would have fallen.

He couldn't fall. If he fell, he'd never get up again.

She didn't need further instructions. Drake was blessed
in having fallen in love with an intelligent woman. She
didn't tempest him with questions or idle comments. His
strength was ebbing second to second, and he had to con-
serve it.

They were in deep trouble. She understood that and didn't
waste their resources.

If he'd had the strength, he would have kissed her.

The bottom dropped out of the world. The elevator was an
emergency exit and had been designed to fall as fast as possible, faster than safety regulations allowed. In seconds they
were in the basement.

Drake kept his fleet of vehicles in a walled-off section of
the basement to the right that only he or his men had access
to, but kept his secret getaway vehicle separate. Slot 58 was
to the left.

He opened his mouth to croak out *Go left*, when he saw
that Grace had already figured out the number system. The
slot was close by. It was pointless having a quick getaway car
far from the emergency elevator.

Even moving sluggishly, feet dragging, they were at the Tahoe in seconds, Grace unlocking the doors with the key fob from five feet away. Instead of heading for the driver's side, she opened the passenger side door first.

Drake shook his head, resisting.

If enemies were coming after them, she had to get in first and, if necessary, pull away without him.

He tried to say it. "Get . . . in . . . first." His lungs were heaving, his voice was hoarse. He was clinging to the door-frame with shaking fingers.

She didn't pay any attention at all, simply pushed and prodded until he half fell in. She shoved his legs in, threw the trolley in, slammed the door behind him and ran to the driver's side.

He kept the vehicle completely serviced, with a full tank of gas, at all times. It roared to life at the turn of the key in the ignition and Grace backed out of the slot immediately, wrenching the wheel and shooting for the exit.

After several tries, Drake managed to buckle his seat belt. Everything was dimming. He needed to do the next things fast.

As Grace shot up out of the underground garage onto the street, skidding wildly, barely missing an oncoming bus, Drake brought his cell phone up, squinting to make out the numbers. Shaking, he punched in a number he knew by heart. All the numbers he needed to know—cell-phone numbers, bank-account numbers—he had memorized. They were not written down anywhere—they only existed in his head.

The call was picked up immediately. "Boss," said a deep voice.

The relief nearly wiped Drake out. Grigori, his best pilot.

It was snowing heavily and cell-phone reception wasn't very good. Drake had about a minute or two of consciousness left, but what he had to say was very simple.

"Grigori—"

A heavy chunk of metal fell on the hood, bounced heavily, then rolled off, leaving the hood badly dented. Grace screamed and lost control of the vehicle for a moment. Another piece of red-hot metal fell from the sky, then another. A long steel rectangle clattered down. The blade of a helicopter rotor.

Someone had blown up the helicopter on the roof. Drake had instinctively made for the ground, and his instincts had once again proven sound.

Grace was weaving erratically down the street, wide-eyed and white faced. "What's happening?" she cried.

Drake stretched out a hand to touch her arm, failed, tried again. She turned slightly at his touch, then turned her attention back to the white, icy street ahead of her. She was sitting forward in her seat, terrified, clutching the wheel with white-knuckled fingers. She wasn't a very good driver, but she would have to do the driving. Drake was in no condition to take the wheel.

"It's okay," he said to Grace and squeezed her arm. She didn't answer, just pressed her lips together and nodded, eyes on the dangerous street ahead.

Drake brought the cell phone back to his ear. It felt like it weighed ten tons. "Grigori, listen. Keep . . . the Gulfstream 4 . . . ready to go. I'm coming down with a passenger. Don't— don't know when I will make it. Stay by the plane."

"Yes, boss," came Grigori's deep voice and Drake was reassured. If it took him a year to make it down to the Tampa airfield, Grigori would be there, the plane serviced and ready for takeoff in a few minutes' time.

Streaks of black crossed his field of vision.

His hand was still on Grace's arm. "Grace. My love."

She didn't take her eyes off the road, trying to hold the wheel steady, but she nodded. She was listening.

"We need to make it as fast as we can to Tampa, Florida. Don't stop unless you have to. I have a plane waiting for us there."

"No! Are you *crazy?* You're wounded, Drake. You're losing blood. I'm sure the stitches in your shoulder have been torn and your back is ripped open. And you're concussed, probably badly. I'm taking you to Ben, right now. Which hospital does he work in?"

He was fading, his voice so weak it could barely be heard over the noise of the engine. He had to make Grace understand how important it was to get out of New York as fast as she could. To linger was to invite death.

"Promise me." His hoarse voice cracked as his fingers tightened on her arm. She chanced a glance at him, wide-eyed at the tone of his voice, then looked back at the street. "Promise me you won't stop as long as you can stay awake. We must"—he coughed, something in his chest exploding with pain—"we must get out of New York and make it down to Tampa. Promise me you won't stop unless you must."

The darkness was almost complete. He could barely see, barely think.

His fingers tightened even more, the last dregs of his fading strength. "Promise me."

"I promise," she sobbed, risking another quick glance at him. He saw from her face that he looked bad.

"Won't . . . die," he promised, hoping he could keep it.

He fought the weakness, with everything in him, but it won.

The world turned black.

Pizdets! Shit!

Rutskoi looked at the message he'd just paid another fucking hundred thousand dollars for.

Drake and woman gone. Blood on floor, walls. Living room full of bullet holes, room completely burned.

It had been almost impossible to see anything in the thermal imager because of the fire that witch started. Against all the odds, Drake and his bitch were still alive.

Cocksucker had made it out, but at least Rutskoi had wounded him. Or the woman. *Or both,* he thought viciously. Let it be both. Let them be bleeding their fucking hearts out on the street.

When he understood that Drake and the woman had probably made it out of the room, Rutskoi had sprinted to the rooftop and had taken out the helicopter on the opposite roof with ten incendiary rounds, watching with satisfaction as the helicopter exploded and fell in burning pieces through the snow to the street thirty stories below. Just to vent his frustration, Rutskoi had shot the pilot who had come out of a small, warm shed on the rooftop. It had given him immense pleasure to take Drake's pilot down.

Shit.

No, control. He needed control. He waited a moment, forcing himself to move into the sniper's mind-set of dispassionate detachment, then descended the stairs.

Rutskoi went back into the empty apartment and calmly broke down his Barrett, placing the pieces in their foam cutouts with steady hands that didn't in any way betray the turmoil inside.

Drake had escaped. Okay. But the game wasn't over yet. He was wounded and he hadn't been able to escape with many resources.

And he was running with a woman he cared for. She would slow him down, force him to make mistakes. Drake was an operator, a clever, ruthless man. He would do what was necessary to survive. But with a woman to drag along behind him and protect, Drake would slip up. And Rutskoi would get him.

Rutskoi knew exactly how to track him down.

Terabyte.

Twenty genius hackers working out of Estonia, who provided around-the-clock services to anyone, for the right price. They could find out anything on anyone. Need dirt on your new boss? In 24 hours, Terabyte will deliver a dossier including video footage of the boss fucking a call girl. Need to know someone's bank password? Easy. Terabyte can get classified information in a day, top-secret information in a day and a half.

Word had it that one of them had been the NSA's top cyber expert and could hack into the array of military satellites ringing the globe.

For the right price, they would monitor the entire world for any appearance of Grace Larsen or Viktor Drakovich, in any of his incarnations.

Rutskoi had known Drake long enough, had studied him long enough, to know many of his pseudonyms, which he'd feed to Terabyte, together with a database of the companies Drake owned that he knew of.

It was entirely possible that with Terabyte's help, he could track Drake to earth very soon.

The woman would slow him down, make him vulnerable. She would be the death of him.

Fifteen

Bed. He was lying on a bed.

It was raining.

Drake opened his eyes briefly, then shut them against the pain in his head. But not before he'd seen a ceiling. Gray, low, cracked. The cracks ran diagonally across the tiny room like a big river with tributaries running off it.

He opened his eyes again, ignoring the sharp pain, taking stock.

Small room, maybe five meters by five meters. Walls painted a dusty tan a long time ago. A small television set high up on a wall bracket, chained to the bracket. A cheap plastic wardrobe missing a handle on one door. A desk, a chair. An open door giving on to a small, white-tiled bathroom.

The mattress under him was as soft as a sponge, guaranteed to provide a restless night's sleep.

Where were they? In a cheap motel room, obviously, but *where*?

He turned his head to the bedside table and had to wait for the room to stop spinning before reaching out to the notepad next to the old-fashioned rotary-dial telephone. It took him a couple of tries to coordinate his hand's movements. Finally, he had the pad in his hand and brought it to his face, trying fiercely to focus.

JORDAN'S MOTOR COURT, he read. WALLIS, SOUTH CAROLINA.

He'd never heard of Wallis, but he knew where South Carolina was.

Where was Grace? That he was alone in the motel room could be seen at a glance.

He had no memory of how he got here and understood that he must have been out for at least eight hours, probably more. If Grace had stopped, it was because she was too exhausted to go on.

So . . . where was she?

Drake felt a sharp ache in his chest that had nothing to do with wounds and everything to do with missing her. He would survive his wounds. His body was already knitting itself up, he could feel it. The headache and muscle pains were nothing.

But he needed Grace like he needed water and air. Ferociously.

Where the hell was she?

He rolled over in bed, relishing the small surge of strength he could feel returning to his body, and that was when he saw it.

The trolley, lying by the left-hand bedside table.

Open.

She hadn't even bothered to close it.

Drake's heart gave a sharp blow in his chest. Pure, lancing pain, such as none he had ever felt before, exploded inside him.

She'd left him.

Of course.

He was a hunted man. His enemies had almost killed her twice, had killed a dear friend and driven her out of her home and out of her life. She must have thought his enemies would eventually get her, too.

And there was the trolley, full of enough money to support someone like Grace for two lifetimes.

He didn't even blame her. Any other woman would have done the same. If there was anyone in the world who understood the imperatives of self-preservation, it was Drake. Grace would have to be crazy to stay with him, a hunted man, a criminal. Wounded, perhaps dying, for all she knew.

He understood, completely.

So why did it fucking hurt so much?

It was a pain unlike any he had ever felt before, more than torn tissues and broken bones, much more. Something essential in him felt broken, blown apart—something at the core of his being, something that medicine couldn't help and that would never heal.

Grace had left him and he felt completely adrift, untethered to the world. Even in his darkest days as a homeless boy on the streets, he had never felt this . . . hollow. The life force that had sustained him forever had somehow vanished.

He was probably capable of sitting up, even of getting up and walking. He needed stitches and some antibiotics, but he could function. He'd managed to get out of bad situations before in worse shape than this.

He knew what he had to do. Lack of money right now meant nothing. He had his cell phone and could start the process of accessing his funds. It would take a little time and a little trouble, that was all.

Grigori was waiting for him. The plan was a good one. Foolproof, almost.

Grigori would be waiting close by the Gulfstream 4, in a small, private airfield not far from the Tampa airport, which had heavy traffic in cargo flights. Grigori had access to all the flight plans out of Tampa. He'd fly them out at night, within 800 meters of a cargo flight headed for Eastern Europe, keeping directly below the jet blast of the engines with the collision lights off, completely invisible to radar.

They would fly across the Atlantic tailing the cargo flight and no one would ever know. It was standard operating procedure for Drake's flights.

They'd land in Montenegro, where the deputy premier was one of Drake's best customers, be carried over by boat to Apulia, the boot heel of Italy, where a car would be waiting to drive them to Rome. Grace had wanted to go to Rome, and by God he wanted to take her there.

That had been his plan—a few days in Rome, showing her the sights, then they would take their jump to the final destination—Sivuatu, a thousand miles from Fiji and a million miles from nowhere.

Even without Grace, the plan was good. He actually needed to go to Rome, where the second-best forger in the world lived. He'd had to run without any documents, and Signor Caselli could get them for him. A Belgian passport, a Maltese passport and perhaps a Croatian one.

But then again—if Grace was gone, why leave the country

at all, why seek a new life? He was shedding his old life and creating a new existence to protect *her*. If she was gone, he could go back to his old life.

So okay, his security had been breached. He'd just tighten it. Put stainless-steel plates behind the windows, shuffle his bodyguards, hire new ones, upgrade his videoconferencing facilities.

Find the fucker who'd betrayed him and make him pay.

Hole up. Hell, he could do most of his business over a webcam connection, no need to ever leave his premises again.

Drake lay on the filthy bed, counting the cracks in the ceiling, telling himself to get up, get going, yet he lay unmoving on the dirty bed. Why did the thought of going back to New York and living under enhanced security conditions make him feel already dead and buried?

He couldn't get his muscles into gear. He had the strength, but not the heart. For the first time in his life, he had no desire to get going. His chest felt hollow, empty, as if his heart had been ripped out, leaving a gaping hole.

Whatever he decided—move forward to the new life or fall back on the old—he needed to decide fast.

But he couldn't move. He lay on his back, watching the lights of the passing cars outside the window, flumes of water thrown up by their tires, listening to the sleety rain pounding at the thin window pane, and tried to find it in himself to care enough to get going.

Nothing worked. He lay, thinking of nothing, feeling nothing, wanting nothing, hardly breathing as the clock in his head marked half an hour, an hour.

A heavy vehicle braked recklessly outside the motel room in a shower of gravel. A door slammed. A few moments later, the motel room door opened and Grace rushed in, arms full of packages.

She was pale, exhausted, completely soaked. Dumping the packages on the chair, she rushed to his bedside, placing a hand on his forehead.

"You're awake. Thank God. I *hated* leaving you unconscious, but you needed medicine and we needed warm clothes and some food."

Drake angled his body up on his elbows.

Grace. By some miracle, Grace was here. Tired and bedraggled and worried looking and more beautiful than ever. Oh God, she was *here*.

"Came . . . back," he managed to choke out through a tight throat.

She threw him a wry glance, hands busy pulling things out of paper bags. Gauze, disinfectant, bandages, cheap warm clothing. From one paper bag came the enticing smell of hamburgers. "Yes, I made it, without killing anyone, too. I know I'm a lousy driver, you don't have to rub it in. I've never owned a car and—" She stopped, sucking in a shocked breath, turning her head to study him, a frown between her eyebrows. "Oh my God. You don't mean that. Oh, Drake." She sat abruptly on the bed, as if her legs wouldn't support her anymore, hand cupping his jaw. "Oh, my darling, you thought I wasn't coming back at *all*." She studied his eyes and he dropped his. "You thought I'd abandoned you."

He couldn't speak. He could barely breathe. Tight bands constricted his chest, clutched his heart, squeezing.

Now that his head was higher, he could see that the trolley was still completely full of money. She'd only taken enough to make the purchases.

Oh God. Surely she would leave now. He'd just dealt her

a monstrous insult, how could she stay? He couldn't even open his mouth to beg her forgiveness, because every muscle he had was locked down in pain and sorrow. He could barely breathe through the constriction in his chest.

The room was utterly silent except for the pinging of sleet against the panes and the far-off hiss of tires on the wet road.

"My darling," Grace whispered, her other hand cupping the back of his head. She bent forward until her forehead touched his. "Know this. I will never leave you. I couldn't. I love you."

Drake turned his head, nestling against her, nose in that glorious hair. She smelled of woman and smoke. He wanted to clutch her to him, but his hands wouldn't move. They were shaking.

He was shaking.

A huge ball of something, some violent emotion, was working its way up his chest and throat, like sharp knives slicing him open from the inside out. He opened his mouth to let it out. It sounded like a sob, but that couldn't be.

Except his cheeks were cold. Something was making them wet.

His battered brain took several minutes to realize that, for the first time in his adult life, he was crying.

Rome
December 2

Grace leaned against the stone balustrade of the luxurious apartment at the top of the Spanish Steps, drinking in the glory of a Roman sunset. Though it was December, the evening was balmy, the setting sun somehow bigger and redder than any sun that had ever set over Manhattan.

From Florida they'd flown to Montenegro in a luxury jet that was like a boutique hotel room. During the flight, Drake started healing right in front of her eyes. Almost hour by hour, he improved.

She'd been so frightened on the horrific drive down to Tampa. Drake had been barely conscious, bleeding from multiple wounds and, worst of all, dazed and disoriented. For a horrific moment, she had thought he might actually die.

And yet, by the time they'd landed in Montenegro, been taken across the Adriatic in a speedboat to land north of Bari with a Mercedes waiting, he felt well enough to take the wheel. Grace had made a token protest, but he'd simply looked at her with a crooked smile, holding the passenger door open. She'd slid inside with a sigh of relief. She hated to drive. The nightmare journey to Florida through a storm with a wounded man beside her had been horrible enough. Driving in *Italy?* No thanks.

Trust Drake to find the most sumptuous apartment in Rome, across the street from the Hassler Hotel, at the top of the Spanish Steps. She'd gasped as they walked in, the Roman skyline glittering just beyond the enormous terrace. The travertine-stone lintel over the huge one-story carved wooden street door had had a coat of arms with 1537 engraved on it. A Renaissance palazzo, with a penthouse apartment that seemed to be theirs, frescoes and all.

She'd been worried about the toll all this travel was taking on Drake. The evening they arrived in Rome, Drake had come naked out of the huge marble bathroom, having taken the stitches in his shoulder out himself. He put a finger to her lips before she could say anything. "It's okay, my love," he'd said. Then kissed her.

A naked Drake kissing her . . . she could barely remember her own name after that.

She'd wanted to see Rome and he'd taken her, everywhere she wanted to go. Dressed in a long cashmere coat, which managed to mask his unusually strong physique, and a black watchcap pulled low over his forehead, with wraparound sunglasses and dark stubble blurring the line of his jaw, he passed unnoticed in the crowd, almost unrecognizable even to her.

This was her time, he made that clear. They did what she wanted, went where she wanted, saw what she wanted. She lost herself so much in Raphael's *La Fornarina* at the National Gallery that the guards had to shoo them out at closing time. When with a start Grace realized she'd kept Drake standing for over three hours while she mooned over a painting by Titian at the Borghese Gallery, she started to apologize.

"Did you enjoy that, duschka?" he asked. "Did it make you happy?"

"Oh yes," she breathed.

"Then I'm happy, too," he said simply.

He stood quietly by her side as she spent an entire morning at the Sistine Chapel, his dark eyes taking everything in. Though he knew very little about art, Grace wouldn't have been surprised if he were now able to describe from memory each and every one of the hundreds of paintings she'd dragged him to see.

It was all so . . . liberating. All her life, she'd had to disguise how passionately she loved classical art. Most people could get a little worked up about modern art, the trendier and more expensive the better, but classical art . . . bleh.

And of course, conversely, she had to feign an interest in the things most people were crazy about—money, fashion and gossip.

With Drake, Grace didn't have to hide any aspect of her nature. After a couple of days, she was surprised to find that she was even unconsciously standing straighter, and realized she had lived her life slightly hunched, waiting for disapproval. Not with Drake. She could be herself, completely, and he loved it.

He loved *her*.

Exactly the way she was.

He loved her. It was there, in his touch, in his rare smiles, only for her, in the way he looked at her.

He rarely left her side, and then only to take care of business. Like now. And she knew, like she knew that the sun setting in a blaze of glory before her would rise again in the east tomorrow, that he would come back to her.

Behind her, a light switched on inside the sumptuous living room fit for a prince and she smiled.

Drake was back.

In a moment, he was at her side, strong arm around her waist. She leaned her head against that massive shoulder and sighed. The sun was disappearing behind the glorious golden cupola of St. Peter's, turning all the buildings a luscious, deep red. The Spanish Steps, below them, were full of people—tourists, students, families enjoying the warm evening, their voices a soft hum on the gentle evening breeze. Grace waved an arm, encompassing all of Rome. "This is so beautiful, Drake. Thank you for showing it to me."

He turned his head to look at her. "Your pleasure has been mine. But our time here is drawing to a close, duschka. I wish it weren't true, but it is. Europe is too dangerous for us.

Soak everything up and commit it to memory, because the sad truth is that we can never return here again."

She knew that. It had been made clear to her, which was why she'd been so greedy to see all the artwork she could.

He pulled something from his overcoat pocket, then tossed the overcoat onto a wicker chaise longue. "Here." Two burgundy passports. "These are our new identities."

Intrigued, Grace opened them. She and Drake were now Maltese, she saw. Victoria and Manuel Rabat. She fingered the identity page, covered in plastic, touching her new existence. "Victoria," she murmured. "It's a pretty name."

Drake shrugged. "I like Grace more. But she is now gone."

"Have you figured out where Victoria and Manuel are going?"

He smiled. "Yes. An island called Sivuatu, a couple of hours' flight from Fiji. It is very lush, warm, but in the path of the trade winds, so the heat is mitigated. I have already bought a home for us. It is very beautiful. One wing will be set aside as your studio. I hope you will like it there."

Grace met his dark gaze. "I'll love it." Her voice rang clearly with the force of her conviction.

He nodded gravely. "I hope so, for we will rarely leave the island. It will be our new home, in every sense, for the rest of our lives."

"When will we leave?"

"Soon, as I said. Everything is ready, just one more thing has to happen and then we go, as fast as we can. But before we go, there is something else we must do."

Grace watched, intrigued, as he pulled two small boxes from his pants pocket, holding them to her in the palm of his huge hand.

Two shiny black lacquer boxes, with BULGARI embossed in

gold on the covers. He put one in her hand. "Open this one first."

Smiling, she opened the box. Inside was a thick band of red gold inset with brightly colored gemstones. She lifted it out, the gemstones glittering with life and vivid color. Amethyst, topaz, aquamarine, peridot . . . she held the ring up to the light and drank in the glorious colors.

"It's beautiful, Drake. Perfect. It's just perfect." It was. The design was clean and exquisite, the gemstones bright and flawless. Exactly the kind of ring to appeal to her.

"Open the other one," he said quietly.

"Two rings," she smiled. "That's a little extravagant, don't you th—" She stopped and gazed, puzzled, at the simple, enormous gold band in the second box. "Drake, that's much too large for my hand."

He smiled. "It's not for you, duschka, it's for me." He extracted it from the velvet holder, placing it in the palm of his right hand. Intense dark eyes stared into hers. "Put it on me, my love. You know which finger."

She did. Her heart began a deep, excited thudding in her chest.

With shaking fingers, she picked up the big gold band. It felt heavy and warm in her hand. She picked up his left hand and slipped it onto his ring finger. It fit, perfectly, just as hers had.

Once the ring was on his finger, he caught her hand, lacing his fingers through hers.

"We will arrive in our new home as man and wife, so we will never have a marriage ceremony. Therefore we will have our wedding now, and here." He indicated the beautiful, terra-cotta-tiled terrace with the elegant wickerwork and iron furniture, the city of Rome laid out before them with its bustling crowds and elegant shop windows all lit up, the domes of the Renaissance churches rising up like dreams made of stone and tile from the forest of rooftop gardens. He brought her hand to his lips and kissed her fingers. Grace nearly cried at what she saw in his eyes, blinking back the tears, because this was the most solemn moment in her life, a moment that would split her existence on this earth into two. Before Drake and After Drake.

"Grace Larsen," he whispered, "I promise to love you and protect you for the rest of our lives." He swallowed heavily. His hard face, normally so impassive, showed signs of emotion, nostrils flaring white, deep brackets around his mouth, muscles rippling along his jawline.

Grace was shaking all over. Deep down, she never thought she'd ever get married. She was too odd, too eccentric, too out of step with the modern-day world. At times she hadn't even minded, because the thought of a fancy, expensive wedding with tons of drunken guests, followed by a marriage in which she had to constantly pretend to be someone else, was almost too much to bear.

This was . . . perfect. So *perfect* for her. The man of her dreams in the city of her dreams. Just the two of them, vowing to love each other forever.

"Viktor Drakovich," she whispered, her throat almost too tight to get the words out. She waited for the trembling to die down, for her voice to steady. Such a solemn moment, it deserved the best she could give. A deep breath. Another. When she finally spoke, her voice was calm. "I promise to love and care for you for the rest of our lives." She bowed her head over their joined hands. "We are now truly man and wife."

His hand jolted a little in hers and she looked up, startled. She barely had a chance to see his face, muscles tight, eyes ferociously fixed on hers, before he took her head in his big hands and started kissing her wildly. Eating at her mouth, tongue deep inside, breathing her in as if he were dying and her mouth contained the elixir of life.

"Mine," he moaned into her mouth. "Mine forever."

It was a hard kiss, almost violent, but Grace met his mouth with equal force, trying to meld with him, hands clutching at him in an effort to get closer, closer. Skin to skin. Loins to loins. Heart to heart.

He walked her backward into the living room, shedding clothes as they went. He lifted his mouth from hers for a nanosecond to whip his sweater off, then impatiently ripped away the underlying shirt. In a second, trousers and briefs and shoes and socks were on the floor and he pulled her to him, hard, still kissing her deeply.

Grace tightened her arms around him, his shoulders so broad her arms couldn't meet. He was so hot, it was like holding warm steel in her arms as she settled heavily against him. His erection was huge and hot between them. She couldn't resist the temptation to roll her hips against it, delighted to feel him swell, grow even harder and longer.

He wasn't the only one affected. She could feel herself growing moist between the legs, her body readying itself for him.

He growled in her mouth, hooked a finger in the pale lavender silk shirt he'd bought her at Valentino and the La Perla bra beneath it and pulled, hard. The pearl buttons pinged as they bounced off the ancient terra-cotta tiles and the shirt and bra drifted to the floor. Grace moaned as his naked chest met hers, the feel of his skin against hers electric and almost unbearably exciting.

He walked them to the plush rug in front of the open fire

in the huge, intricately carved hearth and, still kissing her wildly, eased them both to the ground. She could feel against her breasts the strong play of muscles as he brought them down, laying her gently against the priceless antique rug, then coming down on top of her.

He was shaking with the effort to control himself, but he didn't have to. She needed this just as much as he did. She needed this wild coupling, this drive each of them felt to get inside the other's skin. There was no such thing as being too close, not at this moment.

Her tongue licked deeply in his mouth, her arms strained to hold him as tightly as she could. Desire blossomed in her, a hot unfolding and swelling, until her skin felt too tight to contain her. It was almost painful, this intense desire, and she whimpered.

"Now, Drake. Don't wait."

It was as if she had lashed a whip across his shoulders. In seconds, he had her pants unbuttoned, sliding them down her legs together with her panties, and as soon as her legs were free, he was kneeing them apart.

He didn't need to do that. They separated of their own volition, eager to twine around his hips. Oh God, his weight felt so delicious on top of her, heavy and warm, grounding her, making her whole.

It seemed insane to her that she'd spent almost twenty-eight years without this. How had she survived all those lonely nights?

Drake pulled back a little, face harsh, eyes closed to slits, as he reached down and opened her with his fingers.

"Have . . . to . . . *now*," he gasped. He was always so careful entering her, making sure she was ready for him, but she could tell he couldn't wait. She didn't want him to.

In answer, she opened her legs even wider and lifted her hips, in an invitation as old as time.

He entered her on one hard thrust, muscles hard and straining. She was ready, soft and wet and welcoming. Her entire body embraced him, held him, arms and legs and sheath, as tightly as she could.

He moved inside her heavily, thrusting so hard she was going to get carpet burn, but she didn't care because she needed this, needed it desperately. She needed his hard possession of her body, since she'd just given it to him, together with her heart.

He was straining, hips slapping against hers, the sounds of their panting loud in the hushed quiet of the apartment.

The intense friction caused a firestorm of heat in her loins, her vagina clenched once, twice, rising toward an orgasm . . .

Drake stopped, panting, head hung low between his shoulders. Every muscle stood out in bold relief. He was so huge inside her, she knew he was close to orgasm, too.

"Why—" she whispered.

"No . . . protection," Drake gasped. A drop of sweat ran from his forehead down over the hidden scar, to drop off his chin and onto her shoulder.

Instinctively, Grace tightened her legs around his hips, her hands pushing down on the ironlike muscles of his buttocks, pulling him closer.

"We're married," she whispered to him and it was as if those two words set off a firestorm. He bucked, hard, then started thrusting jerkily, fast and hard, in shallow, irregular strokes. Shuddering, he swelled inside her, then started coming on a low moan, almost of pain, setting off her own contractions.

For the first time in her life, Grace felt a man come inside her and not inside of latex. It was glorious. She could feel the hot washes of semen pulsing inside her, her vagina becoming wetter than it had ever been before, so that he could slide in her more easily.

Even after coming, Drake didn't stop, though he gained control over the strokes, slowing swinging in and out of her in measured movements, moving so easily inside her now that she was wet with his semen.

He groaned with pleasure, eyes tightly closed. Grace's legs and hands rode his buttocks, completely attuned to his movements. She felt herself become one with him, felt his movements inside and out of her, his body a part of hers . . .

With a high cry, she started coming again in tight, almost painful pulses that seemed to come from her entire body. He rode her through the contractions, prolonging them, finally coming once more with her.

At last, spent, he collapsed onto her, huge chest moving like a bellows to pull in air.

His limp weight was enormously heavy, so heavy Grace had to work to be able to breathe, so heavy she could feel her joints stretching where he lay atop her.

But she relished it, held him to her as tightly as she could. It was like his weight grounded her, made her feel she was truly a part of this earth for perhaps the first time in her life.

As consciousness returned, she took stock. She'd substituted romance novels for romance in her life, and in the books, it was never this . . . earthy.

The smell of their sex was sharp in the air, sharper than the smell of wood smoke. Her hair was all tangled and sweaty— *she* was sweaty all over, as was Drake. Her entire groin area was wet and undoubtedly they had created a wet spot on that incredibly expensive antique Persian carpet under her, the one that had given her rug burn.

Her muscles ached and she had to open her arms, legs falling limply open, too, as she let Drake go. One part of her still held him, though. He was still inside her, softer than before but still semi-erect.

She shifted a little to find a more comfortable position, finding it hard with all that weight on her. The instant her hips moved, he stiffened a little inside her and she nearly laughed.

Not right now, ace, maybe later was on her lips, but she didn't have the breath to say the words.

Grace was squashed, uncomfortable, wet and sweaty and totally happy.

Finally, Drake turned his head, eyes half closed, a small smile on his face. He kissed her ear and whispered something in a language she'd never heard before, three short, liquid syllables.

She had no idea what he'd said, but there was only one possible answer.

"I love you, too, Drake," she whispered.

Sixteen

Rutskoi reluctantly killed the outboard engine and gazed with loathing at the rippling black water under him.

He was an army man, through and through. Put him on land and he could fight his way through anything. The Russian army had saved Russia from Napoleon and from Hitler. What had the Russian navy done? Nothing.

It didn't help that he couldn't really swim. He could paddle around in a pool without drowning, but that was about it.

He had imagined his final confrontation with Drake on dry land, walking away the victor, Drake slumped on the ground in a pool of his own blood. Not on the roiling sea. But here he was, on water, the unknown element.

He had supplied Terabyte with a list of all known Drake aliases, including a couple he'd only used a few times. And fuck him if they didn't get back to him within seventy hours, that a credit card in the name of Serge Blansky had been used in Ostia, a small port city just outside of Rome.

It was the name Drake had used in Ossetia, when he'd been supplying the rebels. As far as Rutskoi knew, Drake had only used the name during the month he'd spent negotiating in Tskhinvali. Still, Rutskoi had remembered and had included the name among the twelve known identities of Drake.

So here was a Serge Blansky, booking a room in Lido di Ostia at a fancy five-star hotel that was just Drake's style, and buying a Lamborghini from a local dealer. How many Blanskys had that kind of money?

Rutskoi had kept the hotel under surveillance from a hundred yards away, but somehow Drake came and went right under his nose, because he never saw him come and never saw him go. Rutskoi was very aware of the fact that a surveillance op like this required a team of five or six men operating around the clock, but he was alone. *Deal with it*, he told himself.

Good luck came in the form of an SMS sent to his cell phone from Terabyte.

Subject hired 150-foot yacht from company at Lido di Ostia. Name of yacht "Bella Mia." Pays €10,000 per day for hire.

Rutskoi had raced to the marina, and there she was, half a kilometer out—150 meters of sleek white hull with brass so brightly polished it hurt his eyes through the binoculars. *Bella Mia* was written in cursive script on the hull.

There was no time to assemble a team of divers, Drake

could disappear at any moment. And in any case, Rutskoi worked alone. He found a quiet spot far from the marina and settled in to observe. Drake wasn't in the hotel room, he was on his yacht; Rutskoi would bet the $10 million on it.

Probably fucking the woman right this instant.

That's right, Drake, Rutskoi thought, as he kept the yacht in the lens of his binoculars, *enjoy the pussy while you can.*

It was dark now. An hour ago, at sunset, all the internal lights of the yacht had lit up. Oh yeah, Drake was on the yacht.

Rutskoi had night-vision capability and could see on deck as clearly as if it were noon. The decks were deserted. It was entirely possible that—in a fit of testosterone-induced madness—Drake had dismissed the crew.

Rutskoi pulled out a set of oars and began rowing clumsily toward the left-hand side of the ship. Port side, apparently, it was called. Though it was dark and he'd carefully dressed in non-reflective clothing, he was aware of his vulnerability as he quietly, slowly rowed his way toward the yacht. If there were guards on board, all it would take was a casual look over the railing with night vision and he was a dead man walking. Dead man rowing, actually.

Finally, after what felt like forever, he pulled up beside the bow. He reached out a hand to touch the sleek wood, still warm from the day's sun. He'd pulled up next to a rope ladder. This was more like it. Rutskoi was agile and athletic. He tied the boat to the rope ladder and then climbed the ladder like a monkey, happy to get off the small, rocking boat onto the much more stable yacht.

He climbed carefully, utterly without noise. He had a Glock 17, which a former Spetsnaz officer living in Rome had given him, together with the night-vision goggles. A cold gun, no identifying marks. He had three magazines in case the yacht was heavily guarded, but he thought not. Peering carefully over the gunwale with his night-vision goggles, he saw that the deck was still deserted. No guards.

Drake felt safe, running away with his mistress. Not expecting the trouble that was right now slowly rolling over onto the deck.

Rutskoi also had half a pound of C–4 if the gun didn't work out, together with detonators and a timer. Set the timer, get in the small boat, fire up the outboard and watch from a safe distance as the fucking yacht blew right out of the water.

Rutskoi stood carefully and slowly from a crouch, tensing when he heard voices. A woman's light trill of laughter, the deeper tones of a man. Music. All belowdecks.

Belowdecks was very good because it gave Rutskoi all the advantages of high ground, room for maneuver and surprise.

Quietly, Rutskoi followed the sounds of music and laughter. Noiselessly descending the shallow steps, he felt alive, on the hunt.

This was going to be much easier than he thought. So far he'd seen no one. It seemed that the only people on board were the woman and Drake, whose voice he recognized as he approached the closed door of the salon.

No guards, music, the woman. Drake thought himself safe, had abandoned all caution.

Oh yeah, love turned men into fools.

Rutskoi eased closer to the door, placed a listening device against the shiny wood. It piped sound into an earpiece.

The same as before, only startlingly clear. Background music and Drake talking to a woman. Relaxed voice. His defenses were down.

The door was a sliding one. Rutskoi checked it, ever so carefully, moving it by a hair.

It was unlocked.

God, Drake *deserved* to die.

Rutskoi toggled the door a little to get a feeling for how much strength it would take to slide it open, fit his hand into the space between the door and the jamb and crouched down.

If this had been a dynamic entry with his men, he'd have arranged for a four-man unit. Two high, two low. Two right, two left.

But he was alone, so he went in low. If Drake had a weapon close at hand—and however insanely besotted he was, Rutskoi found it hard to believe that Drake wouldn't have a weapon close by—he'd automatically aim for the head.

Rutskoi gave the door a hard shove to the left and moved through the opening swiftly, gun in a two-handed grip, ready for anything, and found . . .

Nothing.

The room was empty. Large, beautifully appointed and . . . empty.

Yet Drake was still talking, music still playing.

What the fuck?

The music and the woman's voice cut off abruptly. "So, it is you, Rutskoi," Drake's voice said, and Rutskoi whirled, seeing no one, just the back of an open laptop on the table. "I guessed as much."

Rutskoi rounded the table.

Shit! Drake's face filled the screen. Fucker was somewhere else. With a webcam.

It was a *trap.*

"Ah, Rutskoi," Drake said softly. "You disappoint me."

Ten million dollars, slipping through his fingers. Rutskoi could feel it, like sand. His only hope was to rattle Drake, somehow scare him into making a mistake.

He leaned forward into the screen, staring into the tiny webcam attached to the cover. "You got away this time, Drake," he growled, "but I'll get you eventually. You and that bitch with you. You can count on it." He slapped his Glock for emphasis.

Drake didn't reply, but pulled out a cell phone. He punched in a number.

Who the fuck was he calling?

Something started beeping. A big metal box on a counter. With—Christ!—a small LED display, counting down. 10, 9, 8, 7 . . .

Rutskoi leaped, slapped the laptop off the table.

. . . 6, 5, 4, 3 . . .

"Drake," he screamed. "Son of a bitch! I'll get you if it's the last thing I do!"

"I think not, Rutskoi," Drake replied softly.

Rutskoi's world exploded in a fiery ball of white heat.

The sounds of the explosion carried to the city center of Rome.

Epilogue

Sivuatu, Oceania
One year later

His charge slipped into the backseat of the black Mercedes 500 S class and smiled at him. Jim Stanley smiled back into the rearview mirror and ignited the powerful engine.

"Take me home, Jim," Victoria Rabat said, "as quickly as possible." Then she looked out the smoked side window and smiled secretly.

Jim knew what the smile was for. He'd have to be blind not to notice the discreet bronze plaque by the side of the plate-glass door of the doctor's office she'd just visited. DR. RAJAV SINGH, GYNECOLOGIST-OBSTETRICIAN.

Jim put the car in motion. It rolled smoothly, testimony to superb German engineering, because it was steel-plated and weighed more than ten tons. He didn't hurry, though his employer had urged him to. If anything, now that Jim suspected she was pregnant, he drove as if carrying a load of eggs, because his *real* boss, Manuel Rabat, would have his hide if she arrived with even a scratch on her.

Jim had been hired ostensibly as a driver, but it had been made very, *very* clear to him that he was being paid five times the going rate to be the missus's bodyguard, not just her driver. It had been also been made very, very clear that if anything happened to Mrs. Rabat, his ass was grass.

At first, the salary and the fact that his employer—who was no one's fool—had never once mentioned his dishonorable discharge from the U.S. Army, something that had been the big job-killer up to now, seemed too good to be true.

Jim had been a Ranger, and a damned good one, too, until he'd broken the jaw of a candy-ass colonel who'd ordered his team on a suicide mission. Jim had lost two of his best friends, his temper and then his future.

But Manual Rabat hadn't mentioned it once. He'd given Jim three tests. First, he'd taken him down into the second sublevel underneath the enormous home built on a cliff, inaccessible from three sides, accessible on the land side only by one gate that was manned 24/7 by three guards.

The entire subbasement was a state-of-the-art gym, the best-equipped Jim had ever seen. And Rabat used it often, too, as was visible when he stripped to put on his gi. There was a gi for Jim, too, and it was clear that he was expected to show his prowess as a fighter.

Fuck yeah. Jim had been trained in hand-to-hand combat by the best. His only problem was going to be not breaking his prospective employer's arms.

Fifteen sweaty, exhausting minutes later, Jim was on the mat, immobilized. Rabat released him and sprang up, sweating but otherwise unruffled. Jim realized he'd gone three rounds with a world-class fighter and that he was lucky they weren't enemies, because he'd have been dead.

Drake knew all the martial arts moves Jim knew, and some he didn't. Clearly, Rabat had been trained in the Russian art of SAMBO, and he was adept at *savate*. When he stripped to shower, Jim could see the thickened shinbones that came from thousands and thousands of hours of kicking either sand-filled bags or ass. He suspected the latter.

When they were dressed, Rabat had congratulated him. It was the first time anyone had lasted fifteen minutes with him.

He'd passed the first test.

The second came five minutes later, on a mile-long shooting range, where Jim was tested on handguns, machine guns and rifles, at varying distances. Well, at least he got that right. With each weapon, at each distance, he was able to put ten rounds in a nickel. Something told him, however, that Rabat could place them in a dime.

The third test was on a race track, where he was put through a grueling series of tests. A bootlegger's turn at 80 mph, evasive driving and combat driving.

At the end of the day, he was offered a job for enough money to make him rich in ten years' time, and lodgings on Rabat's compound. He was introduced to Mrs. Rabat as her new driver, but Jim was clear on what he was.

The money was worth it to be lackey and bodyguard to a rich bitch. He'd do his duty, no question. But it turned out that the lady was no bitch. Inside of a month, Jim had half fallen in love with her, as had everyone else on the staff.

She was gorgeous, but then that went with the territory of rich, powerful men. If they couldn't have beautiful women, who could?

There was something else about her, though, a sweetness, a

gentleness mixed with a skewered sense of humor that made Jim realize that he'd defend her with his life, even without Rabat.

The woman was magic. Not to mention a highly gifted artist. For Christmas, he'd gotten two watercolors of a puppy who'd adopted him, and they were small masterpieces that he'd framed himself and put up on the wall at the foot of his bed so they were the last things he saw at night and the first things he saw in the morning.

She ran a small, highly successful art gallery in the center of town, selling mostly her own works. She strongly encouraged local talent, but prospective buyers zeroed in on her stuff and didn't have eyes for anything else. Apparently, she sold everything she ever showed, within a week.

And still, there was enough left over to cover every inch of wall in their huge mansion. He'd heard Rabat was planning a new wing just to house all her stuff.

"Jim . . ." She smiled into the mirror. "I know you're a careful driver, but could we please . . . speed it up? I have some good news I want to share with Mr. Rabat."

Well, maybe that wing was going to be used for something a little more lively than paintings. Jim raised his speed by five miles. Rabat was already insanely overprotective. If anything happened to his *pregnant* wife . . .

Jim shuddered at the thought.

Behind him, she drummed long, delicate fingers on the armrest but said nothing more. She wasn't the type to insist or whine.

Finally, they were at the big steel gates that were only one aspect of Rabat's perimeter defenses. There were motion sensors, thermal imaging cameras, trip wires. Discreet, hidden, but definitely there.

Oh yeah, Rabat was an operator. A fucking *rich* operator.

Rabat had appeared out of nowhere a year ago and in a month had become the proprietor of the three airlines that flew in and out of the Sivuatu airport and the owner of the four shipping companies and two cruise lines that operated out of the port.

Jim glanced in the rearview mirror. Victoria was sitting on the edge of her seat now as they drove through the gates, gathering her things, smiling a secret smile. The smile reserved exclusively for her husband.

And there he was, waiting for his wife, as always.

Jim drove slowly down the drive, waiting for the moment that always twisted his guts.

He pulled up, aligning the back door exactly with where Rabat was waiting. Rabat opened the door himself, lifting his wife out of the backseat and . . . his face *melted*.

It never failed to amaze Jim.

Rabat was a hard-ass. It was hard to imagine that look could be on the face of a man like him. All that hardness and toughness and cold detachment, gone.

Victoria whispered in her husband's ear and he picked her up and twirled her, her happy laughter loud in the tropical evening air.

This was happiness on a scale that almost scared Jim. Rabat put his wife down, touching her cheek gently. The expression of yearning and tenderness on his face was so raw, Jim looked away, chest tight.

Some things are too much for mere mortals to see.

Like looking into the sun.

LISA MARIE RICE is eternally thirty years old and will never age. She is tall and willowy and beautiful. Men drop at her feet like ripe pears. She has won every major book prize in the world. She is a black belt with advanced degrees in archaeology, nuclear physics, and Tibetan literature. She is a concert pianist. Did I mention the Nobel?

Of course, Lisa Marie Rice is a virtual woman and exists only at the keyboard when writing erotic romance. She disappears when the monitor winks off.